FOR THE *Thrill* OF IT

SAMANTHA M. THOMAS

Contents

DEDICATION

To headstrong woman like Willow: Greatness is around the corner. Don't let anyone tell you to hold back or back down. We need it now more than ever.

And to my love of true crime: Thanks for making the morbid parts to easy to write.

CHAPTER ONE

WILLOW

I've written and killed off almost everyone in Bluebell Falls.

They're not bad people, but it's cathartic to throw them in one of my books when they annoy me, just to kill them. It's sure as hell better than doing it in real life, right?

I sigh, sitting back in my office chair, and stare at the blinking cursor on the blank page.

I have an idea for this book, but for some reason I'm just stuck. This has never happened to me before, and I'm frustrated as hell. Can I write myself into this book and send me to my own demise? Writer's block has never been in my vocabulary, and my stubborn ass refuses to accept it.

For clarity, I write thrillers—the "emotional, jarring, twists-and-turns galore, and keeps you guessing" type of books. Usually, I'm pretty damn good at it, but today? Today, it feels like I'm in a big, dark hole in the middle of a desert, sinking further and clinging to the remnants of an idea that's slowly slipping away.

And I have a deadline to hit in two months.

Yeah, totally doable and not stress-inducing at all.

Leaning forward, my forehead thumps on my desk. *Thump, thump, thump.*

Music. Maybe music will help.

I pull up my favorite playlist full of everything, from eighties' hair bands to current pop stars to soothing instrumentals. Clicking through the first five songs does nothing to inspire me, and after a further five, I grip my hair in frustration.

What the fuck is happening?

A conversation from a couple of days ago pops into my head. Sheriff Arlo came by my brother, Ledger's, house asking about some rumor Alice and Mabel were spreading. Now, I usually don't take anything Alice and Mabel as truth, but maybe I'll get some inspiration from their tall tales. I don't remember what they were hung up on, but I do remember the word "assassin" being thrown around. And that's just intriguing enough for me to go find them to see what fables they're spinning.

I'm not holding hope to anything assassin related because there's no way in hell anything like that will ever happen in Bluebell Falls. Our small town is more likely to see a bingo hustle than anything as dangerous as an assassin.

I throw my laptop into my backpack, along with a pen and paper in case my computer is the problem, and head out to Main Street.

Small-town life has always been my greatest source of inspiration. I've been making up stories about everyone in Bluebell Falls since I first learned how to write. They've continued and grown in the years since, and when I decided to do online college for creative writing and English, it felt like a natural career path.

I've never regretted that decision once, until today. Writing has always been the easy part. It's the marketing and promotion that I don't love or thrive on. But writing is my escape. I've been successful enough to pay my mortgage and bills, and keep a steady stream of income, but this book might just cause all of that to crash down around me.

A few months ago, I woke up from a dream with this vague thought of creating a series about a badass woman. That's it. Just a badass woman. I don't know if she's the good guy, the bad guy, or both. Initially, I was going for an *Only Murders in the Building* vibe but tossed that out almost immediately. In the months since that dream, I haven't garnered any more clarity. And now it's crunch time if I want to stick to my publishing schedule.

The walk to Sal's is exactly eight minutes. I chose to live closer to downtown because it makes it easier to pop in for a change of scenery while I write. My siblings—Ledger, Rina, and Lennox—live on the outskirts of town because they all wanted their space to grow their business, or in Lennox's case, to be antisocial and live closer to the wildlife.

I just wanted access to everything because I never know where inspiration will come from.

Walking into Sal's gives me a view of everyone in the place. When I see it's mostly empty, except for Old Man Walter, I immediately turn around and head to Grind Time.

"Good to see you, Willow!" Kelly, the owner of Sal's, yells at my back.

I throw a wave at her. I hear her chuckle, and a smirk tips up the corner of my lip. She's used to me just dropping by and being in the zone. It's nice to not have to make small talk all the time.

Grind Time is much busier, and I check my phone to see that it's ten o'clock in the morning, so that makes sense.

I usually avoid the popular coffee shop because the owner, Oakley, is way too damn distracting. I can still remember when he first opened up Grind Time a little over a year ago. I was so excited to have a coffee shop to write at, to create a little office away from home.

And then I saw Oakley.

He's unnaturally tall. At my five-foot, two-inch frame, he towers over me by at least a foot. His dirty blond, almost brown hair is a little shaggy, like he doesn't care enough to get it trimmed regularly. And his eyes. Dear God, his brown eyes have every shade in the spectrum. From gold to the color of the espresso I love so much, they mesmerized me the first time I stepped foot in here.

And it was when he had to ask for my order three times that I knew I couldn't regularly come in here to work. I would never get anything done if I did. So, I've saved Grind Time as a reward for finishing a book. I get to come in and drool over Oakley's gorgeousness without worrying about a deadline.

I look around, and spot Alice and Mabel gossiping in the corner. I take a step to head in that direction when a voice stops me in my tracks.

"Good morning, Willow. Can I get you your usual?" Oakley's rich baritone seeps into my bones, and I have to close my eyes to focus.

"Sure, that would be great," I tell him with an overly large smile pasted on my face. The man remembers every single person's "usual", regardless whether you come in every day or once a month. It's unnatural.

I make my way to the table next to the tall tale committee and sit, carefully pulling out my notebook and laptop. I make sure not to look over at Oakley making my latte with his dark grey Henley sleeves pushed up to his elbows. I definitely don't look at the geometric tattoos covering his left forearm that flexes every time he reaches for something.

Nope, I definitely don't do that.

Shaking my head, I turn my attention to the ladies at the table next to me.

"And he just walked down the street like nothing happened," Mabel says in disbelief.

"Unbelievable," Alice *tsks*. "What happened to helping your neighbors?"

I roll my eyes, not even caring about whom they're referring to because I would bet my next book they're offended by something that didn't actually happen.

"Did you talk to the sheriff about that man again?" Alice says in a loud whisper.

My ears perk up. Anything that has to do with Arlo might be something up my alley.

"I did, but he told me he would handle it. I don't believe that for a second. We need to keep vigilant, Alice. Who knows who is really walking around our town."

I almost burst out laughing and have to cover my mouth in an effort to stop it.

"Here you go, Willow." Oakley startles me as he places my latte on my table along with a slice of lemon loaf.

I look down at the cup and see he's tried to make one of those foam hearts with the steamed milk, but it looks more like a blob, and I roll my lips inward in an attempt to not smile at his effort.

Listen, the man makes killer drinks without the fancy foam artwork, but it's adorable that he tries. I look up at him to tell him thanks and see his cheeks are tinged with pink.

He's so fucking handsome it's ridiculous. The embarrassed blush only makes him more attractive.

"Thanks, Oakley, I appreciate it. How much do I owe you?" I try to keep it cordial because I know if I think too hard about talking to him, I'll be a mess of awkward conversation and run-on sentences. I don't do well with men, especially ridiculously attractive men.

I much prefer my introvert status.

"On the house today. Haven't seen you in a while, so it's my treat." He bows his head and then snaps it up when he hears the bell above the front door. "Sorry," he says, his tone more apologetic than necessary.

"No worries." I wave him off and try way too hard to appear busy writing nonsense on my notepad.

"Long time, no see, Oak." The voice of the man who just entered the door is friendly but unsure.

I peer up at Oakley and see the color visibly drain from his face.

"Follow me," Oakley says, all business, and from his tone, I'd say he's pissed.

"Oh my God, it's him."

Mabel's hurried whisper draws my interest as I watch the two men walk to the back of the store, where I presume Oakley's office is.

"Him, who?" Alice asks.

"The assassin."

My eyes move to the door both men are now behind, and I am more intrigued by the minute.

"He doesn't look like an assassin," Alice muses, and I tilt my head back to stop from laughing out loud.

I wonder what an assassin looks like in the eyes of the older women. Because there could be a case for Oakley looking like one with his muscled build and tattoos. I, for one, would be cool with it. It would be like one of my books come to life.

"Well, he seems to know Oakley, so that's concerning," Mabel dismisses Alice.

"We should just call the sheriff." I hear Alice shuffling around, presumably grabbing her phone.

The bell above the door rings again, and Arlo walks into the unsuspecting barrage that is Alice and Mabel.

"We were just about to call you. Oakley is in the back with that man we were telling you about." The overdramatic concern in Mabel's voice almost does me in.

"The man you think is an assassin," Arlo deadpans.

"The very same!"

I bite my lip so hard I'm shocked I don't draw blood. These two will make anything front-page news, I swear.

"And he knew Oakley, so maybe they're both assassins."

The women talk over each other and my laughter bursts from my chest, unable to keep a lid on my amusement.

"Willow Marie, I know you are not laughing at your elders," Mabel scolds, and I turn to face her.

"I would never." I place my hand over my chest in faux indignation. "I was just laughing at something Rina texted me." I look up at Arlo and see the side of his lips tipped up in a smirk.

I arch one eyebrow, daring him to call me out, but he wisely refrains. We've known each other since we were little kids. With him and Rina being friends for most of my younger years, he acts more like a big brother than Ledger does some days.

"I'll talk to Oakley when he comes out," he offers the tall tale committee before walking to the counter to order his coffee.

"Miss Willow, will you make sure the sheriff talks with Oakley? We've got to get to the Bluebell Center for bingo."

"I absolutely will." I smile.

Watching them as they walk out the door, still huddled together, chatting about a possible killer in our midst, pulls at the tendrils of a storyline but nothing sticks.

"You really shouldn't encourage them," Arlo says as he sits in the other chair at my table.

"But it's just so much fun. Who could blame me?"

"So, what's this situation really about?" he asks before he takes a sip of coffee.

"Not sure. A new guy came in, and Oakley appeared to know him. Took him around the back, and that's all I know."

"I swear, sometimes I wish there was real crime here instead of this made-up bullshit."

"You'll be eating your words on that one, I'm sure. They do make for some great material for my books, though."

"When's the new one coming out?" he asks.

"If I can get my ass back on track, it should be out in four months."

"Well, I look forward to it."

Oakley and the new guy emerge from the back office, drawing Arlo's attention.

"That's my cue. Good to see you, Willow."

"You too, Sheriff." It's still weird calling him "Sheriff" because I've known him since I was a little kid, but he does a damn good job dealing with the made-up drama this town naturally produces.

I observe the interaction as I finish my coffee, watching their body language to gauge any information I can.

The only thing I can tell for certain is that whatever Oakley said to the sheriff has him interested.

Oakley doesn't need to be more interesting to me, but this situation is holding my interest enough to want to dig a little further. Maybe there is something I can use in my book, but I'll never know if I don't dig.

CHAPTER TWO
OAKLEY

W ell, today has gone to shit faster than an avocado.

It started off well enough. The morning rush was easy, and then Willow came into the shop and made everything a little brighter, as she always does when she comes in.

Until Kellen Woodcroft walked through my front door.

It's not like he couldn't find me easily enough, but when I left my job as a U.S. Marshal on the Fugitive Task Force, it was with the understanding that I would be left alone.

Part of being left alone was completely disconnecting from the pain and trauma that comes from a failed case. And the case we fucked up on was more than that. It was, and still is, every nightmare come to life.

It's why I settled in Bluebell Falls, where no one knew me or my past and I could just be Oakley, Grind Time owner and not-so-pretty latte maker. Not James Oakley, Fugitive Task Force Commander, catching one terrible human at a time yet unable to catch the one man that haunts every happy moment of my life.

I'm currently walking Woodcroft back to my office, with a million things running through my mind. *Why is he here? Is there a development in the case? I thought I finally had some peace.*

He quietly shuts the door as I lean against my desk and cross my arms.

"We had a deal," I say through gritted teeth.

"I know, and you know I wouldn't be here if it wasn't something big."

"I don't care how big it is. I got out. We are no longer partners. I no longer have clearance to hear any of this, nor do I care." My anger is betraying my anxiety. My entire body feels like it's vibrating, and my fingers are digging into my biceps so hard I know there'll be bruises tomorrow.

Woodcroft stares at me for an extended second, seeing a little too much. He sighs in exasperation, before walking up to me and clapping my back in as much of a hug as he can with my fuck-off stance.

"It's good to see you, Oak, really good. You look better, healthier."

"Well, I was until you walked through the damn door," I grumble before running my hand through my shaggy hair. *I need a fucking haircut.*

Walking around my desk and plopping down into my chair, I motion for Woodcroft to take a seat.

"We have a lead." He says it so simply, like it doesn't send me into a cold sweat and has my heart rate doubling.

"I'm out, man. There's nothing I can or want to do. Does boss-man know you're talking to me?" I didn't leave on the best terms. Having a full mental breakdown and screaming at your boss will do that. They treated me better than I deserved when I left, but that chapter of my life is over.

"Whose idea do you think this was? I told him you wouldn't be interested." He shrugs.

I hate everything about this, but potential answers are right in front of me, too tempting to ignore.

"What's the lead?" A statement, not a question or a commitment.

"Word is the Tennison Strangler is traveling west. Someone spotted him on Interstate 40 in Tennessee, and we just received a call from authorities that a victim came into a hospital in Knoxville."

Bone-chilling. When people use the phrase to describe movies, it's child's play to this. Alfred Tennison eats horror movies for breakfast and giggles about them.

He was my breaking point and someone I'm not sure I'll ever recover from.

And now, Woodcroft comes to tell me he's attacked again. Left another victim with lifelong damage and an existence that will probably never be happy again. This is worse than dangling the forbidden fruit.

"Kellen, I can't." My voice breaks as I clench my eyes closed.

"I know, but I was given an order to come talk to you, so I have. I'm not here to convince you to come back. I was there last year. I never want to see a friend, a brother, go through that again."

"Shit, you could have just lied, man. I don't want anything remotely to do with that case touching my life here. No one knows that part of my life, and I want to keep it that way." Scrubbing my hand down my face, I'm exhausted. Just the thought of the Tennison Strangler gets my adrenaline pumping, and now I'm crashing.

"It's been a year. Selfishly, I wanted to check in and see how you were doing. You cut everyone out of your life, including me, and I just wanted to make sure you were okay." He looks me in the eye the whole time, and I feel like a shitty friend. We weren't just partners. We were best friends—practically brothers—and I just cut him out of my life like he was nothing.

"I just needed time," I mutter.

"I know, man. I'm not trying to guilt-trip you. I was there for every-thing, and no one blames you for stepping away."

"I can't help you, Kellen. If they tell you to come back here again, don't." I abruptly stand up and walk to the door, ripping it open and standing aside, wordlessly telling him to leave.

He looks at me, opening and closing his mouth a few times like he wants to say something, before he stands up and walks to the door.

Clapping his hand on my back, he says, "Don't be a stranger, okay? I miss when Oak and Wood took over the world."

"We should have punched anyone who called us that. It's fucking ridiculous." I crack a smile at our stupid nicknames.

Following him down the hallway, I do a quick look to see only a few people hanging around today, which is a good thing because I need some alone time to get my head together.

"Good to see you, Woodcroft. I'll make more of an effort to keep in touch."

He nods before throwing a wave over his shoulder and walking out the front door.

"Just the man I was hoping to talk to. You got a minute, Oakley?" Sheriff Arlo's voice pulls me away from my spiraling thoughts.

"Uh, sure." I look over at Brittany, who's manning the front counter. She waves me off as she wipes the counter down, and I turn to make my way back to my office for the second time this morning.

Silently walking down the hallway, it feels like my two lives are crashing together. I'm not sure what Arlo wants to talk about, but it can't be good. He isn't aware of my former life, but I have a gut feeling that will no longer be the case.

"Have a seat," I say, motioning to the seat Woodcroft just vacated.

"I won't take up too much of your time. I'm just following up on the rumor mill. There are reports of a suspicious new guy in town, and I'm banking on the fact it's the gentleman you just conversed with."

His formal tone almost makes me laugh. I've never once heard the man, who looks to be no older than forty, sound anything other than a friend. It doesn't make me feel great that I've lied to a man who's been nothing but welcoming to me, but it was born out of necessity. Now, it all comes crashing down.

"Let me guess, Mabel and Alice made some outlandish claims?"

"I'm not going to confirm one way or the other," he says diplomatically, but the small smirk tells me I'm right.

I sigh. *Fuck*, I don't want to let the ugliness out, especially not in this quiet town that's starting to feel more and more like home.

"That was my old partner, Kellen Woodcroft."

"Partner?"

"U.S. Marshals, primarily working the on the Fugitive Task Force."

His eyebrows shoot up his forehead.

"Woodcroft was just here to update me on a case, but as I told him, I'm no longer a U.S. Marshal. There is nothing to be concerned about, Sheriff."

"Yet he came all this way even though you're, what, retired?" His challenge to me sets my hackles up.

"Not retired, no. Resigned."

I know if I told anyone my reasoning, he would be the best one to do so with, but I can't bring myself to say any of it.

"And then you came to Bluebell Falls to open a coffee shop." He arches an eyebrow.

"Yes."

"So, your partner just came to update you on a case, in which you have no jurisdiction over and no hand in anymore, just for shits and giggles?" A statement, not a question. We're more similar than I care to admit.

Gritting my teeth together, I try to take a deep breath before responding. "Yes."

"Listen, I'm not telling you I need to know this information because if you say there isn't a problem, then I believe your word. However, if your old partner is bringing things to you that could affect the citizens of Bluebell Falls, I'd like to be, at the very least, prepared."

I hear him, but all his concerned tone does is set me on edge. It brings me right back to over a year ago, when I failed one too many times. When I wasn't capable of doing my job and had to resign out of sheer self-preservation.

"Oakley, I promise not to tell a soul. And I don't need to know all the gory details, but at a minimum, I'd like to be informed so I can be here for you if you need anything. Hell, just to talk. The Task Force is no joke, and I know you've probably seen the worst of the worst."

I scrub my hand over my face, knowing the right thing is to fill him in. I doubt any trouble will come to Bluebell Falls because of me, but Woodcroft showing up has me doubting all of it.

"I was the commander on a case, the Tennison Strangler case..."

CHAPTER THREE
WILLOW

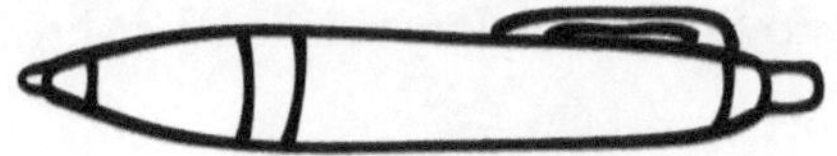

Is eavesdropping wrong? Absolutely. Is my curiosity stronger than my morals right now? Yep.

In my defense, I really did need to pee. When I passed by Oakley's office and the door was open just a sliver, allowing Arlo and his conversation to be heard, I may have leaned against the wall to get the good gossip.

"I was the commander on a case, the Tennison Strangler case, and things went nuclear about a year ago. I don't know if you're familiar with it…"

"I am," Arlo responds.

"The last victim we found was the worst. They were tortured the most. Honestly, death would have been welcomed. And it … it broke me. I had been on the Task Force to track down Alfred Tennison for years, and we never got close. He was always two steps ahead. Victim after victim wears on you, but seeing the aftermath year after year really wore on me. The fact that he leaves his victims alive is the biggest mindfuck out there. The last one, though… Something in my mind cracked. I *couldn't* be on the force anymore. I didn't know how to function properly. This guy had become my life, and I had the realization that I wasn't good enough to catch him. And if I wasn't good enough to catch him, then there was no point in staying on the job. So, I left. Woodcroft came to tell me they had a lead—the first since I moved away, I believe—but I sent him on his way. He won't be back, and my past will stay away with him."

A gasp works its way up my throat, and I slap my hand over it.

I never would have guessed he had a connection to the Tennison Strangler. When he moved here, it was random, yes, but he told us he was some big chef from New York and wanted a quieter life. No one questioned his background. Small-town people take a minute to warm up to people, but when they do? You're in for life, and Oakley's been in for almost as long as he's been here. Everybody loves him.

I don't even hear Arlo's response because my focus turns elsewhere.

My head is screaming with the inklings of a story. *A fucking story!* Plot lines bounce around my head, characters making themselves known, and my fingers itch to start typing it all up.

I speed-walk back to my table before I get caught and open my laptop to start writing. I create a bible of sorts, plugging in characters, settings, and basic plot points. I make sure every little detail floating around in my head is documented, hoping it all adds up to a book.

The next time I look up, the sun is setting and I look around in a panic. Grind Time is completely empty, except for Oakley sitting at a table in the corner. I realize that he's usually closed up shop by now.

"Oh shit. I'm so sorry, Oakley!" I call over to him and start packing up my things frantically. I drop my pen three times before I calm down enough to pick it up and throw it in my backpack.

"I didn't want to interrupt the flow you had going. It's no problem, Willow." The way my name rolls off of his tongue makes my skin prickle.

"You totally should have interrupted me! I'm sure you have better things to do than sit here and wait on me to come back to the real world."

My family is used to this side of me, the zoning out and losing track of time. Most of the time, I'm doing it in the comfort of my own home, so it's not a problem.

"Nah, it was no trouble. I wouldn't want to pull you from such important work." His small smile—God, his smile, however small—makes my fingers tingle with the need to touch those plump lips. So damn useless on a man while I'm over here with thin lips that look like shit with lipstick on.

His words register in my very distracted head, and I snort out a laugh. "Important work, sure."

Writing may be my passion, but I'm under no illusion that I'm making a difference in the world. I may have some die-hard readers who make me feel like I'm changing the world, but I write for me. Because I have to get these stories out of my head and throw them into the world.

He gives me a hard stare, like he wants to make a rebuttal, but chooses to keep quiet instead.

"Can I help you clean up?" I offer instead of pushing him to tell me what he's thinking. He's had a hard day from what my eavesdropping heard, so if I can help at all, I will.

"It's already done. Thank you, though. I just need to wipe down your table." He moves to the counter and grabs a rag before heading my way.

His imposing height should be intimidating, along with his bulky frame, but somehow, it feels like more of a comfort to me.

He quickly wipes down my table as I swing my bag up to my shoulder. Tossing the rag in the sink by the espresso machine, he snags the handles of my backpack before I get it settled. Like a giant, muscled teddy bear. *Jesus… did my vagina decide to take over my life today?* This is why I don't come here often.

"It's getting late. Would it be okay if I walk you home to make sure you get there safely?"

I'm about to tell him this is Bluebell Falls and I'm the scary writer of the town, so no one will mess with me, but then I remember the conversation with Arlo. He's ex-law enforcement, so it's in his nature to be overly protective. Will it be extremely distracting and turn my thoughts to him instead of the book I should be writing? Yes. But a little eye candy never hurt anyone, right?

I could use this as research for my main male character. They have similar features, after all. And now that I think about it, that was probably subconscious. Having Oakley on the brain is clearly having an effect on this story, but why not run with it? It's not like he reads them, and even if he does, he won't put two and two together, will he?

"Willow?"

My head jerks up at hearing my name, and I see Oakley with his eyebrows furrowed in concern.

"I'm sorry, what?" That's the downside of being a writer who doesn't get out much—I'm always in my head and rarely realize it.

"Can I walk you home?"

That's right. What a turn my thoughts took on that one.

"Yeah, that'd be perfect. Thanks." I see my bag in his hand and take a peek at my hands, remembering he took it while I was distracted by my overly hungry libido.

God, my focus is all over the place. Being so far behind on this book has turned me into an airhead. But the smile that spreads over his face is well worth all the overthinking.

He leads me to the front door, shutting and locking it behind me before walking in the direction of my small home. I've never really seen him outside of Grind Time, but I'm not shocked to find he knows where I live. Knowing his real background now, it makes sense that he knows more about this town than he lets on.

The late spring air is already warming up for a hot Texas summer, but at least for now, it's not unbearable.

"Thank you for letting me stay and work, even when you were closed up," I tell him when we're almost to my house.

"No problem. It's not like I have anything going on. If it meant you got done what you needed to, then I made the right decision."

I think I can physically feel my ovaries melting. Such a simple statement, and maybe it says more about my lack of experience with men than anything, but his words have an impact on me.

I stop in front of my house on the sidewalk and hold my hand out. "Well, thank you again, and for walking me home."

His eyes flicker back and forth between mine, like he wants to say something more but decides against it. Removing the backpack off his shoulder, he gently hands it to me and then waits.

"Umm, I'm good from here." I'm confused by what I'm supposed to do right now.

"Just want to make sure you get inside okay. Then I'll head back," he says as he shoves his hands in his pockets.

"Oh, sure! That makes sense." I slap my hand on my forehead and can feel my cheeks heat in embarrassment. I'm so fucking bad at interacting with men that aren't my brothers. Lennox and Ledger definitely don't count.

Skittering to my front door, it takes me three times to get the key in my lock before my door finally opens. I throw a wave over my shoulder before slamming the door and leaning back on it.

Holy trainwreck, Will. Yes, Oakley is hot as hell. Yes, he may have sparked some inspiration for my new book, but he was just being a gentleman. None of this means he's into me, so I need to chill the hell out.

Besides, with this deadline looming large, I don't have time to worry about what Oakley thinks of me.

I head back to my desk and get myself set up to work until I can't keep my eyes open.

I wake up with a start, the drool pooling on my desk making my cheek stick to the surface.

Gross.

I look around to get my bearings and realize I fell asleep after a late night of trying to plot. The buzzing of my phone starts up again, and I realize that's what woke me up.

Rina Calling

"Hey, what's up?" I clear my throat after I realize how groggy I sound.

"Are you just now waking up? It's noon," she says.

I pull my phone away from my ear to confirm she is, indeed, correct. "Shit. I don't know how late I stayed up, but I fell asleep trying to write this damn book."

"Still no luck?" Her sympathetic tone grates on my already frayed nerves about this project.

"I've got a direction." My sharp tone makes me instantly feel guilty. "Sorry, I need more sleep. Or a gallon of coffee." I sigh.

"No worries. I was just calling to see if you wanted to head to Rosedale to get a change of scenery." Rina's hard, outer shell is something she's never aimed my way. She's my best friend in every way conceivable, not just my older sister. She stepped up a lot when our parents died in a car crash when I was still in high school. She helped our oldest brother, Ledger, who became Lennox and my guardian while we finished school, and we both wouldn't be here without the two of them. But Rina and I have always been close.

"Wish I could, but I need to work on this. It feels like I'm right on the cusp of a breakthrough, so I want to stay the course and hope I make a break in it today."

"Sounds good, Will. I'll be back in a few hours, so if you need a breather, let me know."

"I will. Love you."

"Love you too."

I put the phone down and stare at my black computer screen. I need coffee, but after last night, I need to steer clear of Oakley for a while. He's a great inspiration but way too damn distracting for my deadline.

Coffee at home it is.

I brew a whole pot and pour it into the biggest mug I have before I sit back down at my desk and go over everything I did last night.

Five hours later, and I haven't added shit to my outline. I realize the only time I was productive was at Grind Time yesterday, and I don't have time to be choosy about where inspiration is hitting.

Thumping my head onto my desk, I try to come up with any solution that doesn't involve being around Oakley so much. My underused libido can't handle it, and I need to focus. It may be a self-implemented deadline, but I already announced it to my readers. There is one thing I promised myself I would do when I started this career, and that is delivering what I promise to my readers at all costs, but I'm dangerously close to going back on that promise.

I'll just have to ignore the sexy ex-Marshal.

Totally doable.

CHAPTER FOUR
OAKLEY

Willow has been coming by Grind Time every morning and staying until I close up shop for a week and a half.

It's wreaking havoc on my already-frayed mind, thanks to Woodcroft showing up and having to tell the sheriff who I really am.

The day after he showed up, she didn't come in, and I honestly can't tell you if I was more relieved or annoyed by that. Then, she showed up the next day and just kept plopping her sexy ass in the same chair right when we opened.

Now, it's not just that she lights up the room, it's the way her brown hair falls in her face when she's concentrating and she blows it off with a puff of her breath. It's the way she frantically types when she's onto something—you can see the excitement in her movements. It's the way her blue eyes zone out, not really focusing on anything, but it gives me a chance to study them from behind the counter. To see the flecks of gold that catch the light every so often.

Fuck. I need to get a grip.

My life consists of running the coffee shop and then working out until I can barely walk. It's the only way I can get some sleep every night. Woodcroft showing up has brought the nightmares back, just when I was going weeks without one. The fact is, I can only look at Willow, nothing more. I'm in no place mentally to even entertain the idea of something more.

But damn, do I wish I could.

It's not only her appearance either. Her brain is equally fascinating. When I found out she was an author, not too long after I moved to Bluebell Falls, I decided to check out some of her books. Now I own and have read them all. She's incredibly gifted, and there are days I just want to pick her brain. To see how she comes up with her storylines and how she keeps her light when she writes such dark things.

I could use a little of that.

But it's not in the cards for me. I came to terms with that a few years into my Marshal career. The realization that my job was extremely dangerous made me stop dating entirely, and I've never regretted my decision.

Until Willow.

I was able to keep my want pushed down because she rarely came in here. But the last week and a half? It's hard to relegate her to anything other than charming.

Where the fuck is all this poetic nonsense coming from?

Scrubbing my hand over my face, I turn away from the woman currently taking over my thoughts.

I don't know what changed in the last week and a half to prompt her to be here every single day, but my paranoid brain thinks it has something to do with Woodcroft's visit. The timing is too fucking suspicious.

God, I thought I was past the hyper-paranoia. In the course of less than two weeks, my nightmares have resurfaced with a vengeance, and I'm obsessively looking at every single person I can get a visual on.

It's fucking exhausting.

"You okay?" I hear Brittany ask.

"Great. You can head home now that the rush is over," I say automatically.

"You know, I can just stay here until we close and you can take the afternoon off." She's offered more times than I can count, but I'll never agree to it. What the fuck would I do anyway?

"I know. Thanks, Brittany. I'm good today, though."

She holds eye contact for a second—possibly trying to change my decision by hypnosis; who's to say—before shaking her head and undoing her apron.

"You're stubborn as hell," she mutters under her breath. I barely hold in the bark of laughter. She's never outright called me on my shit, but maybe she's finally warming up to me.

"See you tomorrow, Brittany," I call to her as she walks to the front door.

Willow's head pops up from her laptop when she hears me call out, and my attention is pulled back to her.

I hold up a mug, asking without words if she'd like another latte.

She nods then tucks her head back down behind the lid of her laptop, and I get started on her new latte. I've been working on the fancy shit at the end with the foam to make it pretty for her, but I still suck at that. My expertise lies in the food I serve here, not necessarily the coffee. But they didn't have a coffee shop, so it felt like a natural progression for the town. It's not like making basic coffee is difficult to learn, and Brittany has added some different seasonal shit that I've run with.

I don't know. I'm probably overthinking the whole latte art shit because Willow fucks with my head. And my need to impress her just irritates me more.

Being the stubborn ass I am, I decide this one won't have my sorry attempt at artistry. I also grab one of the homemade pop tarts she loves so much and take them over to her.

I place them on the table and silently back away.

It takes her twenty minutes to realize I dropped off sustenance for her and when she finally sees it, her entire face lights up like the North star. Heart pounding in my chest, I know I'm in trouble with her. When she makes eye contact with me before taking a bite of the pastry and then licking her lips? Well, I'm thinking about how that gorgeous mouth of hers could really do some damage—mainly, to my dick that's trying to rip a hole in my jeans. Thank God for the counter covering the obscene tent I'm sporting. Can't have the people of Bluebell Falls getting their hands on that kind of gossip.

I just need to get through the rest of the day, then I can wear my ass out and jerk off in the shower later.

The last two hours before I closed up shop were fucking hell. Willow's little moans of pleasure while eating what I've baked and drinking the latte I made for her almost did me in. The good news is that my apartment is upstairs, so I can immediately strip out of my clothes to stroke my cock. I can't even wait until after my workout, that's how much I'm worked up from that woman.

Collapsing onto my bed as I grip my dick, I think about what she would look like with her hair all wild from my hands. Her cheeks flush with lust, not embarrassment this time. *God, she looks good like that.* My strokes get a little faster as I conjure up the image. I don't even know where I would start with her if I got the chance. I know kissing her would be top of the list, though. Her rosy pink lips draw my eye every single time she talks, and I wonder what other parts of her body are that color.

That's all it takes.

Pathetic.

Cum pools on my abs as I throw my head back with a sigh. I need to stop doing this. There's nothing between us—there never can be anything between us—so there's no use in daydreaming. Hell, she doesn't even know who I am ... not really.

And that thought is depressing as hell.

Climbing off my bed, I rinse off in a quick shower before putting on my trail clothes. The place my head is at makes me feel like a long-ass run on the trails in the national park that borders our town is the best course of action. Sam Houston National Park is one of the biggest perks of moving here. Getting lost in nature has saved my overly depressed and anxious brain more times than I count.

Walking out my front door, I lock up before heading east to the park. I know this is a small town and they're supposed to be ultra-safe, but old habits die hard, and I've seen way too much fucked-up shit to ever chance it.

My mind starts to swirl between images of Willow over the past week and Woodcroft showing up. He left town the same day we spoke, and I was selfishly thankful for that. It was painful as hell to see him after I got over the initial panic. I left that life knowing I would never see my best friend again. Never go to a bar and shoot the shit to decompress after a fucked-up case. Never go to a barbecue at his house after we caught the shitbag we were after. I never really stopped to question my decision until he showed up in Bluebell Falls.

I walked away from a life I had worked my ass off for. Thirty-seven years of the only life I knew, given up because of one man. Shit, I can't even call him a man; he's a piece of demented shit that doesn't deserve to see the light of day.

But I couldn't catch him.

My only job was to catch the worst of the worst, and I was damn good at it ... until Alfred Tennison. He's made me question everything about myself. Everything I thought I was made for suddenly felt like a mountain too tall to climb. I was losing oxygen, unable to breathe, and I knew I needed a change to survive.

Can I even call life in Bluebell Falls surviving?

My pace picks up when I hit my favorite trail, the existential questions pounding in my head causing my anxiety to skyrocket.

I never used to be this way. I was clutch under pressure, never second-guessing my decisions, and always confident.

Now? In the last year, I haven't gone longer than two weeks without a panic attack of varying degrees. It's exhausting, and it makes me feel weak. I fucking hate it.

The challenging hill I'm climbing doesn't even phase me. A perk of constantly being caught up in my head means I'm in the best physical shape of my life.

I check my watch and realize I've been hiking for just about two hours, and I'm on the final stretch that will send me back to town.

I wish this had cleared my head, but if anything, today's given me too much time to think about everything in my life. I'm so lost in the never-ending doomsday that is my mind, I don't realize there's another person on the trail until they're right next to me.

Another reason I quit. I've lost my edge.

"Hey, Oakley, how are you doing today?" Lennox's voice pierces through my self-loathing, startling me. Although, it makes sense since he is a park ranger.

"Hey, man. It's going."

He matches my pace, sending my hackles up. I'm not really in the headspace for small talk, but it looks like I don't have a choice at the moment.

"I've noticed you on this trail a lot, but if you ever want some new paths, let me know. There are a couple that are a real workout." He smirks, sending a subtle challenge my way.

Fucker.

"A real workout," I deadpan.

"Yeah, I mean, how do you think I look so good all the time?" He chuckles, gesturing to his flexing bicep. We've crossed paths a few times but never really talked before this.

I have no doubt he's in great shape, but I also see how often he comes into Grind Time, eating his weight in pastries and paninis.

"Alright. I'll bite. Next week? Name the day, and I'll be there."

"Hell yeah! I'll stop by and let you know when my schedule calms down a little."

"Sounds good, man. I'm going to head home. Gotta be up early to make all the pastries you demolish on a regular basis."

"They're good as hell. I'm not apologizing for keeping you in business."

Laughter burst out of me unexpectedly. Who knew Lennox was funny as hell, but maybe immersing myself in the small-town life will help with all the insecurities that have slowly been demoralizing me. That was the goal in moving here. Might as well follow through on it.

"So, I'll see you in the morning then?" I ask.

"Bright and early." He claps a hand on my back before heading in the opposite direction.

Maybe I just need to put the Task Force fully behind me and embrace this life I was so keen on creating a year ago.

CHAPTER FIVE
WILLOW

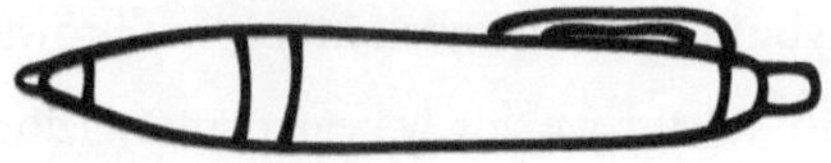

I t's been almost two weeks.

And I'm stuck. Again.

I had some good momentum—finished half of my outline—and now I'm sitting here in my usual seat at Grind Time, staring into the abyss.

Fuck. This book is going to be the downfall of my entire career. Ten years of working my ass off, and it's about to collapse because I can't get a handle on this fucking book.

A shadow interrupts my spiraling thoughts, causing me to blink and refocus. My eyes trail up the imposing man—in a forest green Henley today—up to his brown eyes staring at me with concern.

"Are you okay, Willow?" Oakley asks softly.

"Umm, yeah. Perfect. Why do you ask?"

"Because I've been closed up for twenty minutes and you didn't notice."

"Oh shit. I'm so sorry! Again!" I frantically start gathering all my things, irritated at myself that this has happened twice. It's not his responsibility to stay open because of me.

"Hey, hey, it's okay. I didn't mean you had to leave, but you were staring at the wall, so it didn't seem like you were in a writing zone."

"Yeah, definitely not in a writing zone." I let out a self-deprecating laugh.

"You can stay. I'm not trying to force you out." He rubs his hand on the back of his neck as a red tinge creeps up his cheeks.

Well, he's as fucking adorable as he is hot.

"It's okay, really. I'm not making much progress, so going home is probably the best option. I'm sorry you couldn't close on time because of me. Next time, just kick me out." I'm dead serious too. My writing is not more important than his time, and I never want to take advantage of his hospitality.

"Yeah, I'm not going to do that," he says with the shake of his head. He reaches behind him to the counter and grabs a paper bag, dropping it on my table while I finish throwing all my shit in my bag.

"What's this?" I stand up and push my chair in.

"Lunch. Dinner. A meal, since you haven't really eaten since eight this morning." His gruff tone tells me he's a little uncomfortable, and I have to bite my lip to not smile at that.

He's keeping track of me.

"That's very thoughtful. Thanks, Oakley," I tell him instead of teasing him since I can already see how uneasy he is.

He bows his head with a grunt, and I almost laugh.

He would be so much fun to mess with, but he's feeding me, so I'll be nice. Plus, I like this shy version of him.

"I'll see you later. Have a great rest of your day, and thanks for letting me basically live here lately." I smile at him before heaving my backpack over my shoulder and snagging the bag that I just know will have an Italian panini in it.

"See you later, Willow," he says faintly as I walk out the front door.

I woke up this morning groggy and angry at myself. Last night was pure torture. After getting home from Grind Time, I demolished the panini Oakley packed up for me and saved the second one he sent for dinner. I stared at my computer for hours and didn't get anywhere.

I was so convinced that the little burst of inspiration at learning a little about Oakley's past would sustain me for the entirety of this book, but I was so fucking wrong. I'm even second-guessing what little I have done for the outline.

I made a decision last night that caused me to toss and turn all night long, making me a grumpy asshole this morning.

I need to talk to Oakley about his past life. I need insight into the cases he worked on and how he felt during them. The inspiration for this book, after all, is him. A scorned special agent, working the case of a lifetime, full of politics and twists.

God, even summarizing it makes it sounds fucking pathetic. I have no real plan to move forward, and time is ticking away.

So that leaves me with one option: work up the courage to tell Oakley I overheard things he doesn't want people to know, hope he forgives me, and then beg to pick his brain.

What could go wrong?

Everything.

Everything could go wrong and I could turn Oakley into an enemy, forever relegating me to Sal's Diner for food, and never having another perfect panini and latte again.

Shit, that would suck ass.

But it's the risk of alienating Oakley or failing my readers, and that's not much of a decision for me. My livelihood is what I need to be focusing on.

Packing up all my gear yet again, I give myself the day to figure out how to talk to Oakley about this. I'll wait until closing time before broaching the subject because I know he doesn't want word about who he really is getting out.

Heading to Grind Time is the usual affair it always is. I wave to Mabel, Alice, and Jim, who are standing outside of the grocery store and look like they're up to no good. And a couple of minutes later, I'm walking into the coffee shop.

I head over to my usual spot, and see a muffin and a latte already sitting there. I look around to see who could have taken my spot. When I catch Oakley's eye, he nods to the table then looks back at me, letting me know he left it for me.

My heart pounds in my chest at the gesture. He keeps taking care of me in the background, and it feels strange. New, and something I'm not used to, so my awkwardness doesn't let me just accept it. I walk up to the counter, backpack still on.

"What do I owe you?" My sharp tone is a reflection of how uncomfortable I am and not because of the kind gesture I'm reacting poorly to. It's not his fault I don't know how to handle this level of attention from a man.

"On the house," he counters, not caving to me at all.

And it does something to me. Him standing up to my attitude that's all over the place is attractive. My mind envisions what he would be like in the bedroom. Would we fight for control? He could physically overpower me, and I would be A-okay with that. *Holy shit. Focus, Will.*

I have to turn away, skittering back to my table, otherwise I'm going to blurt out a whole lot of words that would make both of us uncomfortable.

When I sit down, I realize that my abrupt departure because I was in my head was rude.

"Thanks, Oakley!" I call out and see him smirk at my chaotic actions.

Deciding I need to refocus my brain, I take my time eating my muffin and drinking my first latte of the day, before turning back to my book.

About halfway through the day, I cling on to a string of thought about making my main character fall in love but using the woman against him somehow. I have no idea how to make it all work, but the thought won't leave me.

My books don't have a shortage of sex in them, but it's never the primary focus. They are, at their heart, thrillers. For some reason, creating a relationship within this book feels like an important part of the story, sex included. *Huh, maybe it's a romance?* I have no fucking clue right now, and that's scary. Only having a very basic premise for this book when I'm down to a month to write feels insurmountable. And I still need to work myself up to talk to Oakley about his former job.

"Hey, Willow, we're closing up soon. You need anything else?" Brittany asks as I am startled at her voice.

"Nope, I'm good. I do need to talk to Oakley, though, so I can help you close up." It's honestly the least I can do with how much space I'm taking up here daily.

"Oh, no—"

"I insist," I interrupt her refusal as I take the rag from her and move to the table beside me.

Together, we clean the small dining room, Oakley nowhere to be seen.

"Well, I'm going to head out, but I'll tell Oakley you're waiting for him," Brittany says before heading back to the office.

Awkwardly rocking on my heels as I wait in the empty coffee shop, I'm second-guessing this whole thing. I don't know how Oakley is going to react when I tell him what I overheard. He's taken a lot of care to hide his past, and I'm about to blow it wide open. Not that I would tell anyone else in town, but even one person knowing might cause him to freak out.

I figure this could go one of two ways. He'll either calmly hear me out before losing his shit, or go in full-on panic mode and kick me out for good. No more lattes with foam on top he's been trying really hard to make pretty. No more delicious paninis. *Fuck, if this book wasn't so fucking important, I wouldn't be jeopardizing my access to the best food in town.* What an irrational thought. Sometimes, even I amaze myself.

Before I can do any more back and forth in my head, Oakley's voice sounds from behind me.

"Brittany said you needed to talk to me. Is everything okay?" The genuine worry in his voice makes me feel like shit for what I'm about to tell him.

"You should probably lock up and make sure no one accidentally comes in." I know it sounds cryptic, but I know without a doubt he doesn't want this getting out to anyone. This is just extra security.

"Umm, okay." He moves to comply and then takes a seat next to my usual spot.

I join him and start wringing my hands together, unsure of how to approach this. I'm scared of his response. Scared I'll lose this very precarious relationship we've been working on over the last month or so.

"Willow, you're freaking me out. Is everything okay? Are you in trouble?" Gah, those protective instincts of his never stop working.

"Everything's fine. Well, I hope they stay that way after I tell you what I'm about to tell you," I ramble.

"Will. What. Is. Wrong?" he says through clenched teeth.

Will. That's the first time he's ever used my nickname. Focus.

"I overheard you talking to Arlo after that guy came in here, and I know you're an ex-Marshal and worked on the Tennison Strangler case, and I desperately need to pick your brain for this book, and I promise to not tell a single soul anything. I haven't told anyone, and I'm on a tight-as-hell deadline and I'm stressed out, but I think you could help me." I say it all in one breath, looking down at the table the entire time.

When he doesn't respond, I peek up through my lashes and see his jaw clenched so tight I worry about his dental health.

I want to say more, but I think the best course of action is to let what I said sink in before I say anything else. I don't want to make it worse than it already is. Lord knows, I have the tact of a toddler right now.

My mind is running through every possible scenario, and they start to look worse and worse for me.

I open my mouth to say something that could help my cause here but close it just as fast, because I don't think there's anything I could come up with to ease this situation.

I go back to staring at the table as I see Oakley in my periphery, tapping his index finger on the back of his other hand. The beat he taps gets faster, and I think I'm done for.

No more delicious coffee. No more perfectly grilled sandwiches. And no more book.

Fuck. I have no other option. This feels like the only way to get out of my writer's block, and I just fucked up the entire thing.

"You didn't tell anyone?" Oakley's voice is so quiet I barely hear him.

"*No!* No, no one," I say quickly.

His stare drills through mine, and I hold it. If there is a chance he'll talk to me about his past, I need to be committed to doing anything.

"What did you hear exactly?"

CHAPTER SIX
OAKLEY

The relief is evident in her body. Her huge exhale does nothing to settle my pounding heart. If I thought my anxiety was high before, hearing her say she knows anything about my past sends me nearly to the ground, curled up in a ball in a cold sweat.

"I was going to the bathroom when you and Arlo were talking. The door wasn't shut all the way, and I stopped to listen. I know, it was so, so wrong, and I'm sorry. But it finally sparked some inspiration for this book I've been so blocked about. And I know it's not a reason to betray you, but that's my only excuse. I only know what you and Arlo talked about, just about what your past job was and the Tennison Strangler case. Then I booked it back to my table to start planning." She says it all so fast, it's hard to keep up with her.

But what I focus on is that she knows my past. She knows I'm a fuck-up who couldn't catch one of the worst criminals in our history.

And I panic.

"Get out."

"Oak—"

"Get out!" I yell.

The color drains from her face, and for a split second I feel like the biggest asshole, but I can't do anything to stop the freight train that is my fear. I need her out of here before I do something I can't take back.

"I'm so sorry, Oakley," she whispers before unlocking the front door and quickly departing.

I slump against the chair, feeling the weight of my past hitting me like an anvil.

What does this mean now that Willow knows my deep secret? Do I need to move again? Can I still keep my life in Bluebell Falls without word getting out? She said she didn't tell anyone, and I believe her because if she had, everyone would be at my door asking questions.

Fuck, I hate this so much. Every fear I've held on to for so long is rushing to the surface, and I feel like I'm about to break.

I stumble up the stairs to my apartment, feeling the beginnings of a full-blown panic attack in my lungs. Barely getting the door open, I slam it shut before dropping to my knees, clutching my chest. Everything feels tight, like I can't breathe, can't pull in enough air to function. My shirt sticks to my chest from the sweat, and I clumsily try to get it off, struggling with every movement.

I finally rip it off my body, using the momentum to get my jeans off too. Everything feels too constricting, and I need any relief I can get. Once I'm finally in just my boxer briefs, I lie flat on my back on the floor.

Using some of the tools my therapist gave me, I breathe in to the count of ten, and out to the same. I repeat this several times before my chest starts to loosen up enough for me to think clearly.

I haven't had a panic attack this bad since I decided to quit the Task Force. As much as I thought I was moving past all this shit, Willow's words prove I'm not even remotely in a better place than I was a year ago. And it fucking sucks to realize.

Before I could actually walk away from the Marshals, they set me up with a therapist to see if we could figure out what was going on. I will say, it helped, and I thought that I had made a clear decision—the right decision.

And now that my peace has been interrupted, I feel like I'm right back to the day I decided I needed out.

A year ago, I was standing at a crime scene. This wasn't your average crime scene; it was apparent when we showed up that it was Alfred Tennison's work. The poor man sitting in the ambulance was proof enough. He had shallow cuts on every appendage—not enough to do real damage, but enough to make a person miserable. You could see the rope burn around his neck from the repeated strangling cutting his air off until he almost passed out. But the worst of it was the branding. Alfred Tennison never killed anyone, but he took every single victim to the brink and brought them back, time and time again. And when he was finally done with them, he would brand them with his calling card—a partial quote from Alfred Lord Tennyson: *'Tis better to have loved and lost.* You can't unsee any of it, and I can only imagine what it would be like to live with the symbol of your every nightmare on your body for the rest of your life.

The thought still sends a shiver down my spine.

I shakily stand up, trying to get my bearings before heading to the shower. I need to rinse off the reminder of a past life. Stripping off my boxer briefs, I walk under the freezing spray. It feels like a cleanse of sorts, clearing my head of the past and bringing it back to the present.

Willow, *fuck.*

I wonder what she thinks of me, knowing how I failed so many people. Knowing I couldn't catch him, knowing I failed at the most basic level of what I was supposed to be good at.

And then I yelled at her.

I lean against the tile in the shower and close my eyes. *I yelled at Willow.* How fucking insecure do I have to be to take it out on her? Deep down, I know I took it out on her because I was scared. I want her to see me in this perfect light, and that's gone now.

But it's been gone for almost two weeks, and she doesn't look at you any differently.

God, I wish I could believe that.

Self-loathing is a weird thing. Reality can be right in front of you, but you can't see a damn thing, too lost in the negative with no way out.

I turn the shower off—angry with myself—climb out of the shower, and dry off before collapsing on my bed.

This is not how I pictured the day going. I know I should get my ass up, and sweat the doubt and fear in my head away, but I can't seem to get myself to move.

All I can see now is Willow's face when I yelled at her.

She's the last person I'd ever want to hurt, and yet I did so with hardly any effort.

This is probably a sign I need to call my therapist and start back up with him. I'm clearly not as well-adjusted as I thought I was.

This brings my thoughts to what Willow asked of me. I've been so caught up in my insecurities that I haven't actually thought about it.

She said that she got a burst of inspiration after she eavesdropped. That could be a good thing, right?

Then I remember the reason this whole conversation started was her thinking I could help her with her book.

Could I help her? I know she would probably want to pick my brain about all the cases I worked on, not just the Tennison Strangler. If I could steer her away from that case, I think that maybe I could do it. I'd do a lot if it meant helping Willow.

Damnit, am I actually considering this?

My eyes shift around the bare walls of my bedroom. If I have a chance to help, shouldn't I do that? It's always been in my nature to help when needed, and somehow I've lost that. Tennison took it away, along with my faith in humanity.

But maybe this is my chance to change. Helping Willow could help me move past some of my hang-ups. And if anyone can make me feel comfortable talking about shit I'd rather keep buried, it'd be her.

My mind runs through all the possibilities, but the only thing I keep coming back to is the fact that helping Willow would be worth it.

Decision made, I hoist my weary body up from my bed, completely unaware of what time it is.

All I know is that I need to talk to her. I need to make sure she's okay and apologize for my rash behavior, and explain a little of why I reacted that way.

I'll bring her dinner.

The idea sticks and I get dressed quickly, throwing on an old flannel and jeans before heading downstairs to Grind Time's kitchen to make her favorite panini. I load it into a bag with some chips and extra pickles before heading out.

I take a brief look at my watch and realize my mental breakdown lasted for hours, and it's nearing ten o'clock at night. But I know I need to do this now, or I'll never agree to help her. I'll overthink more than I already have and cower away in my apartment, avoiding her as much as possible.

And strangely, I don't want to avoid her. She's been a constant light for weeks, and I don't want that to disappear.

It takes me no time at all to reach her house. I only hesitate a moment before knocking on her door.

When she opens up the door, an oversized sweatshirt hangs off her shoulders and lounge shorts barely cover her ass.

"Oakley?"

"James. My first name is James, and I'd like to apologize and talk. I brought food." I quickly hold up the paper bag.

Her eyes dart between mine and the bag before she holds the door open and steps to the side to let me inside.

My body sags with relief, and I know this is the right decision. No matter how hard it is for me to work through.

CHAPTER SEVEN
WILLOW

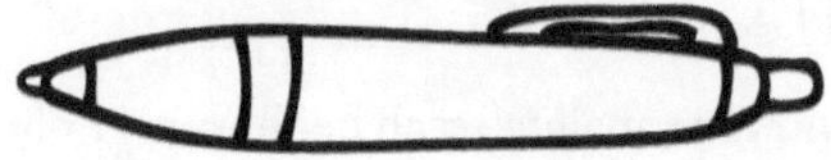

*J*ames.

I always thought Oakley was his first name and he's never told us any different, but now that I've learned the truth, I love it even more. It somehow suits him better than Oakley does.

I eyeball the paper bag one more time before going to sit at my small, dining room table, letting Oakley—*James*—follow me at his own pace. I'm not really sure how this is going to go.

When I came home, I knew I fucked it all up. Blindsiding him like that was not my intention, but I see where my mistake was. I don't know how connected he is to the case, how he feels about it, and my assumption that he would just be okay to talk about it was self-centered. I was thinking of my own gain and not what it would potentially bring up for him. I've written enough shit dealing with the psyche of a person to know there are many facets, and it's not a cut-and-dry thing. Especially if he was lead on the case. I can only imagine there is a reason he's here and not chasing down the Tennison Strangler.

"I'm sorry," he says again softly.

"Nothing to apologize for," I offer, and I mean it.

He slides the sandwich over, and I waste no time tearing the bag open and seeing the chicken pesto panini he made for me. It's my second favorite and my stomach lets out a loud growl, expressing its hunger. I may have eaten the one he sent home with me a few hours ago, but stress makes me hungry.

"Eat, please, while I explain." I shove a bite in my mouth as he continues. "You … surprised me. I think that's about the last thing I expected you to talk to me about, and I was caught off guard. I've done a lot to keep that time in my life hidden. It's not something I like to dwell on." He takes a deep breath, and I take another bite to keep the focus off of him. I don't want him to stop talking.

"The last victim that I saw was the worst, and it broke me in a way I never thought would happen. I've run the whole gambit: therapists, ignoring the problem … you name it—I've done it. But it all came back to the fact that I couldn't do my job anymore. I had failed for years to catch Tennison, and each new victim was like a gunshot to the gut. But that last one…" He visibly gulps, and I put my sandwich down, putting a hand on his arm.

"You don't need to explain. I understand, and you don't need to tell me all of this." Do I want to know about the actual case? Hell yes. But I don't need to know about how the case has affected him if it puts him in a bad headspace. And if talking about the case in general does that, then I'll figure something else out because I can't put him in that position.

It may mean pushing my book back, but I'm human and it's not the end of the world, as much as I despise doing it. That's a hang-up I would need to get over.

"The last one was the worst of all. There were things we kept out of the media because it was so horrific," he continues, ignoring my words. Hell, this may be cathartic for him, so I'm letting him lead. "Two weeks after we found the victim, I found out he killed himself. Whatever Tennison physically did didn't kill him, but whatever Tennison said affected him so much he didn't want to live anymore."

Fuck. No wonder he left. I've kept up with the case, but what I see is what the media releases. This is actual insight into the case, the people working the case where Alfred Tennison keeps kidnapping people and then releasing them forever changed. People always think about the victims in these cases, but no one ever thinks about the people who work the case. The people who see the damage day in and day out. The failure they feel when another victim is found, knowing they haven't been able to stop it from happening.

My heart breaks for him and everything he's been through.

Maybe I should scrap this whole idea. It's selfish to ask him to do this for me. It's selfish to ask him questions about protocols or how a murderer would act, when he's just trying to live his life away from all of that.

"I'm sorry," I murmur. I don't know what to say to make any of this better. I suspect nothing will ever make him feel better about any of it. He carries the weight of it all every day, and his no-nonsense personality suddenly makes all the more sense with this new information.

"You have nothing to be sorry about. I just never expected my two lives to meet if that makes sense. Woodcroft kind of fucked things." He lets out a self-deprecating chuckle. "Because not only does Sheriff know, but now you as well."

"I promise I won't tell anyone," I quickly tell him.

"I know. If you were going to, you would have already."

We both sit silently. I'm lost in thoughts about how to make this arrangement work without causing him a full-on mental breakdown.

He's probably wondering why he came here in the first place and thinking this is all a terrible idea.

"I think I'm going to change the premise of the book," I blurt out, the thought of causing him any pain making me second-guess everything.

"So, tell me about this book," he says at the same time.

I giggle awkwardly, not knowing how to act. He leans back in his chair, shoving the sleeves of his flannel up his tattooed forearm, and I have no brain power. It's like all productive thoughts flee my head because his delicious forearms have distracted me.

"Don't change the book, Will. I'm fine, I promise. Tell me what you're working on." His words take a minute to register.

"So, I really only have a half of an outline, and I'm not even sure if I'm keeping it. But so far, I have a CIA agent as the main character, and he's forced to work with ... someone not in the field." I cringe at the lack of information. "The main thing I've come up with is the CIA agent is the killer," I say bluntly. Hearing the premise and just how little of the main plot I have makes my cheeks heat, and I feel embarrassed at how lame it all sounds.

I make my living off of this, and I sound like I have no idea what I'm doing. But that's exactly how I feel with this book. It's been so unlike my usual process that I'm not sure how to get back on track. But that's why I'm talking to Oakley, because he sparked the inspiration I was desperate for.

"That's different." He leans in closer, appearing interested.

"Umm, yeah. Maybe that's why I'm struggling with it so much."

"What else do you have?" he asks, excitement in his eyes.

I jolt back, wide-eyed. "That's it," I whisper. My outline consists of how the two characters meet and the details of how the CIA agent kills, but as far as the story is concerned, I have nothing.

"Gotcha. Well, I don't really know the process of writing a book, but you're more than welcome to stay after closing at Grind Time, or we can meet somewhere once it closes, and you can pick my brain about processes and cases."

"Just like that?" I ask.

"Just like that. I'd like to help, Willow. If this helps you, I'm in." He shrugs, but he doesn't realize the amount of relief I feel right now.

Sure, I still have a shit ton of work to do, but I think this will help. *God, I hope it helps.* And his sheer selflessness makes me need for this all to be worth it.

"Okay, then. Let's plan on me being at Grind Time when you close up. I seem to have a clearer head when I'm there for this project." I won't tell him it's only clearer because I'm imagining him doing all sorts of things to me when the coffee shop closes up.

Jesus, I need to focus. This is why my deadline is up my ass and I'm begging Oakley for help.

"Sounds great. I'll see you tomorrow, then." He stands up, wiping his hands on his jeans.

I scramble to follow him, remembering to be polite. "Thank you. For helping me, I mean."

Our eyes lock, and I see so many emotions in his—understanding, fear, and some heat that makes goosebumps pop up on my arms.

"Anytime, Will." With that, he turns around and walks back to Main Street.

It's one in the morning, and I'm wide awake. Not just wide awake but horny as hell.

After Oakley left, it took a while for my head to clear and realize that he said yes to helping me. I felt uneasy the entire conversation, and I am still genuinely shocked he wants to help my introverted ass.

The overthinking began when I first lay down. I was thinking about how to keep all the personal stuff out of it, so it was easier for Oakley, before moving to what kind of details he could give me on other cases he's worked—the closed ones that aren't an open investigation. Would they be super gory? I kind of want to hear all the gross details. I like that kind of stuff. And then my head took a drastic turn, wondering what he looked like in uniform. Did he wear a uniform? Would he roll up his sleeves like he does at Grind Time? Show off the tattoos on his forearm? Where else did he have tattoos, I wonder? Do they have any symbolism to them?

And now, I'm here thinking about stripping him out of his clothes in order to study the intricate artwork on his body while also examining his well-built muscles.

I am a writer; it's only natural that my imagination is top-notch. What it's not helping is my resistance to get off to thoughts of Oakley—James.

I should start calling him James.

Fucking overthinking. Maybe I should just cave and have an orgasm in the hopes it knocks me out.

I watch the ceiling fan create a pattern as it goes around, trying to get my brain to quiet.

It never works. I've tried everything in the book. And usually, I just get up and write when I feel like this, except I have nothing to write. Because I'm stuck, and Oakley is the only one who helps.

What an absolute clusterfuck.

Oakley is hot as sin, though. It's not just the tattoos; the man is just straight muscle. Well over six feet, but he isn't super bulky. It's like he has the practical muscles that blue collar workers have, except he runs a coffee shop. I wonder how he stays in shape.

Does he have a whole setup somewhere that he spends hours in after work? Doing pull-ups, shirtless and all sweaty?

My hand snakes down my soft stomach, under the waistband of my panties. Closing my eyes, I picture walking in on him while he's working out. Leaning against the doorway, just watching his muscles flex with every new exercise. Hell, he wouldn't even need to acknowledge me. I think watching him would do it for me.

Kind of like it's doing it for me now.

I see an imaginary drop of sweat trail down his abs, into his workout shorts, and my fingers circle my clit without my permission. If he wasn't so damn attractive, this wouldn't be an issue.

But because he is, I'm already so fucking close to coming, and I'm just picturing him working out. Jeez, desperate much, Willow?

I pull up in my head the image of him at my door earlier this evening , wearing jeans that clung to every muscle. I'm a little sad I haven't made it a point to remember what his ass looks like, but I imagine it's got a nice roundness to it.

I circle my clit one more time, and that's all it takes. A weak and not at all satisfying orgasm pulses through me, and I sag in disappointment.

I need to call this a one-off because I have too much to get done and a distraction is the last thing I need.

CHAPTER EIGHT
OAKLEY

Things are going well.

And it's making me nervous. Willow's been coming in every day this week and staying when I close up. She says I'm helping her get shit done, but all it feels like is a conversation about my old job. She asks me questions, and I answer them as she types away on her computer a mile a minute. According to her, she's actually writing the story and has moved on from the outline—whatever that means. She told me something about switching up her style and being a pantser for this book, and I'll be honest, I just nodded and smiled because I have no clue what she's talking about.

If it's helping her productivity, I'll take it.

Tonight, I wanted to switch things up a little. We've been sticking to the shop, with me making us quick dinners as she works, but tonight, I wanted to cook her some real food. Earlier this afternoon, I made lasagna during a lull, and now it's just sitting in the refrigerator, waiting to go in the oven.

I keep eyeballing the door, waiting for her to come in. It's already past noon, and I'm getting worried. She usually shows up after the morning rush, but it's going on lunch and she's nowhere to be seen.

It's not like we have a set schedule; it's just been what's naturally working out. But my overprotective instincts are struggling with being easygoing right this second. It's Brittany's day off today, so at least I have the distraction of staying busy.

"You stare any harder, and you'll start drooling." The sheriff's voice startles me.

I open my mouth to say I'm watching for customers, but he just snuck up on me, so I close it just as quickly.

"What can I get you today, Sheriff?"

"You heard from your buddy again?" he asks instead of ordering.

Gritting my teeth, I try to calmly answer him, even if it pisses me off that he's even asking. Woodcroft should have never fucking shown up here. Now, I'll forever be answering questions like this from the sheriff. Not that I blame him—if I was the sheriff, I'd be asking questions too.

"Nope. You want your usual?" I move to the espresso-maker to make his americano.

"Willow's sure been here a lot."

I don't bother looking up at him because I know it would just give him whatever answer he's looking for. He seems to assume things are happening, but it's not really his business.

"How's Rina doing?" I counter. If he wants to play petty games, I've got plenty of ammo. I set his coffee in front of him as he grunts in response. I don't even trying to hide my smirk.

"See you later, Oakley," he mumbles as he walks out the front door, stopping to hold the door for someone walking in. I see Willow and meet Arlo's eyes over her head. The look he's giving me is indecipherable, so I turn my focus to the beauty that just came in.

"Morning!" she says cheerily.

"Afternoon, actually." I can hear the grumpiness in my tone, so I try to calm it down. "Have a good morning?"

"So fucking good! I wrote three full chapters today!"

I listen to her tell me about everything she managed to get done today as I make her latte.

"I finally figured out what the other main character's job is, and it's made everything run so much more smoothly."

"What did you decide?" I ask, sliding her coffee to her.

"She's a coffee shop owner!" She throws her hands to the side like a ta-da moment, and I have to laugh.

"So, is there anything you aren't using me as an inspiration for?" I smirk.

The apples of her cheeks turn that perfect shade of rose that has my cock tightening my jeans.

"U-umm," she stutters.

"I'm kidding, Will. I think it works perfectly. A coffee shop owner hears everything, and if your CIA guy is using her as an informant, it makes perfect sense."

"Yes! Exactly that!" Her excitement lights up the whole damn shop, and it's infectious.

"Have a seat while I make you lunch, and I'll come sit with you if it's still dead in here. You can tell me all about the last three chapters."

She makes her way to her usual table, and I have to physically tear myself away from watching her. She's so full of life, so excited about every little thing, and it makes me equally captivated and jealous.

I keep an eye on her as I make her favorite panini, making sure to add a chocolate chip cookie to the plate as well before heading over to join her.

"Oh my God, you're a lifesaver. I haven't eaten all day; I was so engrossed in writing." She takes a huge bite of her sandwich, and I sit back, covering my mouth with my hand to hide my smile. I don't want to say anything to interrupt her. Instead, I let her fuel up so she can tell me all about her progress.

I take the time to really drink her in. Tight, black leggings cling to her shapely legs, ending with beat-up, leather sandals showing she wears them most days. Trailing my eyes up, I see a threadbare T-shirt hanging off of one shoulder, and just that tease of skin has my cock twitching. Her brown hair is plopped on top of her head, pieces falling out left and right, but it just furthers the dirty direction my mind has taken.

"Okay." She rubs her hands on her leggings. "Thank you. I needed that." I nod, wordlessly urging her to continue. "So, the three chapters went so fucking smooth. It felt fantastic to finally get productive words in. It's all just basic setting stuff, but I've gotten the two characters to meet."

"That's really good, right?" I want to be able to help her more, but so much of this flies over my head. The topic, I know a shit-ton on, but writing? I'm clueless and feel extremely inadequate. I've read every single one of her books, and I know just how phenomenal her brain is, so I'm just trying to keep up.

"So good! Like, Charlie—that's the CIA agent's name—has gone to a new coffee shop around the area, where the 'crimes' are taking place, and Niya is the bakery owner. She hasn't put up with his shit so far, so I love her already." She beams.

"That sounds interesting." And I mean it. It just sounds far from her usual set up, so I'm interested to see where this goes.

"So, I think I'm going to crash here and try to get some more words in, and then pick your brain when you close. That good with you?" She's already pulling out her laptop, eager to get back to her progress.

The front door chimes, and I start to stand up. "I'll let you get back to it, but I was thinking we could head to my apartment after I close up today." *That sounds fucking creepy.* "I made a ton of food for dinner, so I figured you could eat with me," I add awkwardly and cringe. *God, that was almost worse.*

"That sounds great, Oakley, thanks." Her focus is far from me, and I'm just glad for the new customer, even if it is Jim Mathews.

He is the start and the end of the gossip train here. Mabel and Alice have nothing on him, contrary to what they think. He's also Ledger's soon-to-be father-in-law.

"Good afternoon, Oakley. How's the day been?" he asks jovially.

"Not too bad. Just keeping the lovely people of Bluebell Falls caffeinated and fed. You want your usual?" I ask, already knowing the answer.

"Yes, please. And can you throw on a double chocolate cookie? Don't tell the missus—she's trying to get me to eat healthier."

"Absolutely." I slide his medium drip coffee to him and move to grab the cookie, throwing it in a bag for him.

He picks both up, saluting me as he turns right back around, heading out to go bug someone else around town. I sigh in relief that he either chose to ignore that I was just sitting with Willow, or that he didn't see it. Either way works for me because I don't want to be the center of any attention.

The rest of the day is slow, leaving me ample time to watch Willow work, and daydream about fucking her. And by the time I'm ready to close up, she's deep in the writing zone.

Locking up takes no time at all, and I sneak upstairs to pop the lasagna in the oven. I set a timer on my phone and then head back downstairs to check on Willow.

She's in the exact spot I left her, except her hair looks a little more haphazard, and from what I've learned, that usually means she's getting frustrated.

"Hey, you want to take a break?" She jerks back at my voice, and I feel like shit that I scared her. "Sorry.""No, no, you're fine. I was zoned out and didn't even realize you were waiting on me. I definitely think it's break time, though." She sits back with a frustrated sigh.

"We have about a little over an hour until dinner is ready. You want to head up and talk about it?" I offer, feeling yet again creepy and awkward at the same time. It's not like I'm great with people in general, but damn, it's exponentially worse with this woman.

"God yes." She starts gathering all her stuff, and I hurry over to help her.

Once we've gotten everything collected—she legit has so much shit with her today it's shocking—she tosses her backpack over her shoulder, but I snag it before it makes it onto her back. She eyes with me a strange look in her eyes, almost like she's curious as to what my end-goal is, and honestly, I have no fucking clue what my endgame is. I just know I want to make things as easy as possible on her, so that means carrying her bag in some convoluted way.

Leading the way to the stairs that lead to my apartment, I hesitate. I still don't know if it's a good idea to bring someone into my personal space. It feels like a huge step, and mentally, I'm not sure I'm ready for it.

"We can go back down, Oakley. It's fine." Her soft voice, so caring and full of concern, snaps me out of my overanxious thoughts.

"Nope, this is perfect. Besides, I need to share that big-ass lasagna with someone." I force a chuckle. *God, it's like I can't function like a normal person around her.*

"You made lasagna?" The excitement is clear in her tone.

"It's nothing. Just made it earlier and then popped it in the oven while you were working." I run my hand over the back of my neck, uncomfortable as all hell. I'm not sure why this feels so personal, but I'm starting to struggle with bringing her up here. But this is a good thing. Woodcroft reminding me that I've cut out a lot of my previous life made me realize I'm not really open in this version of my life either. I'm hoping this small step can help change that because the limbo I'm living in isn't sustainable if I'm really trying to get over my issues.

Willow's little body jolts me back against my door as she tackles me in a hug.

"Thank you, that's extremely thoughtful," she mumbles against my shoulder.

Hesitantly wrapping an arm around her middle, I breathe her in, smelling the lingering scent of coffee and fresh air. *Comfort.*

"It's not a problem, Will. Let's get inside so you can tell me about where you're at in the book."

CHAPTER NINE
WILLOW

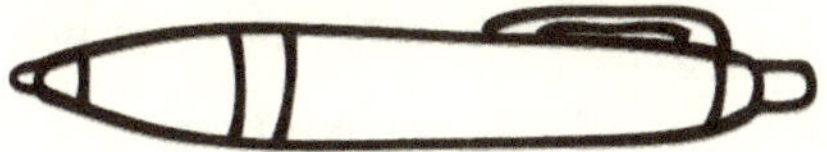

Walking inside James Oakley's apartment feels surreal. It's everything and nothing like I expected. It's both extremely barren and homey somehow. He has a grey couch, a TV on the wall, and a coffee table in the living room. But what pulls my curiosity is the stack of books on the table, as well as the bookcase off to the side.

The bookcase is overflowing with tons of books chaotically lined up two rows deep, and I'm immediately drawn to it. I hear Oakley put my bag on a table before moving to what I assume is the kitchen.

"You want something to drink? I have pretty much anything you can get downstairs."

"Umm, sure. A root beer sounds good," I say absentmindedly because I just found something *very* interesting.

My books. Every single one of them, by the looks of it, lined up perfectly on their own shelf. The only shelf that looks pristine.

My heart rate doubles, and I can't hold my grin back.

Mr. "I'm a loner and keep to myself" isn't so out of the loop in this town, it seems.

"Here you g— Oh, shit."

I turn around just in time to see that super adorable blush take over his cheeks and neck.

"So, were these pre- or post-helping me with the current book?" I ask, genuinely curious but also wanting to mess with him a little.

"Umm..."

"It's sweet, really." I try so hard to reel in my smirk but fail miserably.

"Listen, I got curious one day after I heard someone talking about it and picked one up. I really liked it, so I just kept reading them. Don't go getting all cocky on me." He's trying so hard to make it not seem like a big deal, but to me? This is a huge deal. It's also beyond flattering.

"Oh, I think I'm going to get very cocky about this." The smile on my face is so big my cheeks start hurting almost immediately. But I love this. I love his shyness about this, that he loves my books, and that he took care of my books like they hold a special place in his head and home. It's also the sexiest thing a man has ever done.

It's not like men haven't read my books as a way to get into my pants before, but with Oakley, it's something else entirely. And that was in college, when they were all assholes anyway. Oakley is not an asshole. In fact, he's the exact opposite, and my very Oakley-centered libido is waving the white flag.

He puts the drinks he grabbed from the refrigerator on the coffee table, and it's like his whole demeanor changes.

"You want me to tell you how fucking good of a writer you are?" He arches one eyebrow but there's a playfulness to his tone, and I'm excited to see more of it.

"I would love to hear how good you think I am."

"I think your mind is brilliant. It's fascinating and slightly messed up." Laughter shocks me along with his accurate observation. He smiles at me as he continues, taking a step closer to me. "The woman I know and the writer I know are so different it makes me want to figure out how you come up with the stories you do. It's— You're intriguing as hell, Will."

I close the gap between us, pleased as hell at his analysis of me and more flattered than I'll ever let on. But what I can't stop is my hand moving up to brush my fingertips against his chest, right over his heart, before sliding up and around his neck.

"Willow..."

"I'm not reading this wrong, am I?" I ask sweetly, already knowing the answer if the bulge in his jeans is anything to go by.

He doesn't answer me with words. No, what he does is so much fucking better. He uses one hand as a boost under my ass, lifting me up with zero strain. I wrap my legs around him, gripping his neck as my eyes go wide at the insane show of strength. Being wrapped around him also makes me keenly aware of our size difference.

But then I feel his erection digging into my legging-clad pussy, and all thoughts disappear as an unbidden moan sounds from my throat. I feel us moving, but my mind is too hazy with lust to know where until my back is slammed against a wall. His lips go to my neck, kissing and nipping.

"No, you aren't reading this wrong." He punctuates his words with a sharp thrust of his hips, making me gasp and pull my head away.

That's when I see we're right next to the bookcase, right next to my books, and somehow that little detail lights me on fire. He doesn't just like my body or my sexuality; he likes my brain. *He likes my fucking brain.*

Is there anything sexier than that?

Not to me.

I roll my hips, causing him to growl against my neck before taking those kisses and nips to my collarbone and the shoulder that's exposed. Throwing my head back, I take in how I'm feeling.

Hot.

Impatient.

Sexy.

Irresistible.

Horny.

I have never felt so turned on by a man in my life, and I feel antsy, jittery, and on the verge of being overstimulated. But I roll my hips again because horny wins out above all else.

His big hands slide up my rib cage, under my shirt, before his lips make their way back up my neck and across my cheek into the sweetest kiss that almost breaks me, before he pulls back slightly.

"I did not expect this," he says plainly. No inflection, just facts, and I love it.

"I can't say I'm disappointed," I breathe out as his hips roll again. The grin on his face as I struggle to talk makes me bite my lip with a smile.

"I just want verbal consent before it goes any further."

Well, damn, just when I thought he couldn't get any sexier. His brown eyes shift back and forth between mine, waiting for my answer.

"I'm so ready to take this further. Do your best, James Oakley." I wink then squeal as he spins me off the wall and walks the few steps to a door, which I assume leads to his bedroom.

"I was kind of hoping for wall sex," I pout.

"There'll be time," he says before tossing me onto his bed with no exertion.

His hand moves to the back of his neck, reaching behind him and ripping his Henley off.

Holy Jesus, did I say he couldn't get any sexier? I lied.

Muscles, lean muscles, cover every inch. He's not bulky, but his height causes him to look bigger overall. The faint dusting of dark hair covering his chest makes me squeeze my legs together. What's interesting is that the sleeve on his left arm are the only tattoos to be seen, and I'm more curious about them by the minute. When my gaze travels up to his face, he's biting his lip, trying to hide his smile at me checking him out. He's doing a piss-poor job of it too.

"Go ahead, be proud of yourself. You're gorgeous," I tell him bluntly. I'm not going to hide the fact that he's sexy as hell. I mean, we are about to have sex, right? Why sugarcoat it? It wouldn't be in my nature anyway.

"Never been called gorgeous before."

"Well, that's a damn shame," I mutter, taking another perusal down his body, ending on the very obvious dick outline in his jeans.

"Take your leggings off, Will." A command. So fucking sexy, I can just imagine how he would take control of his team as a Marshal.

I tip my head back, blowing out a steady stream of air in a weak attempt to calm my overactive body.

"Now." His grunt startles me into action.

I fumble to hook my thumbs into my leggings, planting my feet and thrusting my hips at a weird angle to try to get them over my ass. He doesn't move, doesn't help. Just watches the path the offending material takes down my legs.

Once they're off, I reach up and start lifting up my T-shirt.

"No, stop. I have plans for that."

I tilt my head in question, but he doesn't answer me. Instead, he moves his hands to the button on his jeans, flicking it open and sliding the zipper down. He leaves it like that, the fucking tease, slowly walking to the edge of the bed.

My brain starts working overtime. What's he going to do with my T-shirt? Should I have taken my panties off too? Should I try to help him take his jeans off? Is that what he's waiting for?

His hands touch the outside of my thighs, jolting my attention back to him.

"Get out of your head. Be present with me." His voice is low and gravelly.

"It's hard for me to get out of my head," I tell him honestly. This is why orgasms are hard to come by for me. I have a very specific way to get off because it's quick and my brain doesn't seem to factor in.

"Well, let's see if I can help with that." He reaches under my shoulders and shifts me up about a foot before he puts a knee on the bed, in between my legs.

Before I have time to question his words, both hands slide back under my shirt, slowly drawing it up my rib cage.

"I'd like to try something, but if you aren't a fan of restraints, then I won't do it," he says quietly, and his eyes shift up to mine.

"Umm, I've never personally been restrained, but I've read about it." I roll my eyes at myself before continuing, "I'd be interested in trying it."

I don't need to tell him that just him asking me about being restrained pulls my orgasm so damn close to the surface that I'm concerned what will happen when he actually does it.

The earnestness in his eyes shifts to wickedness, and I feel out of my depth.

But I know I'm safe with him. Hell, if there is anyone to explore some things with, it would be this man.

Wordlessly, he drags my shirt up over my head, pulling my arms up as he continues to lift the fabric. When he gets to my wrists, I'm focused on his bare chest pressed against mine, only covered by a flimsy lace bralette. He feels so good; the weight of him feels grounding, and the anxiety and overthinking I usually feel in general are silent.

My wrists feel free again, and he lifts himself off of me. He tips his head down, trailing kisses over all of the exposed skin he just revealed.

It has me squirming, trying to get friction, but I can't because he's keeping himself away from where I really want him.

I feel his hands slide up my ribcage again and tuck his fingers under the lace that's covering my breasts.

"Still good, Will?"

"So fucking good," I breathe out.

The lace of my skimpy bra pops over my breasts before he slides it up and over my head, the same, slow route my T-shirt took.

When he gets to my wrists this time, he twists my bra around my wrists a couple of times, creating a makeshift handcuff.

"Jesus, Willow, you are fucking stunning." He pulls back so his gaze focuses on what he just exposed.

"They're small." It's long been one of my biggest insecurities. I've come to like them for the most part, but him seeing them makes old insecurities come to the surface.

"Oh, I'm going to have fun showing you just how attractive I find them. How do your wrists feel?"

I test the restraint, seeing that it's tight enough to hold but not cutting off circulation.

"Good. It feels good." A rush of arousal runs through my body at the realization that I'm letting this man restrain me.

A devilish smile works its way onto his face, and I know without a doubt I'm unprepared but oh so willing to go along with anything he does right now.

"I just wanted it noted that this feels extremely lopsided right now. You still have your pants on," I deadpan in an attempt to take back a little control.

It's not that I want the control. I'm just so used to it being my default that I don't know how to get out of the mindset.

"You're still in your head," he *tsk*s. "Guess I'll have to try harder."

"Wha—" I don't even finish my question because his fingertips go straight to my nipples.

Soft circles make my head dizzy because it's not enough. My frustration starts getting the best of me when I plant my feet and thrust my hips up to try to get more.

A hand leaves one of my breasts before I feel it shove my hips down. Our eyes never leave each other's during any of this.

He doesn't say anything, but I get the message loud and clear.

He arches his eyebrow in silent question, and I nod my head in response. *I'll behave. I'll let him control.*

His hand leaves my hip and returns to my nipple, both hard and wanting more. A sharp pinch has me gasping.

My head tilts back as he alternates soft circles with more intentional, harder rolling between his fingertips.

"Eyes on me."

My eyes pop open and refocus on him as I nod again.

"This whole time, eyes on me. I need to see your reactions, see that you're okay."

"Okay," I whisper, not knowing how to respond to such care and dominance.

CHAPTER TEN
OAKLEY

The amount of trust she's given me already is humbling. And I've barely begun.

I'm honestly still having a hard time with the fact that Willow— gorgeous, sexy-as-fuck Willow— is in my bed right now.

I've always been a little more demanding in the bedroom—when I had time for sex, that is—but this feels different. I'm not being dominant for my sake; I'm doing it for hers.

So she can get out of her head and really enjoy this. I don't know if this is a one-off or not, so I want to make it the best I possibly can for her. I can't remember the last time I didn't restrain a partner because of some deep-seeded issues, but that's not something I need to think about right now.

God, I hope it's not a one-off.

I don't think I could continue to help her with her book and act like nothing happened between us.

I refocus on her pert nipples, seeing them turning a deep shade of red. The abused flesh shows me exactly how much I've worked her over.

Moving both hands down her rib cage again, I hook my fingers in the side of her panties, slowly dragging them over her ass. Her eyes flicker down for a second—looking at my jean-clad dick, I'm sure. But what she doesn't know is I need the barrier. I need the two layers of fabric separation so I don't blow my fucking load in two minutes flat. She's too tempting, too beautiful, too *submissive*. My control is hanging on by a thread, and I'm not sure she's ready for how depraved I can be.

I need to keep my shit together. And I meant it when I said I wanted to get her out of her head. I can't imagine how hard it is to just clear her head, if she ever does.

Peeling her panties down her legs, I see a little strip of hair leading to such a pretty pussy, glistening with arousal, ready and waiting for me to show it real pleasure.

"This all for me, Trouble?" I brush my fingertip down the strip of hair to her clit, dipping down further and barely pressing inside of her.

Her hands move over her head, forcing me to pin them down with my other hand. I arch my eyebrow at her again, making sure she understands this is how I want her.

At her frantic nod, I continue my teasing.

She may have started this, but I sure as hell intend to be the one to finish it. I pull my finger out of her, circling her clit once, twice, before pulling away completely. Her jaw drops open, and frustration flares in her eyes.

"Close your mouth. I promise I'll make you feel good. Your wrists still feel okay?" I ask, making sure to check in frequently. This is a first for her, and I want to make sure she feels safe the entire time.

"Yes." She whimpers her answer because I thrust two fingers into her at the same time.

"Good." I keep a steady pace, holding eye contact the whole time. She looks and feels like she's close, and fuck if I don't want to make her come this quickly. But I have other plans.

From the moment she kissed me, I knew I wanted to tease her the way she's been unconsciously teasing me for weeks. Cruel? Maybe. Logical? Definitely not.

But the world isn't fair, and I will wring every ounce of pleasure out of her by the time I'm done. It just might take a while to get there.

It also doesn't help that I know for a fact my stamina will be shit once I finally take my pants off, so this is also my way of compensating for that.

I feel the clench of muscles and wrench my hand away from her, bringing my fingers up to my mouth and licking them clean. Tilting my head back, I sigh in pleasure. She tastes fucking amazing, better than I even imagined.

"Eyes on me." Her breathy voice reaches my ears, and I smirk.

Trouble, indeed.

She matches me tit for tat at every turn.

I've never had a woman be at this level, never had someone challenge me in this way. And I have to say, I'm fucking obsessed.

"You feeling a little frustrated?" I tease, waiting a couple of minutes before going back to her sweet-as-fuck pussy.

Edging is one of my favorite tools. It works a person up so much in such a short amount of time and usually ends with a very powerful orgasm. For Willow, I think it will draw her out of her head more and turn her focus to *when* her orgasm will be coming.

Her teeth grit together, not answering me. That's fine. It's written all over her face.

Squeezing her wrists with my hand, my other moves to her clit. I feel it pulse beneath my fingers, and my cock somehow gets harder. Pre-cum wets my boxers, making it uncomfortable, but I won't make a move to strip. Not yet.

I move my finger to her entrance, sliding it in effortlessly. Pumping it a few times, I move it back up to her clit and circle in confident movements. I make sure to watch her reactions, seeing where specifically it feels good for her, and I hone in on that area. Switching back to fingering her, I alternate both for a few minutes until I can feel her clench up again. I pull my hand back again, and Willow growls at me.

"Are you fucking kidding me?!" She tries to arch her hips up, but I pin her down again.

"I did say I was going to get you out of your head. How am I doing so far?"

"You're pissing me the fuck off."

I bite my lip in an attempt to stave off the smile she evokes. I don't want to tell her I think I've been pretty successful in my endeavors, but I do know she won't be able to withstand much more. It's a fine line between being sexually frustrated and just completely done with the moment, and if I try for one more edge, I know she'll be done. And that's the opposite of what I want.

I bend down, dragging my nose along her cheek.

"You're doing so fucking good for me, Trouble. So good. I promise it'll be worth it," I whisper.

I pull back in time to watch her eyes flutter shut, so I take the opportunity to steal a kiss. I miss her lips, and I want one more taste before I'm occupied for a minute.

"I want you to keep your hands above your head. Can you do that for me?" I ask when I pull back.

She nods once more, so I gently let go of them. "They still feel okay?" Another nod.

Sitting back on my knees, I visually peruse her for a moment. Drinking in the image once more of her, naked and restrained for me.

I move my hands under her thighs and shove them up toward her chest before leaning down and wrapping my lips around her clit.

Her musky flavor explodes on my tongue, and I thrust my hips into the bed out of necessity. Groaning, I let her see too much of my vulnerabilities, see how much she's affecting me.

"Oh fuck," I hear her whisper, and it makes me feral.

My hand moves of its own accord, thrusting two fingers inside of her as I keep sucking her clit.

It takes three thrusts, and she explodes. Her orgasm seems to last forever, but it might just be how lost in her I am. She tightens around me so hard I can't help but picture my cock there instead, and my hips press hard into the mattress, trying to get any relief I can.

Incoherent words and screams from Willow's mouth only make me want her more. When her hands grab my shaggy hair, pushing me away, it breaks me out of the haze, making me lean back, removing my fingers from her.

Her chest rises and lowers with each pant. I grab her hands that are still tied up with her bra and carefully extract them. Once she's free, I check her wrists to look for any marks or bruising and find she's clear.

"You are a fucking God, James," she tries to say through her breathy pants.

"And I haven't even fucked you yet," I counter, hiding the insecurities her words bring to the surface.

I stand up, finally stripping out of my jeans and boxers. Pumping my cock a couple of times, I walk around to the nightstand where I put condoms a couple of weeks ago. I was hopeful while never actually thinking this would happen. But damn am I fucking glad for my optimism.

Her head turns as she tracks my movements. She finally gets a good view of what I'm packing, and her eyes widen.

"Holy shit," she whispers.

"Don't worry. You're nice and wet for me. You'll be able to take it all."

Her thighs close—trying to find some relief, I assume—as I open the foil square and roll it down my cock.

I stand back, letting my eyes trail along her body. My mind is trying to decide how to take her. Do I take full control again? Or is she out of her head enough to take her own control?

I decide to let her make the decision instead.

"How do you want your next orgasm, Trouble? You want to ride me so you hit your G-spot just right? You want me to pound into you from behind and make it so deep it almost hurts?"

Her eyes flash at the last suggestion, and I waste no time. I flip her hips over, yanking them back to the edge of the bed. She turns her head to look at me, pure lust shining in them. I smack her ass hard before lining up and plunging in.

There is no warm-up. We don't need one.

Instead, I plunge all the way to the hilt in one steady thrust as my hands grip her hips so hard I know they'll bruise. But that's something I'll have to deal with later.

"Fuck, Will," I breath out. She feels unreal, so wet and tight. I know I was right to edge the shit out of her. I'm afraid I won't last long enough to make it really worth it for her. That's not to say she'll go without—I'll make sure she doesn't.

"Oh my God, James," she wails into the mattress.

It spurs me on, and I set a relentless pace.

James. Something about the fact that she says my first name has me on the cusp in seconds. Reaching around, I slide my fingers over her clit. Her whimper lets me know she's sensitive, so I might be able to get her there with me.

I circle it a few times as I get closer and closer. Her pussy clenches against my cock, drawing up my balls tight and sending tingles up my spine.

Pinching her clit hard, I close my eyes and pray that does it because on the next thrust, I'm coming. I couldn't hold back for anything.

Her hips tilt and thrust back on me as her hands grip the sheets hard. She's coming. *Thank God.* The tight undulation of her pussy sends me completely over, and I moan into the abyss.

I thrust once more, holding myself inside of her, not ready for it to be over yet.

Worthy. That's how she makes me feel right this second.

Squeezing her hips once more, I gently grip the base of my dick with the condom and pull out. I feel the loss immediately, and it's like the sun is behind the clouds. Her hips collapse onto the bed, and I gently rub the globes of her ass.

"You okay, Will?" Concern instantly floods me, unsure if I took this too far.

"So. Fucking. Good." Her voice comes out in a staccato groan, making me smile.

"I'll be right back. Don't move." I wait for her nod of confirmation before moving to my bathroom to remove the condom. I grab the washcloth and turn on the water, making sure it's warm before wetting it.

Making my way back to Willow, I'm struck by the fact that I feel light. The heaviness that's usually surrounding me has temporarily given way to an airiness I'm not sure I've ever felt before.

Willow is in the same spot that I left her, so I spread her legs a little and run the washcloth over her, making sure she's clean before tossing it into the corner. Lying down next to her, I pull her pliable body to mine.

"I think you broke me," she groans.

"I'd say I accomplished what I set out to then, no?"

She half-ass slaps my chest, and A bark of laughter escapes me.

"You sure you're doing, okay? I wasn't too rough?" I'm almost positive I wasn't because I watched her reactions like a hawk, but I never want to assume. Talking to her about it after is a way for both of us to ensure we got what we wanted.

"I've never had sex like that before. Which is probably why I never really loved having sex, because I could never get out of my head enough to let go and orgasm. I'm usually thinking about the next book idea, what kind of character my partner would be in my books…"

She's rambling, but I let her. Sex can be cathartic as hell.

"I— That— Holy shit, James that was … everything," she stutters out.

"I'm glad you liked it," I say softly, stroking my hand up her spine.

"Is that your usual style? Like, are you always dominant like that?"

"Yes and no. I always feel like this, but there are women who aren't into it and that's fine. I don't push my wants on someone if they don't want it. But what we just did? That is my preference."

"The tying up?"

"It's not so much the restraining; it's the control over your pleasure. I like bringing kink into the bedroom because it usually draws the focus away from the act, if that makes sense. You focus less on whether you look right, are placed right, are you actually going to come, and focus more on your senses." I know I'm not explaining myself right, but she has my head so blissfully blank it's the best I can do right now. I also won't tell her she's the only woman I've been with and haven't had tied up the entire time. Ever since that incident so long ago, I've never been with a woman I haven't tied up.

"I liked the tying up," she whispers.

"Then I'll keep tying you up." I press a kiss to her temple.

She lets out a content sigh, and my heart explodes with accomplishment.

I did this to her. And if she lets me, I'll keep doing it as often as she wants.

I wake up with a start, disoriented.

I feel the weight of Willow on my chest, and everything we did rushes to my head.

And then my phone rings. Must be what woke me up. I don't even remember falling asleep, just pulling out the lasagna before climbing back into bed with Willow and feeling content for the first time in maybe forever. I clumsily reach over to the nightstand, feeling for the offending object, hoping I don't wake up Willow.

I finally find it, seeing it's one a.m. and that Woodcroft is calling me.
Fuck.

"What?" I answer quietly, checking to make sure Willow's still asleep.

"Sorry it's so late, man."

I don't answer him, just wait for him to tell me why he called.

"Look, I know you don't want to talk about Tennison or the case, but I think you need to know this." I stiffen instantly. "He's been seen in Shreveport, Louisiana. Looks like he's traveling west and closer to Texas."

"But we don't know any of that for sure," I tell him, making sure to keep my voice quiet.

"Oak, it's a credible source. I just want you to be aware—nothing more, nothing less."

"Okay, thank you."

"I'm just concerned because he always seemed to have a hard-on for you, so I want you to be careful, keep your eyes open."

"I get it, I do, Wood, but I'll be fine. I'll be diligent as I usually am. I promise." I'm not sure if it was the mind-obliterating sex with Willow, but I know he's just trying to look out for me. I was probably way too hard on him when he came to talk to me. But that's a conversation for a day I don't have this gorgeous woman in my bed.

"I just worry about you," he says quietly.

"I know. I appreciate it. I'll call you tomorrow, okay?"

"Sounds good. Sorry to wake you up. I forget you're not used to the calls at all hours."

"All good, Wood. Night."

"Night."

I hang up and stare at the ceiling. I don't like that Tennison seems to be moving closer to Texas, but as of right now, we have no reason to believe he knows where I'm at. I'll stay vigilant.

The day and the epic sex is catching up to me, though.

My eyes get heavy as I check on Willow one more time. My mind's not focusing on my past life, despite the phone call. I start dozing easily, not even remembering when I fell asleep again. But it's the best sleep I've had in over a year, and I have a feeling it's all thanks to Will.

CHAPTER ELEVEN
WILLOW

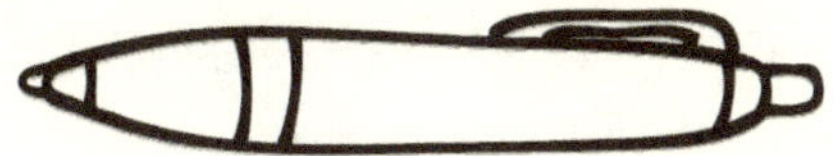

It's been a productive two weeks. I finally feel good about the direction of my book, although it's not anything like my usual stories. This is decidedly more romance-driven than I've ever done before, but I'm liking it.

It's also scary as hell because I have no idea what the reception will be.

But I'll deal with that later because, right now, I'm actually on track to hitting my deadline.

Could it have something to do with the startling clarity I've had since Oakley and I started sleeping together? Possibly, but I'm not going to analyze it at the moment.

The sex, though? Mind-bending. I didn't know sex could be this good, or that I could shut my brain long enough to enjoy the hell out of it. But Oakley isn't your average man either. For as sweet, unassuming, and gentlemanly as he is, he is dominant as shit in the bedroom.

We've been playing with restraints mostly, and I have to say it's not something I thought I would personally enjoy, but now? Now, I can't imagine sex another way.

Shit, am I going to be able to have sex with men who don't do that?
Do I want to?

The thought rings out so loudly in my mind it scares me. Because I don't want to do this with anyone else. I just want James.

Tipping my head back, I let out a sigh. This isn't something I should be thinking about now. Hell, probably ever. Right now, I need to focus on my book, and whatever comes next between the two of us is something I'll figure out after I write "The End".

The smell of freshly made espresso permeates my turbulent thoughts, turning my focus to the very man who's causing the turmoil in my head.

James fucking Oakley.

He's dressed in his usual distressed jeans, and a T-shirt that fits his upper body like a glove and also showcases the artwork I've spent hours studying upstairs in his apartment. I did learn that he got his sleeve because he loved the artist and wanted it on his body. It's why he doesn't have more, and it just adds another layer to this very complex man.

I follow him with my eyes as he finishes up a drink and then turns around, giving me his back and making a panini. I've had to stop coming here early to write because I haven't been getting much done in his presence. My routine now is staying home in the morning, writing my ass off, then making my way to Grind Time an hour or two before closing time so we can take things upstairs.

And by things, I mean sex. Because although we talk and I brainstorm with him, there is no writing.

But there are a shit-ton of orgasms.

You win some, you lose some, and I'm still on pace to finishing this damn book, so that's all that matters, right?

God, I don't even know anymore. I feel like I'm living two very different lives right now, and I know at some point this will all catch up with me. But I can't dwell on that or I'll never finish this book, and then I'll have to think about where James and I are heading, and that's too scary to consider at the moment.

My eyes follow Oakley as he makes his way around the counter, taking a direct path to me.

"Hey there, gorgeous. You haven't had lunch yet, have you?" he asks, setting down my usual latte and a chicken pesto panini. I look around, seeing the place is empty—thank God, because I don't want people speculating about my sex life.

I think I might be in so much trouble with this man.

"I have not. Thank you so much." Anxiety courses through me, trying to make sure I'm maintaining a correct level of disconnect from him while also wanting him so fucking bad. And then there's the fact that he feeds me every single day. Quietly making sure I'm taking care of myself and fueling my coffee addiction at the same time.

My panicked thoughts must be broadcasting all over my face because Oakley immediately starts grabbing the plate.

"You don't want pesto chicken. What are you in the mood for?" he asks quickly.

"No, no, this is perfect, I promise! I'm just a little too in my head at the moment."

His eyes darken, and a sly smirk takes over his concerned features.

"No! Seriously, I need to get more work done today. I'm behind on my word count goal," I refute his dirty thoughts.

"Can we use it as an incentive, then?"

"'It' as in, the mind-blowing sex you've been giving me every evening?" I smirk.

"That'd be the one, yes."

God, he has no shame.

I pretend to think about, like it's such a hardship to have the best sex of my life.

"I guess I can work with that."

He rolls his eyes at my smart-ass retort, and I can't help but laugh. We both know I'm going to cave every single time. It's just a matter of actually finishing my work today.

"Can I help with anything?" He nods to my laptop, and I arch my eyebrow at him. "No, seriously, no sex distraction. I'm genuinely trying to help this time." He chuckles.

I let out a sigh. "I'm stuck." He waits patiently for me to continue. "Well, I have Charlie and Niya screwing, but I'm feeling like it's not actually progressing the story. She hasn't given him any new information in a while, and he's just killing away, acting oblivious at work while getting ass on the side. It feels lopsided, like our baker doesn't really have a huge role in all this yet."

"Okay, so how do we give her a bigger role? Maybe we make her complicit somehow? Maybe she catches him in the act in the next couple of chapters, and it causes a blow-up of sorts? I mean, how likely is it that our CIA agent just sleeps with her without getting close and hiding the fact that he's the very killer he's trying to catch?"

"Hmm," I hum, thinking on it. It could actually work, and it would shift the story a lot. I wanted to have the *Charlie's the killer* reveal as the final twist, but if I go this route, I will need to reveal that sooner rather than later.

"I like it. I would just need to figure out another huge twist toward the end since that was going to be it."

"Okay, let me think on that."

I also haven't missed how he says "we" like we're both writing this book. And I guess, in a way, we are. *Damn, I might need to give him some credit in this one.* The thought makes me smile. I bet he never expected to play such a huge role in a book, let alone one of my books.

I think about the pristine shelf in his apartment that holds all of my books, and it never makes me fail to feel unworthy to have such a special place in his home. As an author, I don't see fans of my books every day. My siblings don't count because they feel like they have to like it, but Oakley? Oakley was reading long before our sexcapades started.

"The other thing I'm stuck on is making sure that Charlie's process makes sense and feels authentic."

"That, I can definitely help with." He leans forward.

"How do guys like this plan? Like, how do they figure out their next move because, right now, his shit feels too random, so it's probably not believable."

"They usually have a pattern, and a lot of the time it stems from something that they interpreted as wronging them. Like childhood trauma, women turning them down. Obviously, that's very cliché, but it's the principle of it. Very few prolific killers do things randomly."

"Makes sense. What is Tennison's pattern?" I ask naturally, not even thinking about the impact.

Oakley's entire body freezes.

"I'm sorry, it was just curiosity. Let's try and think of something unique for Charlie," I quickly change the subject. He meets my eyes with relief in them, and I know this is a big part of why Tennison has eluded him and his entire Task Force for so long. Because everything he does feels random. But it's not random, not to Tennison.

"What about him being more of a vigilante?" he asks.

"Eh, he doesn't feel like a good guy, though. What if he goes after people for things he perceives as wrong, like being rude or shit-talking? Simple things that shouldn't bother a person?"

"That could work. I think you need to refine it a little, but I like it being pettier. Makes it feel more extreme."

"Me too. I'll think more on it, though."

The bell above the door dings, pulling Oakley away from me, and I instantly feel lonely. *Bad, bad Willow. You aren't supposed to be doing anything other than sleeping with him.*

I snort to myself, barely believing my own lies.

"Well, hey there, stranger." Rina comes bounding in and sitting at the seat Oakley just vacated.

"I've been here every day. I don't know where you've been." I give her a knowing look. Most likely building furniture and yelling at Arlo, if she's keeping to pattern.

"Every day?" Her eyebrows shoot up. Damn my big ass mouth around my sister. Now, she'll be pestering me about Oakley until I die.

"So, how's Arlo?" I deflect, knowing it'll piss her off.

"Why are you asking about Arlo?" Lennox asks as he sits down with us.

"No, please, come sit. Let me just move all my shit," I say sarcastically.

"We aren't talking about Arlo," Rina grits out.

"Touchy." Lennox leans back and takes a huge bite of the sandwich Oakley just dropped off.

James's gaze catches mine, and I fight like hell to not blush. My eyes shoot down to my plate to break eye contact, realizing I hadn't eaten the sandwich he made me.

Picking up the half Lennox didn't steal, I shove a huge bite into my mouth, but it does nothing to dissuade Rina's all-knowing stare.

"How's work, Lenny?" Rina decides to ask Lennox instead, and thank God, because I don't even know what to say about Oakley and me. It's not like we've discussed things in between fucking each other's brains out.

"Pretty quiet, actually. No animals giving birth, no trouble out on the trails. All has been good, for once."

"So, no new names to report?" Rina asks, disappointment clear in her tone, and I laugh. Lennox has a history of naming every single animal he comes across, and they are usually ridiculous and immature.

"Nope, it's your lucky day. You're saved from making fun of me for one day." He rolls his eyes.

"It's still early," Rina retorts.

"How's the book coming, Will?" Lennox ignores her.

"It's going. I'm attempting to work on it, but two of my annoy-ing-as-hell siblings decided to interrupt my flow." I act like I'm writing, but It's been a while since I've seen them, so secretly, I missed the banter.

"Are you going to finish it on time?" Rina asks with concern.

They really are the best family, plus Ledger, who I haven't seen in a while outside of family dinner since he and Ainsley got together. But they all know sometimes I hide away, writing day and night to make a deadline, so this isn't that unusual. What is unusual is spending the same amount of time writing as I am in Oakley's bed, but they don't have to know that.

"I think so. It took so long, but I'm finally making good progress. If I stay steady like I have been, I'll finish on time. It's going to come down to the wire, though." I cringe. I don't think I've ever been this close to a deadline before, and it's making me anxious as hell.

"Well, that's good. If you need help with anything, you know we're here for you," Lennox says after he finishes his half of my sandwich. He stands up, tapping Rina's shoulder as he does. "Let's go. She needs to work."

Rina's motherly stare hits me hard—looking for what, I'm not sure—but Lennox pulls her away before she gains clarity. Lennox throws me a wink before dragging Rina out of Grind Time, and I sink back into my chair.

Lennox and I have always been close, and we only got more so when our parents died when we were in high school. Rina and Ledger took over the parental role, and Lennox and I were left to figure out how to navigate high school with the abrupt loss.

"I just need to close up, and then we can head upstairs if you're ready?" Oakley's deep voice cuts into my thoughts.

"Sure. Can I help?"

He shakes his head. "No, just get to a good stopping point with your writing while I wipe shit down."

It takes fifteen minutes to close up. Once he's done, he tosses my bag over his shoulder and fireman carries me up the stairs.

"God, I can't wait to fuck you." His voice is barely discernible from the whooshing in my head from being upside down. But the only thought in my head is: *Me too.*

CHAPTER TWELVE
OAKLEY

Willow's deadline is closing in, and she seems to be okay. After we worked through what her guy's motive could be, she didn't mention it again. It probably didn't help that I immediately took her upstairs and tied her up.

A grin pulls at my lips just thinking about it.

"Morning, Oakley." The sheriff's voice interrupts my memories from last night.

"Morning." I start making his Americano as he continues conversation like I invited one.

"Hear anything else from your old partner?" he asks offhanded, but the question freezes me in place.

I turn around, handing him his coffee and looking around to see if anyone is in, even though it's usually quiet this time of day. I feel like he wouldn't oust me like that, but you never know.

"I have, actually," I say cautiously. I think it's a good idea to keep the sheriff informed if he's worried, even if I don't share Woodcroft's concern.

"Oh?" He takes a sip of his coffee.

"Seems Tennison is traveling west." His jaw tightens. "Last tip was that he was in Shreveport. Woodcroft called me a couple of days ago because he thinks ... he thinks Tennison is coming for me."

"And is there a good reason he thinks that?"

"I don't fucking know. We were like Sherlock and Moriarty. He would fuck with me, but I don't think he has an obsession of me, like Woodcroft does. I honestly think it's just a coincidence."

"But this is the first time he's traveled out of the New England area?"

"That we know of. God knows how long the bastard's been doing this shit." I grit my teeth. This is not what I want to talk about today. Sheriff and Woodcroft are making me fucking paranoid that I'm wrong.

He hums, taking another sip. "Please keep me updated if you hear anything else. I think it's best we both stay extra vigilant."

I nod.

"You ever thought about doing something more, like the Marshals here?" His question throws me for a loop.

"What do you mean?"

"I mean, ever think about not running a coffee shop and coming to work for me?"

He's dead serious, and I have no answer, but my immediate reaction is a hell no.

"Nah, I got away from that life for a reason." He doesn't need to know how badly Alfred Tennison fucked with my head, how I felt like a failure towards the end, and how the guilt of a preventable death and so much suffering will always haunt me. He doesn't need someone like that on his team, and I sure as hell can't even imagine putting myself back into a law-enforcement position of any kind.

He eyes me for a second before turning and walking out without another word, leaving me rattled and pissed off.

My hands are shaking, and I clench my fists to try to drive it away. My skin starts to feel too tight for my body, but I breathe in and out to calm myself down. It takes the edge off, barely. My mind is still racing, thinking about every single person I've failed over the years. Like a PowerPoint, the slideshow is never-ending.

There's only one way to deal with this mood I'm now in, and sadly, it's not fucking Willow. I want to save her from this side of me. She doesn't need to see this unsure, fucked-up version of me.

I pull out my phone and send a text to Lennox.

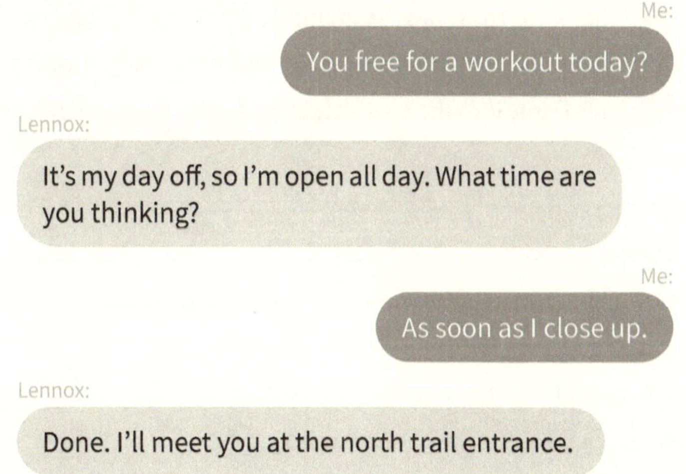

The bell of the front door dings again, and I'm about ready to rip the thing off. My nerves are frayed right now, and that's not helping at all.

Until I see Willow.

But then I remember my workout with Lennox and feel guilty all over again. *God, my head's a mess.*

"I actually ate lunch today, so you don't have to feed me for once!" She moseys up to the counter with a smile. She says it like I hate feeding her, but nothing could be further from the truth.

And I'm honestly upset I don't get to feed her today. Taking care of her in and out of the bedroom is quickly becoming my favorite thing to do.

"That's good. Still want a latte?" I arch my eyebrow.

"Of course." She turns and heads to her usual table, acting like it's a normal day. And I guess, for her, it is. But my mind is a fucking scary place right now, and I need to let her know I need space tonight.

I make her latte from muscle memory, grabbing a chocolate chip cookie from the display case before walking over to her table. I awkwardly drop my large frame into the small café chair and set the goodies in front of her.

"Thank you," she chirps, breaking off a piece of the cookie. "What's up? How's the day been? Any fun stories?"

"Nope." I'm too in my head to elaborate on her questions.

"You okay?" She tilts her head to the side, analyzing my facial features.

"Umm, kind of. Not really." I run my hand down my face. "Sorry, I just talked to Sheriff, and he got me thinking."

"We hate when that happens."

I let out a chuckle. "Yeah. I texted Lennox to go do a workout." I hold my breath, hoping she doesn't take it hard.

"Okay. That sounds like a good idea. I can go home and bust out another chapter." She says it so simply.

I would assume if I wasn't so worked up, it would be that simple, but to me right this minute... I feel guilty, anxious, and so fucking uncomfortable. It's like my skin is clammy, and my mind is making up scenarios where she hates me for ditching her tonight.

I was doing so fucking good too. It's been weeks since I felt like this. I just hope it doesn't devolve into a full-blown panic attack.

"Just let me finish this deliciousness, and I'll head out." She doesn't sound put out, but I don't know if I believe it. I did commit to working out, though, so what could I even do if I told her not to leave?

I open and close my mouth a couple of times, trying to figure out what to say, but come up empty. She just seems so cool about me ditching her, a complete non-issue, that I don't know what to say or how to react, so I don't. I just get up and let her finish her mid-afternoon pick-me-up.

I'm shifting back and forth on my feet, waiting for Lennox. I've already stretched and done a few random exercises to hopefully calm my nervous energy.

Shockingly enough, it didn't work. I roll my eyes at myself for being so fucking ridiculous right now.

"Hey, man," Lennox calls when he turns the corner and comes into view.

"Hey."

"You up for a hard one today?" he asks in a no-nonsense tone, and I appreciate it. No shooting the shit, no catching up, just straight to the point.

"Absolutely."

"Sweet, so let's run this three-mile trail. When we get to the point, we'll do some intervals until one of us feels like puking and then run back." He smirks as he explains, and I kind of love this sadistic side of him. I have no doubt he'll give me a run for my money, but I think I can keep up.

"Sounds good. See you there." I take off, not waiting for him, and set a pretty fast pace. I need to work the anxiety out of my body, and this is the only way I know how.

I'm fucking dead.

I barely made the three-mile run back to the trailhead before collapsing in the dirt.

"Jesus, I knew you were in shape, but damn," Lennox heaves out.

"Fuck you. You didn't puke," I grumble, ashamed he actually kept his word and that I was the one who upchucked.

"Sucks to lose."

"I beat you back here, so therefore, I win," I counter through my labored breathing.

"You're really big on semantics, huh?"

"Winning is winning, Len."

He punches my shoulder, and I laugh.

"How old are you anyway? When someone asks, I need to be able to say I'm badass," I ask.

"Why does my age factor in? And I'm twenty-nine."

"Well, eight years isn't as much as I hoped for, but I'll take it. I beat the youngest Hutton today," I gloat before he punches me again.

"You puked; you didn't win shit. That means you owe me, like, five paninis."

"We made no bet in the beginning. I didn't agree to feed your ass." I would totally feed his ass. That was one hell of a workout. He earned it.

"Seriously, though, good workout." He turns his head to face mine.

"It was. Thank you, I needed that more than you know."

"You know, I'm always here if you want to work out, talk, you know, whatever."

Friendship. That's what he's offering.

Outside of whatever I'm doing with Willow, I haven't gotten close to anyone in town. But this feels nice. There's no obligation to talk. I can just get the shit kicked out of me, and he's cool to leave it at that.

There's the minor problem of me fucking his sister, but what he doesn't know won't hurt him. I inwardly cringe at the thought of him learning about it, though.

"Thanks, man, same to you. Let me know your next day off, and we can do this again." I hoist myself off the ground, groaning in a way that makes me feel every one of my thirty-seven years.

"Sounds good." He stays splayed out, breathing heavily.

I only have one thing on my mind at the moment. The second Willow's name popped into my head, I knew I had to see her.

It's become a routine for us, sure, but it's more than that. My body is clearer since my talk with Sheriff, but my mind needs Willow. She calms me, and I desperately need some of that right now. I just hope I can actually get out of my head and not take it out on her.

CHAPTER THIRTEEN
WILLOW

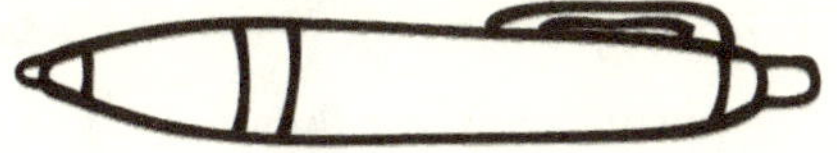

Something is up with Oakley.

It's not like I expect to have his undivided attention every single day, but it was his whole demeanor at Grind Time that has me worried.

The problem is, I can't just barge over there demanding he talk to me just because I'm worried about him. We're just hooking up and haven't spoken a word of anything more than that. He doesn't owe me any explanations.

So, here I sit, leg bouncing uncontrolled on my couch, thinking of Oakley when I should be writing. But I can't focus. All I can think about is what I can do to help him—whether that's getting him to talk to me or distracting him, I don't care.

And that's a huge problem. Because we haven't promised each other anything other than amazing sex. I'm dangerously close to uncharted territory here. Shit, I think I'm already past it if I'm being honest with myself.

I throw my head back against the couch and let out a sigh.

What the fuck am I doing here? I'm supposed to be talking to Oakley to get this damn book done. I was never supposed to fall into his bed, let alone every night after. This whole thing screams heartbreak. He's never gotten close to anyone in Bluebell Falls because of his past, and I get that now, but it also doesn't mean he's going to magically change what he wants just because the sex is that incredible.

And what about what you want, Will?

Another sigh. *Wonderful question, self. Why don't we analyze that?* I roll my eyes. But it's a good question, and the answer is glaringly obvious now that I'm forcing myself to think about it.

I want James Oakley. Not just in his bed, but I want to go on a date, maybe go for a hike. I stop myself—maybe not a hike. I know I couldn't keep up with him. Laughter escapes through my tumultuous thoughts. God, he's messed me up really good if I'm thinking about hiking with him.

A knock at the door disrupts my thoughts.

I swear to God, if it's Rina coming here to pester me about what's going on with Oakley, I'm going to scream.

I take my sweet-ass time walking to the door, deciding that if I'm going to have to listen to her, making her wait is my only petty move.

The knock sounds again, and I groan. "I'm coming. Jeez, chill out."

I rip the front door open and am startled to see Oakley, not Rina, standing on my front porch.

"Oh!" *Oh?* That's all I can say? I mentally chastise myself for my earlier thoughts that are now making me second-guess everything I say to this man.

He stares at me a beat longer than normal and then steps over the threshold, sliding his hand into my hair and slamming his lips against mine. I hear the door slam, but my focus is on the intensity I feel coming off of him.

I run my hands up his muscled arms, up the side of his neck, and into his slightly damp hair, telling me he came straight here after a shower.

His hand not tangled in my hair moves to my ass and picks me up. My legs wrap around his hips, and I hold on while he makes his way to the living room.

Ripping his lips from mine, he almost stumbles over my coffee table. "Bedroom. Where?"

"Hallway on the left."

He barely shifts his eyes from mine before heading in the correct direction. It's wildly attractive how he just muscles me around, keeping all his attention on me.

He once again sends me flying onto the bed the second he gets to my room. I meet his eyes, seeing his pupils are completely blown, lust warring with something else I can't make out.

"Strip." One word, and I don't dare disobey.

It feels like he's in a different mood than he usually is, and I don't think it's a good move to test him. I slide my baggy sweats down my legs with my panties, unceremoniously throwing them to the side. My tank top follows, and I'm glad I had committed myself to a lazy night, so I don't have to contend with a bra right now.

When I look back up, Oakley is shoving his pants and boxers down his legs, having already taken his shirt and shoes off. The man is a piece of art, I swear. The artwork on his arm, mixed with the dusting of hair on his chest, does it for me.

As he crawls onto the bed like a man possessed, I spread my legs to make room for him. He's definitely quieter than normal, but it's honestly hot as fuck, so I'm not about to disrupt the tension he's built. He grabs one of my wrists, pulling it to the side to grab the other, then slams them above my head. His chest rubs against mine, and the friction sends arousal surging down my body.

He licks up my neck before biting at the spot between it and my shoulder. A whimper leaves me as my hips thrust up. His other hand shoves my hips down to the bed before moving to reach to the side. He rips open a condom with his teeth. I didn't even see him toss it on the bed, but I'm glad for the forethought. Briefly letting go of my hands to roll the condom on properly, they return with a strength that has me melting under his touch.

His dominance undoes me. The way I can completely let go with him is beyond euphoria. It's a power I never knew I had, and I love it.

His fingers trail down, circling my clit once before dipping down and pushing inside of me. He must like what he feels because he wastes no time after that thrusting into me.

The stretch causes me to gasp. It feels so damn good, and he knows it too, because he doesn't let me adjust before pulling out and thrusting to the hilt again.

"Oh God, James," I moan.

He holds a steady pace, getting me so damn close before he pinches my clit hard, sending me over. He follows shortly after with erratic thrusts and then collapses to the side of me, releasing my wrists at the same time.

I take a second to catch my breath. When I finally do, I realize he's barely said two words, and the distance now feels like a giant canyon.

Something is very wrong, but I don't even know how to approach it with him.

Rolling over to my side, I tuck my hand under my cheek and look at him. His arm is thrown over his eyes, his chest still rising and falling.

Wordlessly and without looking at me, he rolls off the bed and finds his way to the bathroom.

Cold, that's how I feel right now.

My eyes well up with tears I refuse to let fall because this reaction is ridiculous.

As amazing as that was, it also felt detached. For the first time since we got together, I feel used.

I know there's more going on here, more going on with him, but I can't see past my own hurt to give him the benefit of the doubt right now. Or hell, the support he probably needs, and it makes me mad at myself.

"Will..."

"I really need to get some more writing done tonight. I hope that's cool." I blink back the tears before sitting up and grabbing my clothes. I quickly dress and head toward my office, not caring if he follows right now.

The distance he came in here with is the distance I'm going to make damn sure I keep right now. I knew it was a terrible idea to think we could be anything more, but damn it, I wanted to be right, no matter how unrealistic it is.

I want him.

"I'm sorry." His soft, gravelly voice hits me.

"What happened?" I ask, still refusing to look into his eyes. It feels like if I do, I'll show him too much, let him see too much.

"I-I had a bad day," he finally says.

It's not enough; he knows it, and I know it. There's way more to it, but he's choosing to only tell me the bare bones. I'm not sure why. I'm not sure when I gave him the impression that I couldn't handle the hard stuff, but here we are. And I'm not even sure I want to try to push him. Because what would that really accomplish right now?

Getting closer and falling for him? Being let down easy? Which would lead to me not writing because it would hit me harder than I want it to, leading to a missed deadline and disappointed readers. A petty reason, but it feels monumental to me right now.

This whole night is bringing up feelings I'm not remotely ready for, and Oakley staying here is only making it worse.

"Okay. If you want to talk about it, you know where to find me." I'm proud of how normal I sound.

I plop down in my chair and open my laptop.

"Will, I just don't want to talk about it."

"Yep, I get it. No worries. I'll see you tomorrow, maybe?" I internally curse myself for sounding needy.

"Umm, yeah. I guess I'll see you tomorrow." He pauses at the threshold of the doorway before turning around and walking out.

I wait until I hear the front door shut, then I collapse onto my desk.

Fuck, I hate this.

I didn't even realize I was this far gone for him.

Tonight was hot at first—it always is with him. Then it changed. And a man I never thought would make me feel used and *ashamed* did.

And it makes me sad.

I thump my head on the desk a couple of times in an attempt to rid myself of these feelings. When I lift my head up, I get this weird lucidity.

I open up my Word document holding my newest book, and I write.

I write down every feeling, every hesitation, every want, and I don't stop.

I don't stop when my stomach growls in hunger.

I don't stop when the clock on my desk says two a.m.

And I don't stop when the morning sun rises.

CHAPTER FOURTEEN
OAKLEY

I hate myself.

I did exactly what I told myself I wouldn't do, and I took my messed-up headspace out on Willow. I'm so fucking ashamed of myself I can hardly look in the mirror. She didn't deserve that, and even when she was patient and knew something was wrong, I pushed her away instead of leaning into her and talking. It's not like I don't know she would listen because I know for a fact she would be the best listener. But I'm stuck in my old ways and don't know how to break free.

It feels like I need to resolve all my shit before I can talk to Willow about what's in my head. I don't want to poison her with my failures.

This is exactly why I didn't get close to people, why I moved to small-town U.S.A. and forgot about the life I once lived.

Because I hurt people.

And hurting Willow is like stabbing myself in the eye with an ice pick. But I don't fucking know how to fix it.

After I left her place, I walked home. I tried every trick in the book to sleep, but nothing was working.

I've been pacing my apartment ever since, and now it's time to go work and I'm not in the fucking mood. I'm super tempted to call Brittany and ask her to cover for me, which I have never done before.

But I don't because the distraction might do me good.

Hopping into a cold shower, I rinse up then quickly change before heading downstairs and starting work on the pastries I make daily.

The monotonous work only allows me more time to think.

About Willow.

About Tennison.

About how I've fucked up my life.

About how it's nothing like I had imagined it would be.

I mean, I'm thirty-seven fucking years old, and it feels like I'm starting over. *Because that's exactly what you did.*

"You sure are thinking hard over there."

Brittany's voice surprises me so much that I dump half the lemon curd I was making onto the stove.

"Shit, sorry. I called your name, like, four times." She cringes as I start cleaning up, hurrying over to help.

"Not your fault, Britt." My voice is gritty from the lack of sleep.

"You okay, boss? You can take the day off, you know. You've set up for the day. I can handle it from here."

"I'm good. Thank you, though."

She eyeballs me as she finishes wiping down the counter.

"I'm good, I swear." I'm not good, but I refuse to show weakness to anyone.

The next hour goes quickly, finishing up prep before opening up the doors. The big rush in the morning proves to be more challenging than usual. I can't tell if it's my attitude or if there's something in the water, but everyone I talk to has some sort of attitude, and when it finally dies down, I head back to my office for a break.

"Seriously. Go home." Brittany follows me back.

I sigh. "So I was the problem?"

She winces. "Kind of. We all have off days, though. I can handle it from here. Go take a nap, or work out, or whatever it is you do when you aren't here."

Fuck Willow, my thoughts immediately fill in for her, but then I remember last night.

"Alright, you win. But call me if you need help. I mean it." I point my finger at her.

She rolls her eyes. "Yes, boss," then turns and walks out the door, heading out to run the shop I'm incapable of running right now.

Dropping my head into my hands, I let the weight of the past twenty-four hours rest on my shoulders.

A workout. I need a workout. Not that it ended so great yesterday, but maybe if I go back to my default before I started hanging out with Willow, my head will work itself out.

Before Willow. My chest clenches painfully, and I move my hand to run over it.

Yeah, a workout is needed. I waste no time, running upstairs to change before heading out the back and out to the park. I debate texting Lennox again but decide against it.

Instead, I pull out my phone and call the last person I expected, but it somehow feels like the right move.

"To what do I owe this shocking turn of events?" Kellen Woodcroft says as a greeting.

"Why did you really contact me and bring me up to speed with the Tennison case?" I ask. It's something that's been nagging in the back of my mind. They left me alone for an entire year. And then out of the blue, he comes to visit and gives me information about the case? It doesn't make sense. He *shouldn't* be talking to me about any aspect of the case.

"Shit, man," he curses, and it's more telling than anything.

"What did you leave out when you came here?" There has to be more.

"Tennison switched things up when you left the force."

"Switched things up how?" I'm leisurely walking a trail, but my heart rate speeds up like I just sprinted a couple of miles.

"Captain doesn't want me telling you," he says quietly.

"Fuck the captain! If it has something to do with me, then I have a fucking right to know, Kellen."

Panicked. That's how I feel right now. Worried that I somehow triggered Tennison in a way none of us expected. I've taken care to avoid news surrounding him because I wanted to completely separate myself from the case, but now it feels like a potentially fatal move.

"Fuck. Please don't freak out."

"Too late," I mutter, feeling my palms starts to sweat.

"He's leaving calling cards."

"Calling cards?" I ask, confused. He's never left calling cards outside of the brand he leaves on victims.

"He ... he's been leaving oak leaves ... in the cuts of the victims."

I stop in my tracks and instantly feel nauseous.

"He started shortly after you left, but we didn't see the pattern, so he made it more obvious. Once we realized what it was, he just kept to that method."

I bend over and dry heave, slamming my eyes shut at the images bombarding my brain.

"Then he started traveling outside of his usual haunts. And it seems like he's taking a direct path to you." He says it so quietly I almost miss it over the pounding in my head.

"How?" I barely gasp out.

"I don't know, man. I've been working nonstop on this, and I can't fucking figure it out. I don't know how he's doing any of this, or how he knows where you are. I don't fucking know." The pain in his voice is familiar. It's a helpless pain—constantly seeing your failures in the most gruesome way imaginable. He's where I was a year ago, and I suddenly feel selfish to have left it all to him.

"I'm sorry," I gasp out, trying to get enough oxygen in my body.

"No! Jesus fuck, Oak, this isn't on you. This is one hundred percent on Tennison. I just have no idea how to stop the fucker, and it's eating me alive."

"And now he's coming after me," I gasp out. The panic attack is taking hold before I have time to even realize it or try to combat it.

"We don't know that." He says the words but doesn't believe them.

A humorless laugh escapes me through the gasping breaths. I lie down on the trail, trying to gain some stability. The rough rocks stabbing me in the back give me something to focus on.

"Oak, listen to me. This is not on you, and I will catch this motherfucker no matter what it takes. I just wanted you to be vigilant without telling you all of this. I know he's messed with your head."

"And now he's getting to you," I tell him as my breathing starts to regulate. I shift on my back, causing more pain, but it stabilizes my thoughts more.

"Well, he's going after my best friend, so fuck yeah, he's getting to me."

We both are silent for a couple of minutes, both in our heads.

"How the fuck do we get him?" I whisper.

"I don't know, man. I can't figure out his pattern. And now that he's on the move, which he never has done before, there are too many factors. I'm fucking scared, Oak." His voice is barely above a whisper.

"Me too, Wood." I want to be able to say more, but I can't. Because I already failed. I've wracked every corner of my brain to try to figure out this fucker, but I just can't. The worry now is that he's moving toward Texas, and there's too much that can happen.

"Please keep me updated on any movements." It's the only thing I can offer right now. Besides the panic attack creating a fog all around me, I can't commit to helping or even working on the case. I want to help Kellen, but I just can't.

"I will. I'll catch him, Oak. If it's the last thing I do, I'll catch him." It's a promise he can't make. We both know it, but he says the words anyway. It's no comfort to either of us.

I hear a rustle on the trail and try to perk up, but I'm sluggish.

"I'll talk to you later, Wood. Keep me updated please." I hang up without another word, just as a huge body comes out of the woods.

I shield my eyes against the midday sun and see Lennox dressed in his usual Park Ranger uniform. And he looks fucking pissed.

"How much of that did you hear?" I don't bother beating around the bush, letting out a sigh and collapsing back on the trail, a rock digging into my back again but I don't bother to move it. It helps me feel something, *anything*.

"Enough to know that you aren't a fucking chef from New York."

I struggle to sit up but don't move to stand up. I know from past experience that I'll just fall right over if I try it so soon after a panic attack.

"You wanna sit for this?" I ask.

"No."

Awesome.

"My name is Oakley, James Oakley, and I used to be a U.S. Marshal, mostly working on the Fugitive Task Force."

The color drains from his face, and shocked features take over the angry ones.

"I worked lead on the Tennison Strangler case," I tell him point-blank. He knows this area better than anyone in town. It's wise to fill him in so he can also keep an eye out.

"Holy shit," he mutters before plopping down next to me.

"Yeah." I don't want to, nor can I tell him details of the case.

"Is that who you were talking about coming after you?"

I close my eyes, trying to figure out what I can actually tell him that isn't classified. Kellen breaking the rules for me is different than me breaking the rules for a civilian.

"There is ... concern that he's travelling closer to this area." I keep it vague, knowing Lennox will read between the lines.

"Shit."

"Yeah. I need to ask you something I have no right to ask."

He turns his gaze to mine, and I see a resolution in his.

"I need you to stay hyper-vigilant. Not just keep an eye on things but look for anything that looks out of place. You know this area, and you'll notice things better than I ever could."

"Done." Just like that. Done. No question, no panic, and nothing taken out on me like I expected. I brought this shitstorm here; I deserve a lot more than his ire.

We sit like that, just lost in our thoughts for a few minutes. When my head finally feels clear, I attempt to stand up and only stumble once before I find my footing.

"Woah, man, you okay?"

"Yeah, just the aftermath of a panic attack." I try to go for nonchalance, but he sees right through it.

Concern takes over his face as he steps closer to me.

"I'm fine now, I promise. Just the conversation you overheard shocked the shit out of me, and where Tennison is involved, it usually means bad news for me even if I've been out of the game for over a year."

"You know, you can talk to me if you need to. I assume there is stuff you can't actually talk about." I smile at his knowledge. "But I work in a fucking national park and talk to animals all day. Your secrets and struggles are safe with me."

His pointed stare when he says "struggles" doesn't go unnoticed. Somehow, just the offer makes me feel a little lighter. I'm not sure if I'll ever take him up on the offer, but I do appreciate his support regardless.

"Thanks, man." I give him a nod, then awkwardly start to step back in the direction of town. "Well, I better check on Britt and make sure the shop didn't burn down." I let out a half-assed chuckle, and he gives me a knowing smile in return.

"Next day off is Wednesday if you want to get your ass kicked again," he calls as I get further away.

"You're on." I turn completely and make the walk back to Grind Time. The talk with Woodcroft, now that my panic has subsided, is front and center in my mind. I want to sit down and see if, after some time away, I can figure out any pieces of the puzzle that is Alfred Tennison.

CHAPTER FIFTEEN
WILLOW

It's Sunday, which means family dinner night.

I haven't talked to Oakley in a couple of days, and I just feel down about the entire situation. I've decided that family dinner will be the thing to cheer me up if I can just shut my brain up for a couple of hours.

I walk into Ledger and Ainsley's home, making a beeline for the kitchen, hoping there's wine or a seltzer—I don't really care, just anything to take this depressed edge off.

"Well, hello, kill anyone off lately?" Ainsley saddles up next to me, and I have to laugh at her. It's become a sort of game to her to try to guess who in town I've killed off that week. She's yet to guess correctly, so it's fun.

"Loads. Too many to count at this point," I deadpan. "You're so scary, but I fucking love it." She grabs two vodka sodas from the refrigerator and hands me one.

I take a long swig and take a minute to look around their house.

It always makes me happy to be here. Ledger gave up a lot of himself for so long, making sure us kids were taken care of, and now he's living the life he should have always gone for. All because of Ainsley.

"Whose favorite are you cooking today?" I ask since it is tradition, after all. Every week, at Ledger's house, we all gather and he cooks one of our favorite meals. It's something we did when our parents were alive, and he kept it going. We also go around the table and say something good that happened to us that week. I usually make quips about who I've killed off, hence Ainsley's game now.

"Today is Rina. She's been busting her ass on some crazy custom order, so I felt like she probably needed the pick-me-up."

I don't envy Rina. Her furniture building business has blown up recently, and it feels like she's busy more often than not. We haven't seen a lot of her lately, which is not normal.

"So, burgers then?" I arch an eyebrow. She's very basic, but Ledger makes pretty damn good burgers, so I don't mind.

"Yep." She takes a swig.

The front door crashes into the wall, and I cringe knowing Lennox just put another fucking hole in the drywall. He does this so often; they should really put a stopper or something.

"Shit, I promise I'll fix that," he says with a guilty look on his face as he joins us in the kitchen.

"I mean, honestly. Should we just put a metal piece right there this time? So you literally can't break it?" Ainsley asks in exasperation.

"Oh, bro, you finally fucked up. Ainsley's now annoyed with you. I don't think just fixing it is going to work this time." I chuckle. He's like a giant puppy dog sometimes, I swear.

Ainsley sends me a covert smirk as Lennox's face pales.

"I'm sorry, Ains. I promise I'll do better."

"I'm just giving you shit. What do you want to drink?" She turns to the refrigerator as Lennox sags in relief.

Yeah, family time is exactly what I needed.

"I watched some badgers build a new home yesterday," Lennox tells us as we go around. He smiles fondly, but there's something in his eyes that tells me that wasn't the only notable thing that happened this week.

"I finished one piece of ten for this fucking order," Rina grumbles, and now I see why it was her turn for food.

"I took a day off and spent the day watching movies with Ains," Ledger says with an adorably sweet smile on his face, and my heart trips in my chest.

I don't think I'll ever have that with Oakley.

My thoughts turn to all the what-ifs, and I curse myself for continuing to think about him.

"Yeah, ditto. I don't care if that breaks the rules," Ainsley adds, and we all laugh.

"Will?" Ledger asks.

"Umm." I try to come up with something, but it's been an uncharacteristically bad week for me. "I wrote a lot a couple of days ago. like, more in one sitting than I ever have before," I offer. When I went back to read what I wrote that fateful night, I cut every single word and moved them into another document. They didn't fit my current story, but I didn't want to delete them. They were not only cathartic but something I could possibly use later. Who the fuck knows anymore, honestly.

"Well, that's great! You think you'll make the deadline?" Ainsley innocently asks.

"We'll see." I give her a small smile. A week ago, I would have said hell yes. Now, I'm not so sure. I meet Lennox's eyes, and his brow furrows with what he sees.

The rest of the conversation flows normally. It's a weird mix of super happy Ledger and Ainsley, with a pissed-off Rina, and Lennox and I both stay pretty quiet. But they're my family, and I love them.

An hour later, I'm cleaning dishes when Lennox walks in.

Wordless, he starts grabbing dishes I've cleaned and starts drying them. We work in tandem for a few minutes until everything is done before he grabs us both a drink from the refrigerator and nods to the back patio.

Everyone else is chatting in the living room, but I follow him.

I sit down in one of the rocking chairs Rina built for the house and wait him out. He clearly has something on his mind.

"How much do you know about Oakley?" he asks, completely blind-siding me. I mean, sure, he knows I've been hanging out with him as research for my book, but that's supposed to be all he knows.

"Umm, that he owns Grind Time?" I play dumb, poorly, but it's my only defense.

He eyeballs me as he takes a drink, and I'm desperately trying to avoid eye contact. Which, in hindsight, probably gives me away more.

"You know."

"Know what, Lenny? What are you even talking about?"

"Fuck, I don't like this, Will. You need to be careful around him, and I think you know that because you know more than you're letting on." He runs his hand over his slightly overgrown brown curls, viability flustered, which is very unlike my easygoing brother.

"What exactly do you think you know?" I ask, my curiosity getting the better of me.

"It's not what I think I know; it's exactly what I know. I overheard him on a phone call while he was on the trail."

My blood runs cold. *How much did he overhear? Does Oakley know he heard him?*

"I talked to Oakley about it, so he knows how much I know. Hell, he told me a lot of it himself. I can already see the panic on your face, so you might as well give up the façade."

"I didn't know you knew a word like 'façade'," I quip to hide my rising panic. I don't know what to say to him because it all feels like I'm breaking Oakley's trust.

"Will..."

"Everything is fine, Len. I'm careful; he's careful. Things are fine." It's generic, and I don't even know if it's true, but it's all I can really give him. I'm not sure what they specifically talked about that's freaking out Lennox the most, but I'm a big girl and I can handle myself.

But you can't protect your heart from James. Yeah, but Lennox doesn't need to know that. Although, it does make me think something else happened. Especially if I combine this knowledge with James and my last interaction.

"If something happens, call me please. And be careful around him. I know you're using him for research or whatever, but if you can spend less time with him, you should."

Something in his words makes me angry. Maybe it's the fact he doesn't understand just how safe Oakley is, or that he's telling me how to spend my time, but it doesn't sit right with me. It probably has more to do with my defense of James, but I don't want to think too hard about that.

"Yeah, we're done with this conversation. Please believe that I can take care of myself, and please don't ever tell me how to spend my time again." I abruptly stand up, but Lennox grabs my arm.

"I'm sorry. Shit. Will, you know I just worry about you, and I don't hear from you that often. I just want to make sure you're safe. It's not that I don't trust Oakley, because I do, especially knowing more of his background now, but I don't trust the situation."

"Okay. I hear you, but you need to see that I'm not a child anymore. I write thrillers, for God's sake. If anyone can see the signs of bad shit to come, it's me. Trust that I won't get myself into trouble."

I don't wait for his response because all I want to do is go home. I'm depressed because of the whole Oakley situation, and now my brother is trying to warn me against him. It's too much for my confused mind, and I need to leave.

"Ainsley, Ledg, wonderful dinner as usual. I've got to get back to the writing cave." I kiss Ainsley's cheek and give Ledger a hug quickly, leaving them a little shocked at my abrupt departure.

I know if I stay, the cracks will show. This face I put on in front of them will fracture and all the fucked-up little pieces will start showing through, and I can't handle a well-meaning family talk right now. Hell, I don't think I can handle any attention. Curling up in a ball of blankets and avoiding the world feels like a good move right now.

I get in my car and drive home, since Ledger lives on the outskirts of town, breathing out a sigh of relief to be alone.

The entire drive, my thoughts flip from missing Oakley to thinking about how much of a danger he could actually be. Lennox's words infiltrate what I know and make me second-guess a lot of things. Which

I fucking hate. I'm that person that rarely takes a step back and thinks before acting; I usually just jump. Second-guessing is not in my nature.

But I've been doing a lot of that lately.

The drive home is one of the scary times you forget you're driving. I pull into my driveway and have exactly zero recollection of driving here. If Lennox wants to talk about who's the danger, it's probably me.

The house is dark when I walk in, and I don't bother turning on any lights. I walk to the bedroom and collapse onto the bed. Inhaling deeply, I can smell the faint scent of the very man I'm trying to avoid.

Why is the sex so fucking good? Why can't I just keep my feelings from bleeding into my everyday life and keep him as some fun on the side?

Because he's a good man who treats you like you've never been treated before.

It's the little things that stick in my mind the most. The lunches, the homemade dinners disguised as him cooking too much. It's the never-ending flow of lattes when I'm so immersed in writing I don't even look up to care about my needs.

But James Oakley sees it all. He sees me.

Even if he wants to ignore this connection.

Even if he wants to act like we wouldn't be great together and all the things he does are normal.

Even if he's afraid.

CHAPTER SIXTEEN
OAKLEY

I rest my forehead on my desk and take a deep breath, trying to calm my raging anxiety. It's been like this all week. She's been avoiding me, and I know she has every reason to, but it's still tearing me apart inside.

I know I fucked up. I told myself not to take my bad mood out on Willow, and that's exactly what I did. She didn't deserve the way I treated her. She may have acted like everything was fine, but I saw the hint of tears, the dejection on her face.

Hell, that's the exact reason I can't want more with her. Look what I did when there weren't real feelings at stake.

Keep telling yourself there aren't real feelings at play, buddy.

And that's the problem, isn't it?

I'm already too far gone with her, but I'm not in a place to be what she needs as a partner. And the way I treated her when I showed up to her house? I'm so ashamed of myself. There's no excuse and certainly no reason she should forgive me, even if she does hear me out.

And I don't feel right just barging over to her house to apologize. She's working and doesn't need me to interrupt her with an apology she may or may not want.

A knock at the door startles me, and I look up to see Brittany at the door.

"Hey, I'm about to head out. Do you need anything? I can stay," she offers, and I feel like shit. She's been picking up the slack this week since my head is noticeably elsewhere.

"Nah. Thank you, though. Go home. Enjoy your afternoon." I get up to head up front with her.

The front door dings as we make it to the counter, and I wave Brittany off as Ledger comes in.

"Hey, long time, no see. How are things going?" I ask, trying to not ask anything about how Willow is.

"It's busy as fuck, man. Ainsley's been working nonstop, so I figured I'd stop in here, and grab her favorite sandwich and coffee to slow her down a bit." The pure love in his eyes would normally have me rolling my eyes. But now? I wonder if I have that look in my eyes when I think about Willow.

"I'm on it. Anything for yourself?"

"Yeah, I'll take my usual."

I nod and get the sandwiches going before turning to the espresso machine. "So, how's the family," I ask and try to hide my wince at how obvious I feel like I'm being.

"Umm, good, I guess. I bet you've been seeing more of Willow than any of us have."

His words shouldn't hurt, but they fucking stab me. I *had* been seeing a ton of Willow, but I ruined it.

"Oh, yeah. She's been working in here a lot recently." *But not this week.*

"I'm worried about her. Usually, she cranks out books and it's no big deal, but this book is consuming her. She's stressed and definitely wasn't her usual self at family dinner on Sunday. And she hasn't talked to anyone since then."

I nod because if I say anything, he'll see right through me.

"Will you keep an eye on her? I mean, I know you're probably busy, but if she comes in here, will you keep an eye on her?" What's lower than dirt? That's how I feel. I feel like the scum of the earth I used to track down.

"Of course, man." I bag up the sandwiches and slide Ainsley's coffee his way.

I watch him as he nods his thanks, relief in his eyes, and then turns to walk out. I feel sick to my stomach. This is all because of me, and now he's asking to look after her like I'm not the cause of it to begin with.

The bell dings again, and I almost throw a coffee mug through the window. My nerves are frayed, my mood is completely shot, and I don't want to talk to anyone. But I do have a business to run, so it's time to shove all that shit down, like I did before Willow.

"Good afternoon." Sheriff's voice is like a spark that causes the fire to start.

"Sheriff."

"Haven't seen Willow around lately. Everything okay there?"

What the fuck is with everyone asking me about Willow? I mean, I was glad for a little bit of information from Ledger, but this is just too fucking much.

"Wouldn't know. I'm not her keeper," I almost sneer.

His eyebrows raise, but none of this is his business. He can try to pry and dig all he wants, but I'm not talking to him about it.

"Your usual?" I ask.

"Yeah," he grunts. I wordlessly go about making his stupid Americano before sliding it over to him.

"Something happen between you two?" He smirks, but it disappears just as quickly. Must be the death stare I'm giving him.

"Message received. You know, Oakley, I'm not your enemy. If you want to talk about things or go out to Sal's for dinner and shoot the shit, we can. You're allowed to have friends here." He looks genuine, and I swear it fucks my head up more.

"I appreciate it." And I do, but I'm not in the headspace to even remotely consider this right now. And that's a fucking realization.

How much have I really worked on myself since I moved here? I left my old life behind so that I could start fresh, but what have I really done? Open Grind Time? Know everyone's food and drink order but nothing else? That's not really living.

Maybe this is my sign to make some serious changes. To really think about what I want long-term.

Because what I think I really want ... Is Willow.

"I'm shocked to see you calling," my therapist from when I first left the Marshals, Dr. Ames, says when he answers my phone call.

"Yeah, it's shocking to me too, honestly."

"Is this a friendly phone call, or an 'I need help' phone call?" he asks plainly, and it's one of the reasons I didn't outright hate him at first. He's no-nonsense and doesn't sugarcoat shit.

I take a deep breath and say the one thing that's the hardest to admit. "I need help."

"Okay, you want to start with updating me on what's going on in your life? Last I heard you were leaving the Marshals, but hadn't heard anything since."

"Yeah. I left pretty abruptly. I, umm, I just couldn't stay when I was failing every single day Tennison wasn't caught." I clear my throat to try to shove down the lump in it.

"We didn't get to talk much about how you were feeling overall, more about decompressing from the things you saw and working through that. I apologize for not going big picture with you, but I'm glad you took the step to call me. Do you still feel this way? Still feel like you're failing?"

"I probably feel it more now. Is it possible to enjoy the changes I made, albeit they were drastic, but also feel like I fucked up by leaving the way I did? I mean, he's still out there, still torturing innocent people, and I just ... left. Because, why? I couldn't handle it anymore? That's not really a good enough reason."

God, I know this is what I should be doing, but it's like opening up a wound and letting it bleed out until you're left as just a lukewarm body.

"Why do you think that your life is any less important than theirs? Than anyone else's?"

"Isn't it? I signed up for a job that was to catch the bad guys, no matter what. I was good at it and felt like that's what I was put on Earth to do. My life, at the end of the day, is just a tool to protect the innocent."

And I fucking ran away, so really, how good am I?

"Do you feel that you aren't allowed to be happy?" He asks so calmly, but it blows what I know about myself wide open.

Do I feel like I'm not allowed to be happy because of what I've seen? Because of all the terrible shit I see people go through?

"I think..." Fuck, admitting this makes it real. Makes it so I can't just shove it down. "I think I'm scared of being close to people because of everything I've seen in the Marshals. How much hurt they can cause and how fast you can lose the ones you love. It scares me to not be in control, not be able to protect someone close to me."

"That's a good observation. And I'd venture to say a lot of people in your old position would feel the same. It's hard seeing the worst of people, and for people day in and day out to not be affected by it isn't realistic. Let's go back a little. Do you feel like going back to your old job would make you feel better?"

"Better? Hell no, but could it make me feel like I have more control? Possibly." I lean back on my couch and stare at the ceiling.

"Control, that's a good word choice for you. It sounds like a lot of this comes from control, or rather a lack thereof. But, I gotta tell ya, James, you can't control everything. Trying to leads to things like obsession with catching Tennison, feeling like you're failing no matter what you do, and falling back into old habits. Let me ask you, have you had any more panic attacks?"

Lying on the trail, talking to Woodcroft flashes in my memory.

"Yeah, I, umm, I had one about a week ago. Before that, it had been months."

"And do you know what brought that on in particular?"

"Woodcroft. Well, not Woodcroft specifically. I was talking to him, and he updated me on some details on Tennison."

"So, you've been away from the Marshals for about a year now, right?"

"Yep," I clip.

"Do you think the right move for your life is going back? You said you enjoy the changes you made, but do you think you can be happy? Can you be truly happy with a life going back to your old position and leaving what you've built up there? If the answer is no, I want you to think about what would really make you *happy* with your life. We only get one life, James, and everything you've done with the Marshals has been admirable. But there is no shame in saying you need to put yourself first for once."

"I met someone," I blurt out because all this talk about being happy brings only one person to mind.

"Ah, things are making a little more sense now." I swear I can hear his smirk through the phone call.

"Being around her has brought up a lot of things I probably pushed away when I moved. It was easy to just shove all my issues to the side and work, distract myself, you know. But with Willow..." I pause, trying to decide how much information to tell him. "We have—had—fun together. But I fucked up and took out some of this mess that is my head out on her, not physically," I quickly add. "But I treated her— God, I treated her like shit."

"Because you're starting to get too close," he observes.

"And it scares the hell out of me. What if something happens? What if lose her or can't protect her? I don't think I can recover from something like that," I admit quietly.

"You can't control everything, James. There is always a chance that bad things will happen, and that goes for every single person, not just you because of your past. I think you need to really make a conscious decision about what you want in your life, how you want your life to be. If that's with Willow, you need to be willing to be open and communicate with her your fears and needs. If that looks like going back to the Marshals, you need to make sure you are doing it for you, not because of some sense of failure you need to correct. What is going to make *you* happy and fulfilled?"

"You've given me a lot to think about." I let out a self-deprecating laugh.

"That's my job." He chuckles. "But seriously. If you want to do this more regularly, if you think it helps, just call me and I'll put you on my schedule, okay? There's no shame in going back to therapy."

"I will probably take you up on that," I admit. He's right, as hard as it is for me to admit that. Sometimes, you need more help than you can provide yourself.

"I'll wait for your next call. It was good to hear from you, James."

"Thanks, Doc."

I hang up and throw my phone onto the couch. The realizations in a half an hour conversation with Dr. Ames are a lot to take in.

The biggest one?

I want more with Willow, but I'm scared to lose her, scared to get close only to have my heart shattered.

Can I put in the work to be mentally in a good place to be open to a relationship with her? Would she even want that after how I behaved?

There's only one way to find out.

CHAPTER SEVENTEEN
WILLOW

I can't sleep.

I've tried everything—writing, watching something, my vibrator—and nothing is shutting my brain off.

I look at the time on my phone and see it's just after midnight. Throwing off the covers, I do something I'm sure Lennox would lose his shit about.

I throw on some tennis shoes, not bothering to change, grab my cell phone and a flashlight, and head out to one of the easier trails in the park.

It's Texas, after all, so my lounge shorts and oversized T-shirt will be fine in this godforsaken lack of seasons.

Ten minutes later, I'm moving my flashlight back and forth to make sure I can see around me, and very quickly determining this was a terrible idea.

Sure, Will, just go to the secluded National Park, where anyone could be hiding and no one knows where you're at. Great idea.

The paranoia grows, and my breathing starts to pick up. Hell, I know there are things that go bump in the night—I write about them almost daily—so why I thought this would be the thing to clear my head, I have no idea.

"Stupid, stupid Idea, Will," I tell myself. The silence is eerie, so talking to myself is the next logical step, obviously.

I roll my eyes at myself, annoyed that I decided to come out here and that I'm freaking out. I was better off staying in bed, and tossing and turning all night.

I walk another couple of steps and then spin on my heel to head back home.

"Nope. I may be able to write this shit, but I'm going to call it like I see it—I'm chicken shit."

"You're not chicken shit," a deep voice comes out of nowhere, and I scream bloody murder.

I drop my phone but grip the flashlight with both hands like a bat. I find out really quick that it hinders actually seeing around me when I do that.

"Who's there? I ... I will ... beat the shit out of you with this flashlight!" I yell.

"It's just me, Will. Stand down. I'm sorry I scared you." A phone flashlight pops up on a phone and shines on Oakley's face, where he's standing two feet in front of me.

"What the actual fuck," I heave out as I drop my flashlight and put my head between my legs. The panic is still raging through my body as I desperately try to calm it down.

"Shit, are you okay?" His voice sounds as panicked as I feel, but I don't even have the brain power to worry about him right now.

"*No!* Oh my God, I think I just had a heart attack." I feel his hand softly on my back, circling it while I continue my freak out. Once I finally catch my breath, I stand up and start laughing hysterically.

What a fucking mess I am.

"And I'm supposed to write thrillers. I should be better at this shit," I say through my obnoxious laughter.

"Hey, that was totally on me. I should have turned on my light sooner so you saw me coming." His shaky voice finally pulls my focus off of me and onto him.

I hold up my flashlight to see him better and see he's pale as a ghost.

"Are *you* okay? I'm sorry if I scared you too."

"I ... I'm fine. I saw you but I feel like shit for scaring you."

This man may have unknowingly hurt me, but he's the most thoughtful person I know.

"I'm fine, really. I just couldn't sleep, and it was a stupid move to come out here alone. Thought I'd be a badass and hoped a walk would help me sleep." I grin, trying to lighten to mood.

But he isn't having any of it.

"Why are you out here alone?" His tone shifts to complete seriousness, and the flashlight on his face highlights his clenched jaw.

He looks super fucking hot like this, which is wildly inappropriate right now.

"I impulsively thought a walk could help, and I didn't actually consider what a walk at midnight in a tree-heavy national park would look like." I ramble.

He grunts but says nothing, and it's unnerving.

"You've got to be more careful." His gruff tone catches me off guard more.

"You know, I don't understand you. How the fuck can you act so concerned right now?" I know I'm starting to raise my voice, but seriously? He's going to pull a protective act, like he didn't fuck me and then leave like I was nothing more than a warm hole to fill? No, thanks. I'm not putting up with this shit.

"Willow—"

"No. This is bullshit, James. What did I do to deserve to be treated that way? I mean, sure, the sex is always great, but that last time? Do you know how fucking hurt I was?" It feels like the week I've been avoiding him has finally bubbled over and all my hurt is crumbling at my feet.

"I do." He says it so softly I can barely hear him over my heavy breathing. "And I'm so fucking sorry."

"I— What?" I think I misheard him.

"I fucked up, so badly. I learned some new information about Tennison that I didn't handle well, and I thought my head was clear enough. God, I wanted it to be clear enough to not take it out on you, and I fucked up. I shouldn't have even come to your house. I never want you to feel like you aren't important to me. Nothing could be further from the truth."

"Did you ever stop to think that you could just talk to me?" I don't want to be this vulnerable right now, but I do want to see if maybe, just maybe, he's realized I could be more.

"At the time? No. But I've been forced to do a lot of thinking in the last week—thank you for that, by the way. And I ... I had a phone call with the therapist I talked to when I left the Marshals. He made me step back and realize a lot of things, honestly, but that's not the point. The point is I fucked up, and I really need you to see how sorry I am. Selfishly, because this past week has been the absolute worst."

"You talked to your therapist?" I'm not sure why that little nugget of information is sticking with me the most, but it's huge. I don't really care about the reason he made the call, but what I do care about is that he sounds so honest and humbled right now. I wish I could see his face, see the emotion I'm sure is showing all over it.

"I did. If I want to make my future into one I'm proud of—"

I stop thinking. For the first time in a week, my brain quiets. I step up to him, cutting off his words to pull him down to me and kiss him.

I kiss him with all the feelings I've been shoving down in the recesses of my brain. All the feelings for him that I've been desperate to hide and act like they aren't there. I kiss him because he didn't just apologize; he took fucking action.

And that's the most attractive thing I've ever seen.

One of his huge arms wraps tight around my middle and the other boosts me up by my ass, letting me wrap my legs around his waist.

I will never get over our size difference and how it allows him to just throw my ass around wherever he wants.

I missed this.

I missed him.

And I know we need to sit down and talk more about ... everything, but right now? I need him.

I need the way he knows exactly how to handle me. How he can get my brain to shut off with a well-placed kiss or the restraints he loves to use on me.

I feel him move, but it's so dark I can't really see where he's going. Our lips are still connected in the type of kiss that makes me think I could be a romantic. When my back hits a tree, the rough scrape somehow heightens my arousal. I'm so fucking turned on. I know it's not going to take long.

He rips his lips from mine, nuzzling my neck with his nose.

"I fucking missed you. More than you could ever imagine, Will. You make me want crazy things," he whispers in my ear as he kisses my neck in between words.

"Less talking. Please," I whimper out as he grinds against me.

He nips at my neck. "You going to boss me around tonight?"

"If you don't get to it, fuck yeah, I will. I've already gotten off once tonight, and it totally sucked." I rock my hips into him.

He abruptly pulls away from me. "What did you use?"

I'm mindless with need, so the question doesn't register for a minute until he stills my hips.

"What did you use to get yourself off, Will?" he growls.

"My vibrator," I breathe out.

"It didn't give you the relief you need because it wasn't me, wasn't my cock filling you, was it?"

"No."

My head tips back onto the tree as he kisses along my exposed shoulder, and the hand that's holding my ass moves along my waist as he presses forward with his body weight to hold me up.

I feel his touch slide over my hip, over my shorts, and slip under my underwear.

"I like the shorts." His voice holds a teasing lilt, and it so damn sexy.

Before I can come up with a snarky comeback to try to get a leg up in this spar of ours, his fingers circle my clit once before plunging two inside of me.

"Holy fuck," I moan.

"Put your hands above your head and keep them there," he growls as he keeps a steady rhythm with his fingers, and I comply without hesitation.

The bark of the tree scrapes against my palms as I try to grip it, but I don't feel any pain. How could I when James Oakley holds my pleasure in the palm of his hand?

"God, I missed you. Missed this pussy clenching around my fingers. You close already, Trouble?"

"Shut up," I say through gritted teeth, trying desperately to hold off my impending orgasm.

His chuckle threatens to send me over. The way he can get me there with barely any effort is scary. He has so much control over me, and I just want to tell him to take it all, take all of me.

My serious thoughts are interrupted by him pulling his fingers out of me and lifting me up higher onto his stomach. I whine at the loss, but he shushes me.

"I know, but I need to fuck you. That orgasm you're about to have is going to be on my cock." I hear him rustle a little before he drops my legs, still holding me up, and sliding my shorts and panties off before resuming our position. The tearing of the condom with his teeth is the only thing I can see in the dark forest, and he reaches under me to slide it on. Once it's on, he shifts me again, and I cling to the tree desperately, trying to not move my hands. I don't want to give him any reason to stop because he's right—I am so fucking close.

"Just happen to have one handy?" I joke.

"I've taken to always having one on me because of you. I guess I stayed optimistic this week." He presses a kiss to my jaw, making me smile.

Without preamble or warning, he slams me down onto his cock, and I groan into the silent forest.

"Fuck, Will. You feel too good, too wet, and too fucking *mine,*" he growls.

The possession in his words gets to me, and my entire body clenches up as I come.

"Fuck yes, come all over me. I missed this so Goddamn much. Missed you," he breathes into my neck as he keeps a steady pace. "I'm sorry I messed up. I'm trying, Will."

"I know," I moan out, barely able to speak coherently.

"You make me want things." His hand moves back to my ass as he shoves me closer to him, pushing himself deeper. "Shit, why is it always so good with you?"

His wonderment makes me smile. He never talks this much—not about things like this, at least—and it's sweet and sensual at the same time.

"Because we're good together," I tell him quietly, almost hoping he doesn't hear me because it's too much. I know it's too much, but damn it, it's the truth. I've been a fucking mess this week, and the only change was not being around him, talking to him, sleeping with him.

"Yes. We. Are." He punctuates each word with a hard thrust, and I feel myself getting close again. The arm around my waist protects most of my back from the friction. My thoughts turn to how I can get to my clit without disobeying him since both of his hands are occupied, but I can't figure out a way.

"Focus on me, Will. What do you need?"

"My clit. I'm so close, but I need more stimulation," I moan out frustrated.

"Such a good girl, not wanting to move your arms and defy me." I hear the cockiness in his voice, and I want to call him on it, but the arm around my back moves as he steps back and creates more room between us.

"This what you need? My fingers on you?"

"Oh God, yes!" I scream, and the orgasm hits me hard. It completely catches me off guard with how strong it is as I scream out into the wild.

"Squeeze me just like that. Yes. Shit." I hear his words, but I'm too lost in my orgasm to focus.

The fingers on my clit move away, and both hands grip my ass as he moves me with his thrusts as he comes.

He rests his forehead against mine, and it's the most intimate moment I've ever had. I move my hands to his shoulders and just revel in the feeling.

We're both trying to catch our breath, and I'm doing a very poor job of hiding how much this entire night is affecting me.

"I didn't intend for this to happen," he whispers against my lips.

"Yeah, I'll take the blame for this one." I huff out a laugh, then wince as a sore spot of my back scrapes against the tree.

"Oh shit, your back." He abruptly pulls out of me, sets me down, and spins me around to check on me.

The brightness of a flashlight shines around me as he speaks, "I might have ruined your shirt."

"Worth it." I sigh.

He spins me back around, placing his hand on my jaw before bending down to kiss me.

Pulling back, the light shines over his face just enough to see the emotion on it.

"Can I take you somewhere, or do you want to go home and get to bed?" He sounds worried, and I realize how late it is.

"Let's go." I'm sure the tiredness will hit me, but this feels like a night for vulnerabilities and openness, and I don't want to squander that for something as mundane as sleep.

CHAPTER EIGHTEEN
OAKLEY

This night feels like a dream.

As I lead Willow to the rock formation that overlooks most of Bluebell Falls and is close to the actual waterfall the town is named after, I think about how panicked I was to find her walking along in the park at midnight. It freaked me out so much that I spilled all my anxious thoughts I had been ruminating on.

I sure as hell didn't expect her to kiss me, or to take her against a fucking tree. Her back is all beaten up, and I'll have to take care of it later, but right now, I want to talk. A novel idea coming from someone who actively refused to talk to anyone for the better part of a year, but here we are.

It takes less than ten minutes to make our way to the rocks, and after grabbing the flashlight Willow so smartly brought with her, it makes everything go a lot faster.

Holding her hand, I sit down on one of the flat rocks and pull her onto my lap.

"You know, I don't think I've ever been up here. Lennox would probably be pissed about that." She giggles.

"I doubt most people even know this is here. It's always empty when I come up," I tell her, holding her tightly to me.

She feels so fucking right in my arms.

"Woodcroft called me before I came to your house that night. He was telling me something new about Tennison." I debate telling her or not. It's not that I don't trust her to keep it to herself, but I just don't want to worry her. "When I quit, he started changing his routine." I run my fingers along her arm to try and calm myself. I still don't know how to react to the news Woodcroft told me, but I think talking some of it out with Willow could help. "He's on the move. South, apparently. He's only ever attacked in the same area, leaving his victims to cope while he hid out until his next one. He's never changed things up," I tell her softly.

"Holy shit, are you serious?" She tries to turn around, but I hold her in place. It's easier to tell her all of this when I have a little more perceived control.

"Yeah. After I got off the phone with him, I wore my ass out with a workout. For hours, but my head was still a mess from speculating about every little detail I could. The only time my head is clear is when I'm with you. So, I had the bright idea to go to you, figuring the workout calmed me down enough to not take how I was feeling out on you."

"But your head never cleared. I could feel it."

"If anything, it made it worse. And I should have never put you in that position or treated you that way. I'm such an asshole." I press my forehead to her back and breathe in her comforting scent. It's amazing how she instantly calms me, but I also know I can't take advantage of that. I can't use her as a tool to not face my shit, to not work through all the problems I ignore.

"You were an asshole that one night, but you aren't an asshole in general."

I chuckle at her distinction. "Maybe."

"Is that why you called your therapist?" she asks.

"Yes and no. It wasn't the whole reason. I think I talked to more people this week while you were—rightfully—avoiding me than I have since I moved here. Ledger is worried about you. Sheriff seems to be trying to recruit me."

"Well, that's interesting," she muses.

"Which part?"

"Arlo. Ledger is always worried about someone, so that's not shocking. But Alro wants you to work with him?"

"He's hinted at it, more than anything."

"Huh, is that something you're considering?"

I sigh. "At the moment? No. It feels like Tennison has a block on me, so I can't imagine I would be much help to him."

She hums in response, telling me without words that she doesn't necessarily agree with me.

I press my cheek to her back, closing my eyes and mentally preparing myself to be completely open with her. This isn't something I've ever done with a woman, but Willow is more than worth it. I just have to hope she's open to hearing it all.

"I'm scared, Will."

She starts to turn and I try to stop her, but she moves my hands. Facing me completely, she straddles me and grabs my jaw in both hands.

"You know, it's okay to be scared. It's okay to not have all the answers." she says.

I lean forward, pressing my forehead to her collarbone.

"I should be over so much of this, though. Tennison should be my past, but he's forcing himself back into my life. And you know what scares me the most about that?" I ask her, pulling away and looking into her eyes. "You being anywhere near the line of fire. You're a vulnerability for me, regardless of whether I wanted it or not. I can't put you anywhere near danger. And Will, everything around me screams danger right now."

"I'm a big girl, James. I can handle myself. Not taking into account tonight, I'm usually pretty smart about my actions. I don't go out at night. I bring things in my bag that can be used as weapons. I'll keep my eyes open."

"I appreciate your concern over safety, but my point is that if I get close to you..." I try to think of a way to articulate my thoughts, and I just decide to go for it. "Fuck it. I am getting close to you, and it's scary as all hell. You being close to me makes you a potential target for Tennison, and I can't have that. I have survived a lot in my life, but that is something I wouldn't recover from."

"But what if you're doing all this worrying for nothing? What if we could just enjoy our time together because you never know what the future holds? I don't know that always focusing on the what-ifs in life is the healthiest approach to things," she says softly.

"You could be right, but what if all that worrying saves you? Protects you?"

"I hear you, I do, but what about things you want? You constantly worry about everyone around you. Your old job was worrying about saving people you didn't even know. Who worries about you?"

"I don't have an answer to that." Mostly because I don't really want to do a deep dive into why I am the way I am. "You know, Sheriff made a point to tell me that it's okay to have friends here, and I never realized how disconnected I truly was until he said that. It's hard to let old habits die, honestly, and I've never really been close to people in general. You are the exception to that. Hell, Willow, you're the exception to everything."

She presses a soft kiss to my lips before pulling back. "How about I be the one to worry about you?"

I'm running on far too little sleep right now, but I'm happier than I've been in forever.

Brittany has been side-eying me all morning, but what am I going to say about this sudden change in personality? I'm with Willow, and we fucked in the park her brother works at last night? Yeah, no. I'd rather keep all of that to myself.

Speaking of Lennox, he could be an issue, but I think he'd be okay with me dating his sister, though. We get along, so that has to count for something, right?

Willow's the most important Hutton to me either way, so however he reacts, I'll deal with it.

Brittany starts tapping her nails on the counter, and I can feel her stare on the side of my face.

"Don't even think about asking whatever is on your mind." I shut her down.

"You don't even know what I was thinking about. It could have been about … about Mabel and Alice's new fixation." She huffs.

I hold off my smirk. "You weren't thinking about Mabel and Alice."

"You know, for a coffee shop owner, you're annoying as hell sometimes with how well you know people."

Because it used to be my job.

I grunt in response because not even Brittany calling me on my shit is going to damper my good mood today.

The bell rings above the door and Lennox walks in, looking pissed as hell.

Might have spoken too soon about that good mood.

"Do you have a minute?" he practically growls.

I sigh and motion for him to head back to my office. "I'll be back," I tell Brittany before following Lennox.

I quietly shut the door and cross my arms, waiting for him to tell me why he's pissed.

"Leave Willow alone," he says when he finally stops pacing. My eyebrows shoot up, shocked at the audacity he has right now.

"Leave Willow alone?" I repeat.

"Look, I don't think you're a bad guy, but you have a past that doesn't really seem to be so in the past. Leave her alone and don't put her safety in jeopardy."

"And you think you can just come in here and decide things for your sister—behind her back, at that—and I'll just what? Do as I'm told?" I stand my ground. I see where his head is at, and honestly, I understand it more than he'll ever know. I'm scared shitless to potentially be putting her in danger, but I also recognize that this is as much her choice as it is mine. Lennox coming in here and pulling a big-brother act won't change her mind.

He scrubs his hand over his face. "Fuck. I don't know. I've been thinking about..." He gestures wildly to me. "All of that shit, and it freaks me out. What if something happens? What if that asshole really finds you? That puts Willow in the direct line of fire and, Oakley, I've got to protect her." The worry in his voice brings my guard down.

He's doing what he thinks he has to in order to protect her, and I can't fault him for that.

"Sit." I walk around my desk and plop down as he does the same in the chair in front of me. "First, Willow decides what to do with her life. I don't. If she chooses to be with me, which I'm fairly certain she does, then we have to accept that. She's a grown-ass woman who is more than capable of figuring out what's best for her. Second, I'm just as worried as you are." I lean forward and meet his eyes. "You know I'll protect her with my life, right?"

I need him to see I'm not only serious about her safety but about her as well.

"Fuck. This whole thing has my head so fucked up. How the fuck did you do this shit for a job?" He groans and drops his head back.

"Well, there's a reason I don't do it anymore." I laugh humorlessly.

"I know, logically, she'll be safe with you, but what if something happens? What if that asshole shows up here? I can't lose her, Oakley." His voice gets softer as he talks, and I second-guess every decision I've made in the last week.

Can I protect her?

Am I putting her in more danger by not holding her at arm's length? I still don't know.

"I don't have all the answers, Lennox, but I can promise to do everything in my power to protect her at all times. And if something happens and I fuck up in any way, I give you full permission to beat the shit out of me." I grin in an attempt to lighten the mood. We both know nothing with Tennison is in anyone's control, but I will do everything in my power to protect her from it all, even if in the end that turns out to be from me.

"I will absolutely hold you to that. Fuck, I'm sorry. That was such a dickhead move to come in here and demand shit. Don't tell Willow. She'll skin me alive."

And just like that, the bulk of the tension dissipates.

We both chuckle, knowing she would kill both of us if she knew this conversation was taking place.

"I really like her, Len, and I won't take advantage of the fact that she seems to be on the same page. I just want to make her happy," I confess to him. He's the closest thing I have to a friend here, and with him being her brother, I want him to know I'm not just fucking around with her.

"I know. It's written all over both of your faces. It's really annoying," he deadpans ,and I chuckle. There's the little-brother attitude. I'm glad it's alive and well.

"I'll remember you said that when you get close to a woman," I smirk.

"Yeah, you do that." He stands and walks over to me. Cuffing my shoulder, he looks at me sincerely. "I'm sorry for pulling this shit. I'll admit, I looked up Tennison after we talked on the trail, and it freaked me out."

As it usually does.

"Understandable. Just know, I'm keeping updated on the case, and if something is going to affect the town or your sister, I'll fill you in. I will admit it's kind of fun seeing you in the protective-brother act."

"Whatever. I'm going to get a coffee. Text me if you want to work out later. I'm off today."

He turns and leaves my office, and I slump back in my chair.

My good mood is all but gone because he's not wrong.

If something happens, if Tennison finds me, can I truly protect Willow?

CHAPTER NINETEEN
WILLOW

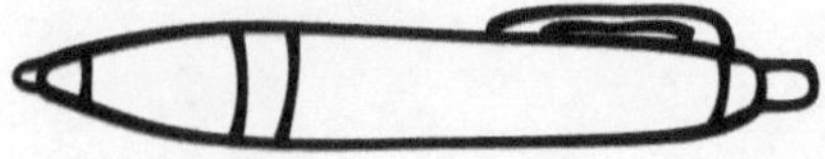

Three days.

I have three days to finish this fucking book, and I feel like I'm drowning.

I wrote for hours after Oakley fucked me in the park and then left. Since then things have been … robotic. I feel like I'm writing what I should and not what the story actually is. It's got all the pieces I usually put in, and yet I fucking hate it.

I've been taking things slow with Oakley as well. After our … park incident, things were intense, and I felt like I had too much going on all at once. We discussed taking things slowly, especially while I finished this damn book. But right now? All I want to do is walk down to Grind Time and be in the same room as him. I need to feel that sense of calm that only he brings me.

So, that's exactly what I do.

Loading up all my shit takes far too long for me, and by the time I'm walking toward the coffee shop, I'm antsy and flustered.

"Good aft— Willow." The relief and happiness on Oakley's face make my heart rate speed up.

Taking things slowly was a terrible idea. Good job, Will.

"Hi." I throw my hand up in an awkward wave. I take a quick look around and see two teens in one corner, but otherwise the place is empty.

Sure, we've talked, but it's been a couple of days since we've actually seen each other, and it suddenly feels like this giant chasm is between us. I hate everything about it.

"What sandwich do you want today, Will?" he says softly, already working the espresso machine for my latte.

"Umm, surprise me."

We stare at each other for a second before I shift and move to sit at a table in the opposite corner from the teens.

Oakley comes over five minutes later and sits down at the table.

"I've missed you," he says with a smile. "How's writing going?"

He's been the most supportive person I could ever dream of. He's been checking in but also giving me time to get into a flow without interruptions.

"It's a nightmare," I say, snagging the caprese panini he made me and taking a bite.

"Anything I can do to help?" I see his arm reach under the table before I feel his warm palm on my thigh. He gives me a little squeeze of support, and I realize maybe he is exactly what I need to get this damn book done.

"Can I stay after close?" I ask before taking a sip of my latte.

"You can always stay; you never need to ask, you know that."

"I know, I just feel so fucking awkward right now and I don't even know why. This book is kicking my ass. I thought staying home in my writing cave would help me figure it all out, but it all just feels wrong. And I missed you. So damn much." I suck in a deep breath, wondering if my brand of manic is going to eventually run him off. All my anxious thoughts are spewing out, and I feel like a fucking mess right now.

"Okay, well, I close up in twenty minutes. How about you just relax, don't think about writing or anything book related, and when I'm done cleaning, we can head upstairs and you can tell me everything you feel like you're hung up on."

I nod and feel my throat constrict with just how understanding he is.

He's unlike anyone I've ever met, and the fact that he just lets me be me makes me think this could be the real deal.

He stands up, leaning toward me to press a kiss to my cheek before standing to his full height and heading back to the counter. He wastes no time and starts cleaning, giving me plenty of arm candy to watch as he does.

An orgasm. Maybe that's what I need to unblock my brain.

I shake my head, making a pact with myself that I can only have sex with Oakley if I hit my word count for the day. I need to keep my priorities, or I'll end up in his bed all night and really miss my deadline.

God, I'm a disaster. I roll my eyes at myself and continue to watch Oakley close down the shop. Before I know it, he's done and kicking out the teens before locking the front door.

"Ready?" I look down at the table and realize—sometime in my mindless thoughts—I finished my sandwich and coffee, and he somehow already cleaned it up. Which makes me sad because I didn't even get to savor it, didn't get to enjoy how freaking good it was. I can't wait until this book is done and I'm able to get out of this damn funk.

"Ready?"

I take the hand he's holding out, and he leads me to the stairs.

I sit on his couch once we're inside and watch him as he fusses around, picking up things, getting me water, and overall being adorable.

"James," I say.

His eyes lift to mine, and I pat the seat next to me.

"Sorry, I just want to make sure you're comfortable."

I lean into him, cuddling into his chest and breathing him in. Instantly, my head is calmer and my racing thoughts mellow.

"I hate everything I've been writing," I murmur.

"How can I help?" I love that he doesn't offer immediate solutions; he just asks me what I need.

"I have no clue. I wrote a shit-ton after you— After we— After the time we were together that kind of sucked." I wince.

"That's a very nice way to put what happened. Continue."

"I wrote all night. I had so many emotions to get out that I just threw them into the book. The next couple of days, I realized none of it worked with what I usually write, so I moved it into a separate document and moved on. Well, attempted to move on."

"Why don't you think it would work within the book?" he asks as his fingertips trail up and down my arm.

"It feels more ... romantic. It no longer became about him killing and hiding it; it became a love story between him and his informant."

"And that's a bad thing?"

I smile at his innocent question. Maybe I am just stuck in my ways and not being open to what the story could be. Too hung up on what works and not pushing myself to do something new.

"I'm not exactly sure. Everything I've been writing in the last week or so feels so canned. Maybe I do need to revisit it. Maybe this isn't a true thriller," I think out loud. "What if I don't label it? What if I market it as a love story with a twist and just see where it takes me? I have a loyal fan base and if they hate it, they hate it. But somehow, my normal routine, normal approach isn't working."

"I love the way your brain works," he whispers.

I look up at him and chuckle. "You mean, a mess of anxiety and a thought process that only makes sense to me? And even then, sometimes I don't understand it."

"Intelligent, on a whole different playing field, with no limitations—take your pick," he says instead of letting me be a downer to myself.

"It's not all that glamourous."

"To you. So, how can I help? Do you want to go home and write all night? Stay here? I'll cook you food and keep you sustained if you'd like."

I let out a sigh and burrow into him more. "Can I set up shop here and just see where it goes? I promise not to interrupt your routine and all that."

"Will." He cups my cheek and draws it up so I'm looking at him. "Interrupt, please. Helping you is all I want to do, so whatever else I had going on—which, admittedly, isn't much—is going on the backburner."

"You're like a mythical creature, you know that?"

His laugh is loud and strong, and it makes me smile. "How so?"

"You're ready to drop everything to basically cater to my every need because I'm on a deadline of my own making. Do you see how rare that is?"

"I'll be honest and say I don't really keep up with how other people handle their relationships, but I do know that if you need help, whatever that looks like, I want to be the one to do it." He shrugs.

"Just that simple?" I ask.

"Just that simple."

I stretch up and kiss him hard. "Thank you," I whisper against his lips.

"Anytime. So, what do you need, Trouble?"

I smirk at his rare use of the nickname he gave me our first night together.

"A place to set up? And possibly the use of your brain?" I smile cheekily.

"Done." He presses one more kiss to my lips before shifting me so he can stand up. He moves to the little dining area he has near the kitchen and clears it off, before grabbing my laptop and notepad, laying them out nicely before turning back to me. I roll my lips inward to stop the smile on my face from spreading.

He really is too adorable.

Standing up, I sit in the chair he's pulled out for me and start up my laptop.

"So, if I shift everything, do I keep the general storyline?"

"What would the endgame be if you move to a love story?" he asks thoughtfully.

"I mean, a happy ending, but more specifically, I think I would like to keep him as the killer and the barista as the informant. Maybe she figures out who he is and secretly loves it?"

"What if she not so secretly loves it and joins in?" He taps his lips with a finger.

"Joins in the killing?"

"Yeah, I mean, why not? If you want it to fundamentally be a love story, wouldn't she be accepting of what he does to an extent? Or are you wanting him to get redemption because of her?"

"Well, damn, you're good at this." I'm stunned. Sure, he reads a lot, so I figured he could help me talk through this, but what I didn't expect was him to break down how to write a love story like it was his job and then give me options.

"Am I?" He looks shocked.

"Oh yeah. I think I like the idea of her joining him. Giving him redemption feels too predictable."

"Will what you wrote and then cut work with that, though?"

I think back to the pages I wrote, think about the emotions both characters went through, and realize this is exactly what I was leading to. I wrote about them getting close, sharing secrets, sure, but I also wrote about her realization that he wasn't who she thought he was. It led to a lot of confusion on her end and even more questions, and I think I could absolutely have her realize that being with him is the right move for her.

"Yeah. Holy shit, I think it'll work perfectly." My mind starts working a mile a minute, and my fingers move to the keyboard without another thought.

A kiss to my temple is the only thing I remember as I buckle into an intense writing session.

A plate hits the table softly, and I see a couple of slices of pizza and a cup of water.

I eat it like I'm starving, and I probably am. I don't know what time it is. I've switched my computer into focus mode so nothing distracts me.

I briefly look up and see Oakley looking at me with a small smile on his face.

"Thank you," I whisper.

I eat everything within minutes and then go back to writing. Things are going well so far.

The next time I look up, the sun is rising. I look down at the document and realize I'm about two-thirds through. One more good day of writing, and I'll actually make this deadline.

My eyes are bleary as I look around and realize I don't see Oakley. Wondering if he's still in bed, I stumble over to his room and find it empty.

He's probably already at work.

I decide to lay down for a minute, and work up the energy to head downstairs to find him, maybe get some coffee in the process.

As my head hits his pillow, I think about how sweet he was last night. How much he took care of me when I zoned out and essentially ignored him.

The last thought in my head is how I think I could love him in time. Hell, I probably already do, and then I drift off to sleep.

CHAPTER TWENTY
OAKLEY

Watching Willow work all night long was something to behold. Sure, I've been with her when she's been in the zone, but not like this. She didn't look up, didn't move the entire time. I would periodically put food out for her, and she would pick at it as she wanted, but it still didn't feel like enough.

I'm yet again running Grind Time on little sleep, but I wouldn't change a thing.

The front door dings, bringing in a welcome reprieve to my thoughts.

"Morning, boss-man. How's the morning been?" Brittany says as she walks past the counter to the back to drop off her purse.

"Slow," I call back to her. It was a light morning for us, but I did hear Jim Mathews say they were holding a huge bingo tournament, so maybe that's why. "Yeah, I heard Ledger talking about Ainsley's dad setting up this thing at the community center. I didn't get all the details, but I assume a good chunk of town is there."

"Bingo tournament," I inform her.

"Of course it is." She laughs.

"Can you run things for a minute? I just need to go upstairs and check on something."

"Absolutely. Take your time."

She walks around, checking things are to her liking before heating up a muffin. I chuckle as I walk away and head up to my apartment. I left Willow while she was still working; she didn't even hear me leave, so I want to see if she's still up.

If she is, I might have to tie her to the bed so she gets some sleep. She's stressing me out with the all-nighter of work, and the need to take care of her is too strong.

I skip steps, quickly making it up to my front door and opening it quietly. Everything is silent, but that doesn't mean much while she's working.

Walking around, I check the dining room and see all her things still splayed out, but no sign of Willow. Making my way to my bedroom, I finally see her spread out over the entire thing. My heart pounds in my chest at seeing her asleep in my bed. Something about it feels so intimate.

She's lying on my pillow, and I'm hoping it smells like her long after she leaves.

I walk closer, realizing she didn't even cover herself up, that's how tired she was, so I move her as carefully as I can, hoping I don't wake her up before covering her up.

Pressing a kiss to her forehead, I whisper, "I will take care of you every day if you let me. Just don't give up on me if I fuck this up." I kiss her once more before quietly leaving the room and heading back down to the café.

"You know, if you want to call it a day, I can handle things here. You deserve to take the day off once in a while, and it's clearly not going to be a madhouse today." Brittany's words reach me as I move behind the counter.

For once, I don't argue with her. I have something more important than Grind Time waiting for me.

"Sounds good. Thanks, Brittany. If it's super dead after the lunch rush, just close up."

She makes eye contact with a smirk on her face. I raise an eyebrow, daring her to say something about what I'm sure is the obvious reason I'm playing hooky today.

"Have fun, boss-man." She twinkles her fingers at me before turning around and finishing her coffee.

I turn right back around and head upstairs.

A free day with Willow, no matter how we spend it, sounds like the perfect day to me.

Once I'm inside, I strip out of my clothes quietly and slide into the bed beside her. Instantly, she moves closer and snuggles into my chest, like she subconsciously knows I'm here. Wrapping my arms around her, I kiss the crown of her head as sleep takes hold.

I wake up to Willow kissing my neck.

"Good morning, Trouble." My voice is gravelly from sleep.

"Good morning, or apparently, afternoon. Why aren't you downstairs?" she whispers as she continues to kiss along my jaw.

"Bingo tournament. Day off. Wanted to spend the day in bed with you." I turn my head to catch her lips.

"Mmm," she hums with a smile. "I think I like waking up next to you."

"We can definitely make this more of a habit," I agree. "Are you hungry?" I ask, knowing it's been a long-ass time since she ate.

"Fucking starving." She sighs as she plops back down onto the bed, and I grin at her response. Good to know food comes before sex.

"Breakfast or lunch?"

"Hmm, breakfast please," she says as she snuggles back under the blankets.

Sitting up, I lean to kiss her one more time before I get up and throw on some joggers, and head to the kitchen.

I look at my options, my hearing hyper-focused on any noise coming from the bedroom, and I decide on an easy breakfast of French toast and bacon. The bedroom is still silent as I get started, and within a half an hour, breakfast is ready.

I grab our coffee first, taking it to the bedroom and seeing Willow has fallen back asleep. The smile that takes over my face hurts my cheeks just from looking at her. She's so fucking beautiful, and right now, she's in my bed. Mine. Let's just hope I'm able to keep her.

Going back for the French toast, I double-check to make sure it looks perfect, then join her in the bed, holding both plates.

"Time to eat, Will," I say softly, trying to not startle her.

She moans as she turns toward me, and my dick hardens at the sound. *Not the time.*

"Food's up, and there's coffee on the side table."

"It smells delicious." She shifts to sit up, snagging the mug and taking a sip. Her eyes close, and she hums contentedly.

This. This exact moment is what I'm going to be working for from here on out. Therapy, putting Tennison behind me, whatever it takes to make sure these moments happen with Willow.

When I look back in time, this will be the moment I remember falling in love with her.

I set the plate of food on her lap as I dig into mine so I don't spill my sappy soul to her right this second. She has so much on her plate right now. I want to ease the load, not add more to it.

"Oh my God, this is so fucking good," she moans, and I'm about two seconds away from saying fuck it and jumping her.

"Stop moaning, Trouble. I only have so much self-control."

She says nothing, but mischief is blazing over all of her features.

Wordlessly, she puts a bite of French toast dripping with syrup into her mouth, and I have to scrub my hand over my face in an attempt to break the sexual tension.

Her laughter reaches my ears, and I smile. "You're bad."

"I am, but you like it." She smirks.

"I do. So, how was writing last night?" I ask, changing the subject because I need her to know this isn't solely about sex to me anymore. I want to know all the details of her day, every day.

"It was ... manic. I don't really know how to explain it. I wrote more over the course of last night than I ever have in a 24-hour period, and it wasn't total shit. In fact, it felt really fucking good."

"Are you still liking the direction you're going?"

"I am. It's so different, but it feels right for this story. I think I only have about a third left, maybe a little less, so I should be fine to make my deadline. I emailed my editor too to give her a heads up on the genre shift. She's optimistically leery." She laughs. "It'll be good ... hopefully."

"That's good. So, what's the plan for today?" I ask. Since I don't have to work, I'm available for anything, even if that involves shutting up and feeding her while she works.

"I think I need a quick nap, and then I'm going to jump right back in. With any luck, I'll finish it tonight. I can go home, though, for that. I always have a weird schedule when I'm this close to a deadline," she adds quickly.

"I'd like for you to stay, but I won't force you if you're more comfortable at home."

She holds my stare for a moment. "I want to stay." Her voice is quiet, like she's unsure of my reaction even though I just asked her to stay.

"Done. I'll make sure you have sustenance while you work." I nod as I take my last bite of bacon.

"You're spoiling me. How am I going to be able to write a book all by my lonesome again?"

By doing this every single time. Staying with me every night and letting me take care of you.

"We'll work something out." I wink at her instead of telling her how I really feel.

"And this was a wonderful breakfast, although, that's not shocking coming from you. Have you always been a good cook, or is that something you learned when you left the Marshals?"

"Always loved it. It felt like a natural transition because I didn't really have to learn anything new. It was an easy shift when I moved here, and it's blown up more than I thought it would. Grind Time wasn't supposed to be this huge attraction in Bluebell Falls, but that's what it's turned into."

"Well, selfishly, I never want you to leave because I'm well fed thanks to you." She takes a sip of her coffee.

"You think I'm going to leave?" I ask, confused why she has that idea.

"Honestly, I have no idea. You fit in well here, but everything I've learned about you makes me think your job isn't finished with the Marshals."

I ponder her words and am a little ashamed to say I'm starting to feel the same way. It feels like I ran away from an unfinished job, and it's coming back to bite me in the ass now.

"Well, I have no intention of leaving. This place has really grown on me," I tell her instead.

Her eyes twinkle as we stare at each other, then she leans forward, pressing the softest kiss to my lips.

I want more.

But I also know she has work to do and a nap to take. My needs aren't important right now.

"Time for that nap," I whisper against her lips.

"Yeah, but can I at least help clean up first?"

"No." I smile.

She flops back down onto the bed with a relaxed sigh.

"I really like you, James Oakley."

"I really like you too, Willow Hutton," I say softly.

She meets my eyes, and the depth of feeling is almost too much. She's like a tornado that came into my life and changed it irrevocably. I couldn't be more grateful for it.

I drag myself away from her as she snuggles back into my bed, collecting our dishes and heading to the kitchen to clean up.

I'm almost done when my phone rings, and I see Woodcroft calling.

"Hey, man," I say after drying my hands off.

"Hey, how are things?" His voice sounds tight, like he's trying to play it cool but he's stressed.

"What's going on, Wood?" I ask instead of answering him.

"There's another one. In San Antionio, this time."

It feels like my entire body is drained of all its blood. It's a shock to the system not only hearing there's been another victim but that it's so fucking close to me.

I open and close my mouth a couple of times, but I can't make any words come out. It's like I'm locked up mentally and physically.

"Oak, I think we need to make local authorities aware."

I clear my throat. "They— They are. The sheriff here is informed."

"Okay, that's good. Can you let him know of this new information? And I'll call you again if I hear anything new."

"Yep." I strain to get it out.

"You okay, man? I know this is a lot to drop on you, but I need you to be safe."

"I'll be good. Let me call the sheriff." I know I should probably talk to Woodcroft more, but knowing that Tennison is in Texas has me in a panic. It was one thing when we just thought he was moving around, but now he's in the same state as me and it's less and less likely that I'm not a part of his reasoning now.

"Call me if you need anything. Just keep your eyes open, and we'll do everything we can to catch him before anything else happens." They feel like empty words because we've been hunting him for years to no avail. Anything's possible, but I have a feeling things will get worse before they get better.

He hangs up, and I stare at my bedroom door. I need to find a way to end this. I refuse to put that woman in any danger.

Scrolling through my contacts, I pull up Sheriff's number.

"I never thought I'd see the day that you call me."

"I have news."

"I'm listening." His playful tone turns serious in an instant.

"Tennison took another victim in San Antonio."

He curses. "We've got to get proactive."

"Yeah, for once, I agree."

"It would be a lot easier if you were working in the department," he not-so-subtly pries.

"I can't," I whisper, feeling more and more useless by the minutes. The realization that Tennison is coming for me is starting to hit, and the panic is rising.

"Just keep it in the back of your mind. I'll start calling some contacts and doing more patrols of the area. I'll call Lennox too, so he's aware and can keep an eye out at the park."

"Sounds good. I'll call you if I get more information."

"Thanks, Oakley. We'll figure this out." He hangs up before I get a chance to tell him it's not that simple. That groups of people have been on this case for years and we're no closer to catching him.

My eyes are drawn to my bedroom door again.

It's time to stop hiding. If that's what it takes to protect Willow, then I'm going to find Tennison and make sure he never hurts anyone again.

CHAPTER TWENTY-ONE
WILLOW

I wake up refreshed and ready to finish this book. Stretching, I roll over and see Oakley isn't in bed, but I didn't expect him to be. He's not the one on a fucked-up schedule right now. Grabbing my phone off the nightstand, I see it's just after noon. Lunch then writing, I think.

Rolling out of bed is more of an ordeal than I wanted it to be. I'm still a little groggy, but I need to get shit done, so lying in bed all day isn't an option.

I walk to Oakley's closet, grabbing the first T-shirt I find, and snag a pair of boxers from his dresser. I'd ask first, but I have a feeling he won't mind me walking around in his clothes all day.

"Thanks for letting me—" I stop in my tracks when I walk out to see Oakley hunched over, head in his hands.

"Hey, you're up. Hungry?" His head jolts when he hears me and puts on a façade.

Something happened while I crashed.

"Yeah. I could eat. Are you okay?" I ask, knowing he probably won't tell me. I can tell when he's going to open up and talk to me about things, and I can tell when he's closed up tighter than Rina's lips when we ask her about Arlo.

"I'm good. Just had a phone call from my old partner. Nothing big, though. Just shooting the shit." He averts his eyes, and I know there's more to it but I won't push him. He'll talk when he wants to; at least, that's what he's been doing.

"Can I make lunch today?" I ask to change the subject.

"No." He smirks. "It's my job to take care of you, so I'll be taking care of all your hunger needs today."

"Just my hunger needs?" I ask with a sly smirk.

"If you finish your book, we can talk about what other things you need, Trouble." He shakes his head like it's such a hardship.

I grin at his reaction, knowing if I finish this damn book, I sure as hell will be having him take care of my other needs.

"What do you want for lunch?"

"Umm, would be it totally cliché to say a panini?" I cringe. He has the day off, but damn it, his paninis are the freaking best and it's the best kind of fuel for a long day of writing.

"Nope. I'll run downstairs and make you one."

I shuffle over to him, and stand on my tiptoes in an attempt to kiss his check but only get up to his neck. Shrugging, I press a kiss to his neck instead. "Thank you."

He smacks my ass before leaning down and kissing me. "Go get set up. I'll be right back."

I stand in a daze as he leaves to make me lunch like some kind of house husband. Who knew there were men out there that went through this much effort for a woman.

I shake myself out of my Oakley stupor and walk over to the area where I've set up my makeshift desk. I make sure I have some water, all my notes are how I like them, and I review where I left off this morning. By the time I'm done with all of that, my sexy man is back with provisions.

I devour it before diving headfirst into the last third of this book.

I come up for air about five hours later and see the sun setting.

"Holy shit, I'm done," I say to myself.

"You finished it?" Oakley's voice draws my attention. He's sitting on the couch, reading one of my books, and I think I fall in love with him right in this moment.

"Yeah," I breathe out.

Relief like I've never felt takes over my body, and I slump into the chair. Tipping my head back, I exhale as I hear Oakley moving.

When I feel his hands on my jaw, I open my eyes and see pride in his.

"You are fucking phenomenal," he says softly.

"That was the hardest book I've ever written, and I'm so damn proud of it." I start tearing up because it's been such an emotional roller coaster and it might just be the best book I've ever written.

"I'm so proud of you, and I can't wait to read it." The sincerity in his voice damn near breaks me. It's incredible to have this support from someone who isn't family.

"Take me to bed, James." His words, his actions over the past few days come crashing over me, and it feels like I need him right this second or I'll ... just cease to exist.

"Gladly." Kissing me hard before his hands move to my ass, he picks me up out of the chair as he stands up, our lips still connected. I grip his too-long hair, controlling the kiss while I can because if I know him, and I think I do, I won't be able to use my hands in a minute.

When he tosses me onto his bed, I bounce a little before he walks to the closet and grabs something. When he turns around, a line of rope is in his hands, causing my legs to clench together. We've never used actual rope, always just what we could find on hand, and I'm more excited about this than I thought I'd be.

"You ready for this?" His voice is deep and hoarse.

"Oh, hell yes." I squirm on the bed.

His wicked grin turns me on more than the prospect of being tied up.

"Hands up, Trouble."

"Yes, sir," I snark.

He arches an eyebrow at me, just waiting for me to do as I'm told.

I throw my hands up before he starts stalking over to me, tossing the rope and a couple of condoms on the bed, and I mirror his arched eyebrow.

"You've worked hard. I'm going to make sure you are completely boneless by the time I'm done with you. If that takes a couple of rounds, so be it."

"Jesus, you're sexy," I whisper.

His hands grip the bottom of his shirt I'm wearing and slide it up my body. "I like you in my clothes, although, I like you naked better. This will do when I'm not fucking you."

"Oh, now there's a dress code?" I giggle.

"There can be. It'll go both ways, Will, don't worry." He winks, and I can only smile at him.

This banter, this playfulness while still being so serious is the absolute best. It shuts my brain off, my only focus on him and what he's going to do to me next. I love it.

Next, he drags the boxers off of me before pulling my leg up and trailing kisses from ankle to thigh.

Gently putting my leg back on the bed, he moves to pick up the rope, undoing it from the neat bundle he stored it in.

"Are you okay if I use rope? I bought it after we first got together. You're the first I'm using it with, and it's bamboo, so it's super high quality and should have low friction," he quickly explains.

I love how thoughtful he is about it all. I would have let him tie me up with anything, but it's nice to know he's really thought everything through.

"Very much okay with it," I say quickly. Later, when my entire body isn't solely focused on getting an orgasm, I'll ask him about his affinity for tying up hands.

"I'm going to make a sort of handcuff, and if at any time you hate it or it doesn't feel good, just tell me."

"Okay," I whisper.

I hold out my wrists to him, and he immediately gets to work. The intricate knots he creates between my wrists are wildly attractive.

He tests the knots, and the space between my wrists and the rope, and deems them perfect. "How does it feel?"

I can't stop squirming on the bed because I'm so damn turned on. The whole time he was tying me up, he was pressing kisses to different parts of my body.

"So good," I moan.

His grin greets me as I look at him, and he takes the long tail from my wrists and ties it to the bedpost, forcing me at an angle on the bed.

"Good." I feel his fingertips along the outside of my thigh, and I fail to keep in my whimper. "Spread your legs for me. You've earned yourself quite the orgasm."

"Because I finished my book?" I can't help but ask. He makes me want to be a little bratty just to see what he'll do.

"Because of that, and because you've helped me see there is more to life than pretending to live."

My body freezes, and my eyes blink open at his words. His soft smile greets me, and my heart pounds in my chest, this time from something dangerously close to love.

When his fingers start creeping toward the inside of my thigh, I adhere to his earlier command and spread my legs. If this man is promising a damn good orgasm, I know he'll deliver and then some. And after sleeping in his bed the past couple of nights without actually having sex, I'm so damn horny I feel like I'm going to combust.

His teasing starts slow, first just his fingertips right at the juncture of my hip, slowly moving closer to where I really want him. He barely grazes my clit, and I flinch at how sensitive I already am.

"Fuck," I hiss out.

"Oh, you really are in trouble this time, aren't you? So needy already."

"James," I whimper as he circles my clit harder before dipping down and barely pushing inside of me.

"God, I fucking love it when you say my name," he growls as he pushes his finger in more.

"What else do you like?" I just want to hear him talk. Everything he's doing is clearing my head from all the stress that's built up over the past weeks. It's like the anxiety disappears with each word he says.

"I like when you're wet and needy for me. When you're so fucking turned on that you're on a hair trigger. I love having you tied up and at my mercy. It calms me, makes me feel invincible."

My back arches as he adds another finger before pulling them out and circling my clit again. He repeats the pattern over and over again, until my muscles are so taut they start to hurt, never quite pushing me over the edge.

"You are incredibly sexy like this," he murmurs.

Without warning, he shoves his fingers back in as his thumb circles my clit, and I go off like a bomb. My mouth opens wordlessly, my arms pull on the rope holding me in place, and my legs shake.

Panting as I come down, James eases me down from it, never removing his fingers. "That's it. We're just getting started, Will."

I collapse on my back, feeling absolutely boneless. It feels like the perfect culmination from all the tension I've carried over the week. The perfect escape and release. And we're just getting started.

Rustling draws my attention, and I look up to see him stripping. His tattoos pop against his golden skin, and if I wasn't tied up I'd be kissing every single one of them.

He shoves my legs apart as he kneels on the bed, and I moan in anticipation.

His hands wrap around the back of my thighs as he pulls me down enough for there to be tension on my arms.

"How are you feeling?" he asks.

"Good, so fucking food. Arms feel fine too," I add, realizing that's what he's really asking.

I feel his hot breath before he sucks my clit into his mouth.

"Holy fuck," I breathe out.

It shamefully takes him no time at all to make me come again as he licks and fucks me with his tongue. The orgasms just compound on each other. All I want to do is grip his shaggy hair as he takes complete control of my body, but he has a proclivity for tying me up. Maybe one day, I'll return the favor and take everything I can from him.

"Fuck, you undo me, woman," he grits out as he stands up and snags the condom, ripping it open and rolling it down his impressively hard cock.

Leaning over me, he cups my jaw, kissing me hard and letting me taste myself. At the same time, he notches himself at my entrance and thrusts with no hesitation. I gasp into his mouth as he sets a punishing pace. Like a man possessed, he doesn't stop until I'm right at the edge again.

One hand supports his body weight as the other moves to tweak my nipple. He starts off softly and then quickly pinches harder, causing my orgasm to come out of nowhere.

"God damn, you feel good coming around my cock," he whispers against my neck before he gently bites it.

I don't think I could talk even if I wanted to. Between the endless orgasms and the quietness of my mind, I've got nothing except for feeling right now.

James quickly pulls out of me, and I whimper at the loss, but then he flips my hips over quickly and yanks them up so my ass is in the air.

Shit, that was hot.

He slams back into me, and my back arches in pleasure.

"I can't hang on much longer, Will. Fuuuccckkk," he groans as his pace picks up.

I can tell he's close because the grip on my hips is bound to bruise a little, and I fucking love it. I've never in my life been into rougher sex like this, but with James? It's sexier than I could have ever imagined.

He reaches underneath me and circles my overstimulated clit, triggering another damn orgasm. I feel tears rush to the surface at the sheer relief of it all. He thrusts in hard and stays there, succumbing to his own orgasm, and I wish I could see the look on his face right now.

Before I even have time for my breathing to regulate, he pulls out and flips me back over. Reaching up, he starts to undo the knotted handcuffs, and within a couple of minutes my hands are free. He grabs them both, inspecting them and kissing any red spots.

"Was that okay?" he mumbles against my wrists.

"It was mind-blowing," I pant out.

"Yeah?" The vulnerability in his voice makes me smile. He cares so much about me, and he doesn't even attempt to hide it.

"Yeah, James." I pull my wrists from his hold and circle his shoulders in a hug.

He shifts to the side so he doesn't put all of his weight on me, but lets me continue to hug him.

My mind and body are blissfully content.

This moment with James is something I didn't know could be a possibility, and I want nothing more than to keep it forever.

CHAPTER TWENTY-TWO
OAKLEY

I love her.

That's the thought that keeps circling in my head as her fingertips run along my chest and stomach. We're lying in bed after I got us cleaned up, just soaking in the moment.

"I've never had something like this." Her quiet words permeate the air.

"Something like what?" I ask, my voice gravelly from not being used.

"A partner, someone who actually puts in effort. It's not like I've done a ton of dating, just a little in college, so I don't have a lot of experience," she rambles.

"I think the last woman I dated was at least a decade ago," I tell her. "And it was maybe a couple of weeks, nothing more. My life has always been work-focused."

"Why did you go into the Marshals?" she asks.

"It's not a tragic story, like some. It's actually a success story for the entire Fugitive Task Force. My parents and I were on vacation when I was eight, and there was a story on the news about the Marshals looking for a fugitive in the area we were in. Didn't think much about it at the time, and we continued on our way, checking out the tourist attractions in the area. What's funny is I can't even remember where we actually were, but we found the guy."

"What?" She lifts her head up to look at me.

"Technically, I found the guy, but I didn't really know what it meant, you know. I told my parents that it was the guy from the news, and they immediately called the authorities. It was a huge whirlwind after that, but I was hooked. These badass guys came into town, looking scary, but they were the good guys. They were pulling a guy who was this really bad guy from the streets. From that moment on, I never wanted to do anything else with my life. So, I made it happen and never looked back."

"That's fucking amazing." She smiles.

"It changed the course of my whole life, and I never really stopped to think if there was more to life, you know?"

"I do know, except I think I took things to the other extreme. My parents died when I was in high school, and Ledger had to step up for Lennox and me. Rina too. I dated some when I was in college, but I decided early on that I would rather stay alone than have to deal with the pain of losing another loved one."

I hold her wordlessly, both of us realizing that these ideals we previously held about our lives are no longer possible as long as we're together.

"I want to figure out this shit with Tennison. It feels like I'm stuck, like I'm not able to fully move forward until things are settled with him. With Woodcroft coming here, it feels like this past year was just running away from the larger problem."

"How can I help?"

This. Fucking. Woman. She has no idea that her simply asking seals my fate completely. It's odd... Every version of a relationship I've seen or dealt with has always been uneven. Either one person is putting in more effort, or one isn't really into it as much as the other person, but with us? Willow and I feel like the definition of equal partners. She's been busy for the last couple of weeks, so I stepped up. I know that if I get busy or need help, she will jump in without question.

"I don't know that there is much to do at the moment. It's basically a giant waiting game, like it has been."

"Are you needing to go back to New York? I have time now that the book is off to edits, and I can come with you," she offers ,and I realize she doesn't know that Tennison is traveling and probably closer to Bluebell Falls than anyone wants.

"No, I need to stay here."

"Okay, that's cryptic."

"There's a lot that's classified, Will. Things I can't tell you. Shit, things that I shouldn't even know right now."

"I get it. Just know I'm here if you need help or a sounding board, or I don't know, if you need an orgasm." She smirks.

"Oh, I'll definitely take you up on that one." I smile, and I poke her side.

She sighs. "So, what about your parents?"

"They are currently living the high life in Arizona in a retirement community. We don't talk a lot, which is mostly my fault, but we've also just never been that close. I let them know when I moved, and we've maybe only talked a couple of times past that. They'd like you, though." I pull her tighter to me as I close my eyes.

"My parents would have loved you," she whispers, and my heart clenches at what she had to endure at such a young age. "We have family dinners every Sunday. I'd like for you to come whenever you feel ready."

"I'd love that." I know immediately I need to figure out this Tennison situation as soon as possible. If I have any chance of keeping Willow and making her happy, I need to resolve this gaping hole in my past.

"What's on your agenda the rest of the day? Night? I don't even know what time it is." She giggles.

"It's about ten at night."

I chuckle at her muttered, "Oh, jeez."

"So, I have sleep on the agenda. But if you're hungry or want to do something else, we can do that instead."

"I think sleep sounds perfect."

Sleep takes us both quickly, and I fall into the best sleep I've had since I was a kid.

A ringing phone startles me and jolts me out of bed. I climb out of bed as quietly as I can, snagging my phone as I head out to the living room. I shut the door behind me, trying to let Willow sleep.

"Oakley," I answer without looking because if someone is calling me this late, it's for a good reason.

"Hey, man." Woodcroft's voice sounds tired. Worn down.

"What's going on?" No need to beat around the bush when we both know he's calling for a reason.

"He's been seen traveling north on I-35, taking a direct line straight to you."

I curse under my breath, trying to figure out what the next steps are.

"Fuck, I've been out of the game too long. I've already informed the park ranger and the sheriff here, so they've got their eyes open. What else do I need to do?" I can hear the panic in my voice, and I count to ten to try and calm down. The last thing I need right now is a full-blown panic attack.

"Well, I'll be there in the morning. I'm at the airport right now, heading your way, and the rest of the team will be joining us in the next day or two, whenever they can get flights."

"Fuck, the whole team? So we're really going to try and catch him here?"

"It's the only chance we've got, Oak. We know he's coming for you, know where he's heading. It's the best chance we'll ever get."

"I know. Fuck, I know. But I can't put the people here in danger. I can't risk it, so we need to figure out a way to draw him out somewhere."

"That's all stuff we need to discuss with the team and the sheriff."

I quickly realize I'm not in charge here. The natural instinct to step in and take control of things isn't my job anymore, no matter how much I feel the responsibility of it all.

"Well, I live above Grind Time, so if I'm not downstairs when you get in, come find me."

"Will do. I'll see you in a few hours."

I hang up without a response, lost in the very real possibility that I'm bringing the devil to the doorstep of people I truly care about.

I have to protect the people of Bluebell Falls. I need to protect Willow, no matter what it takes.

"What the fuck?" Willow's stunned voice shocks me, and I turn around to see her ashen face greeting me.

CHAPTER TWENTY-THREE
WILLOW

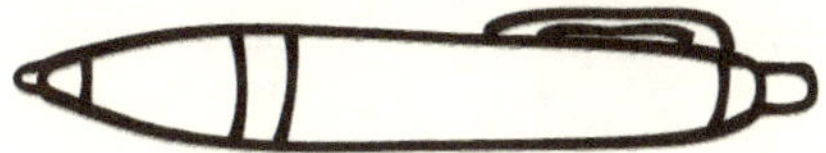

Eavesdropping is bad. I know that. God, do I know that.

And yet, instead of just staying in bed when I felt him leave, I crept to the door to listen to his conversation.

What I didn't expect to hear was that his old team is on the way here. The only reason they would be heading this way is if Tennison was.

I crack the door, trying to hear more of the conversation.

"What the fuck?" I whisper. Or I think I whisper it, but when Oakley looks up and sees me, his face drops.

"Will—"

"What is going on?" I can hear the terror in my voice, but I can't even begin to calm myself down.

"Fuck," he groans, pulling his light brown hair in frustration. "Sit, please," he asks more calmly than I imagined he could right now.

I plop down on the couch, waiting for him to join me, but he starts pacing instead.

"You know the basics of Tennison, but things have changed."

"Changed how?" I ask.

"He's traveling, for one, and he's never done that before. And he's going after one person, specifically."

My eyes widen, confused as to why his modus operandi seems to have changed so drastically. "Who?" I whisper, praying it's not whom I think it is, praying that all of Oakley's fears aren't coming true.

He stops pacing long enough to give me a sad smile. "No," I whisper. "No!"

Stopping his movements, he comes and sits next to me. "He's been slowly making his way to me, and the Task Force hasn't been able to get ahead of his movements, always missing him. He's been ... he's been taking victims along the way and leaving a new calling card."

"James..." I don't know how to respond. I don't know how to feel. The only thing in my head is how to keep him safe, how to keep him out of Tennison's hooks and with me.

"The team is heading here as we speak."

"What's the calling card?"

"I'm not sure what the plan will be, but I know the goal is to try to get him here, set a trap or something. I don't know." He ignores my question.

"James, what is his calling card?"

He lifts his head and stares into my eyes. I see the guilt, the frustration, and the devastation he's feeling right now.

"He's been leaving oak leaves with the victims," he whispers, and my heart shatters.

"Fuck." The guilt must be encompassing his every thought right now.

"When the team gets here, I'm going to do everything in my power to lock this bastard up."

"What can I do?" I ask. I'm not sure I can actually do anything, but I need to help. I can't just sit back and wait to see if Tennison gets his target, crushing my entire world.

"Nothing. I need you safe—that is literally the only thing that matters. I cannot risk you being in his crosshairs." His pleading tone has me starting to feel panicked.

I swing a leg over his lap, straddling him before cupping his jaw in my hands.

"I can't lose you either. Don't you get it? This—whatever we label us as—is special, and I will not let some psychopath come and threaten that. And if he's coming here, then everyone in Bluebell Falls will rally for you. You're one of us now, and we have each other's backs."

"But, Will, I'm not worth protecting like that. Whatever happens to me was set in stone the second Tennison's and my paths crossed."

"You are a noble man, but that's some ridiculous bullshit you're spewing right now." I smirk to lessen the blow. "The second you won everyone over with your delicious coffee and sandwiches, you were stuck with all of us."

"I've seen things, done things, that are horrible, Will. I don't deserve that level of support, and I definitely don't deserve you, but fuck if I don't care. I just need to stop him. The things he's done, the things that are kept from the media, it's something I need to figure out how to stop. Woodcroft isn't supposed to be even sharing any of this shit with me, let alone me telling you, but I need you to be aware and cautious. I need you to be safe."

I nod, telling him I hear him and will absolutely be on my game.

"Oh, and 'girlfriend'. You're my girlfriend. That's the label I want."

"Done." I smile. "You want to try to get more sleep before our sleepy little town gets overrun with a super manly task force team?" I ask with a giggle in an attempt to break some of the tension.

"If I see you ogling any of the men I used to work with, I'm tying you up before beating the shit out of them."

Laughter bursts out of me. "I'd pay to see that show, honestly."

"Don't even start, Trouble," he growls as he tickles my waist.

"Truce! I promise I will only have eyes for you!" I squeal out before he hugs me tight to him. The serious look in his eyes stops my laughter.

"I definitely need to try to get more sleep, but I also need you to know that I appreciate you and everything you do, everything you offer. Thank you. I want to make a real go of this, regardless of what happens in the next few days with Tennison."

"Me too," I murmur.

"I— I just need you to be safe," he relents, and somehow I don't think that's what he meant to say.

"I will be. "

His hands grip my ass again. "Let's try to get some sleep." He stands up, carrying me to the bedroom, where we snuggle back into bed. His arm wraps around my waist, pulling me close to him as he spoons me from behind.

Content. That's how I feel. Even though it feels like bad things are coming. Even though it feels like things are going to get way worse before they get better, I'm content in his arms.

And even though my thoughts are still whirling with the new information, I'm exhausted enough to fall back asleep.

CHAPTER TWENTY-FOUR
OAKLEY

I don't sleep a wink.

Willow is sleeping soundly beside me, and I'm a stone's throw away from a panic attack.

I watch through the blinds as the sun starts to rise, and I know things are about to change today. It's something I both want no part of and know that I need to finish. Tennison needs to be stopped, and Woodcroft and I are the ones to do it. *We have to be the ones to do it.*

I was serious when I told Willow I couldn't lose her. Serious when I said I needed her to be safe. Hell, I almost told her I loved her, but it wouldn't be fair to her. What if something does happen to me? I couldn't tell her that and then not come back to her—that's a whole different level of cruelty.

A sharp knock at my door tells me my time with Willow is up. She starts to stir next to me as I get out of bed.

"That was the door?" she asks with a sleep-roughened voice.

"Yeah." I sigh.

"I'll meet you out there," she says as she swings her legs over the side of the bed.

I nod as I throw on a pair of jeans and a T-shirt. Walking to the front door, I open it, and find Woodcroft and Sheriff at my front step.

"Thought we'd make it a party," Woodcroft says, far too happily.

"Great," I grumble and open the door so they can come in.

As they make themselves at home in my living room, Willow comes out in a pair of leggings and one of my shirts, making it more than obvious what transpired last night.

"Morning, Willow," Sheriff says, not trying to hide his smirk.

"Morning. Coffee?" she asks them both before looking up at me.

I nod and join the men, hoping it will shield her from the worst of this conversation.

"What do we know?" I ask, not beating around the bush.

"We know he was spotted again last night near Austin. A gas station, but he was gone before anyone could get there. He grabbed a bag of chips and filled up on gas before hitting the road again. Paid in cash. We received another tip about the same car on the eastern side of the national park," Woodcroft says.

"So, how do we get him? How do we stop him?" I ponder, still not any closer to a solution.

"Well, I think it's positive you know where he's going. That helps with the end game." Willow's voice reaches my ears.

"Willow, go home. You don't need to be here for this," I say offhand-edly. I just need her far away from this, but I don't think about my actual words.

"Oh, shit," Sheriff mumbles under his breath as Willow cocks her hip.

"Too bad," she says simply before plopping down in the dining room chair she's been using to write. She gives me a hard stare, daring me to tell her to leave again, but Lord knows I can't tell her what to do in any situation.

"I like her." Woodcroft holds out his hand. "Name's Kellen Wood-croft. Nice to meet you."

She takes it with a smile. A growl escapes my throat, and they both laugh.

"Willow Hutton. Lovely to meet you as well."

"I think she's right. This is a leg-up we've never had," Woodcroft says.

"Thank you," Willow says as she tucks her feet and takes a sip of her coffee.

"There are too many places to hide around here, though," Sheriff says.

"True, the national park doesn't help matters. It's acres of woods and trails," Willow says.

"Fuck," I say, running my hand over my head. "It feels like we're right back to a year ago. No progress, more danger, and more threat."

"Why don't you just let the team and Sheriff Arlo handle it? You aren't on the force anymore; we don't need you to be involved, especially if it's going to put you in a bad head space. I'm not trying to put you back there, Oak."

"Kellen…"

"I'm serious. I just got my best friend back. It's not worth going through the mind games, especially if he's targeting you." He looks up at Willow, and she bows her head in a show that she knows all the details, so he's able to talk freely. He arches his eyebrow at me, and I ignore him.

"Maybe we should take this down to the station," Sheriff intervenes. "We can map everything out and get a plan together."

"Shit, I've got the café to run. Brittany isn't coming in today."

"Well, then it's settled. You'll run your business, and we'll take care of Tennison," Woodcroft says so easily it's starting to piss me off.

"I'll run it." Willow's voice is strong and sure.

"What?" I ask.

"I'll run Grind Time. I mean, I'll probably suck at the coffee, but no one in Bluebell Falls will really care. I'll hold down the fort while you guys take this asshole down." She offers it so effortlessly, and for some reason, it hits me hard. She doesn't bat an eye to support me, to step up when I feel like I need to finish this. The guys may not agree, but she understands. *She gets me.*

"I can just close up shop," I suggest.

"Nope, it's already decided. I'm going to get cleaned up, and I'll head down and take care of it." She's already standing up, taking the last sip of her coffee before heading to my bedroom.

"She's fucking perfect for you," Woodcroft says quietly with a chuckle.

"Because she's running Grind Time?" I ask.

"Because she's pushing you to finish what you started, even if I think it's a terrible idea. I know you, and I know you wouldn't listen to me anyway, but she just stepped up and she's feisty. Like I said, perfect for you."

Sheriff is just watching us with a smirk on his face. I get the feeling he doesn't really talk to anyone that much unless it's for a good reason. But his facial expressions give him away if you pay attention.

"Alright, I'm heading down. Call me if you guys need some coffee, and I'll run some over. I assume you'll be at the office for a while?" Willow turns to ask Sheriff as she comes out of my bedroom. She's tied my T-shirt into a knot at her hip and thrown her hair up on top of her head. She looks fucking beautiful.

"We will be. I'll let you know. Thanks, Will," Sheriff says.

She nods as she walks to me, leans down, and kisses me. "Be safe," she whispers, and I can see the fear in her eyes.

"I will."

"Well, great to meet you, Kellen. Arlo, be nice." She bounds down the stairs like this is just part of her everyday routine.

My eyes track her until she shuts the door behind her. I don't want to leave her, I don't want to leave our safe space, but she's right. Her actions tell me more than her words ever could. I need to go after Tennison. I need to close the door on that time in my life so I can put my full effort into being the man that Willow needs and deserves.

The three of us walk into the small sheriff's office. It looks like there's just him and a part-time front-desk person, who isn't currently here. No wonder he's been bugging me to take a job.

We make our way to his equally tiny office and grab chairs, getting settled in for the long haul.

"Okay, so what do we know?" Sheriff pulls out a map of the area, laying it out flat before sitting back.

"We know he's heading north from Austin. He was last spotted there, about" — Woodcroft checks his watch — "fourteen hours ago. And a few hours ago, we got the call about the same car on the outskirts of the park."

"Shit." I scrub my hand over my face.

"I don't know the entirety of the case, just what I could find in the news and other reports, but if he's coming for you, Oakley, then is it not safe to assume he's either setting a trap or watching your movements?"

"Yes. He's stealthy, so I can't imagine he would change up his routine entirely. I would assume he's done a little of both, honestly. I'm sure if he was able to get here last night, he would have been watching Oak to some degree. And that probably will lead to him setting a trap of some kind."

"If he was watching me, he knows about Willow."

Terror. Sheer panic is all I feel even speaking those words.

"I've called in some reinforcements," Sheriff Arlo causally says.

"Who?"

"All the busybodies who have nothing better to do. They'll keep an eye on her and the area. They've been told to look out for any trouble, not whom specifically."

"Smart." Woodcroft nods.

"No use in worrying the whole town if we're able to get him without their interference."

"I'll be honest, as much as I want to get Tennison, I can't let anything happen to Willow."

"Heard." Woodcroft turns back to the map. "It would make the most sense that he's hiding in the national park. Do you have anyone well-versed in that area?" he asks Sheriff.

"Lennox Hutton is the park ranger. Knows the park better than any-one."

"No," I say immediately, heart clenching. Not only is he now a good friend but he's Willow's brother, and I won't bring him into this.

"Oak... If this is our only chance, we need to try," Woodcroft says.

"It would be up to Lennox anyway. We can bring him in, but if he wants nothing to do with this—and I understand if he doesn't—then I'm not forcing him."

Woodcroft and I nod at Sheriff's assessment. It's not our decision to make, it's Lennox's.

"I'll send him a message. I'm not sure if he's working today or not. If I don't hear from him within the hour, I'll call him, maybe run by his house." The sheriff pulls out his phone, sending a message before tossing it on the table.

"Okay, so here are some obvious spots..."

The three of us look at the map and attempt a plan of attack.

CHAPTER TWENTY-FIVE
WILLOW

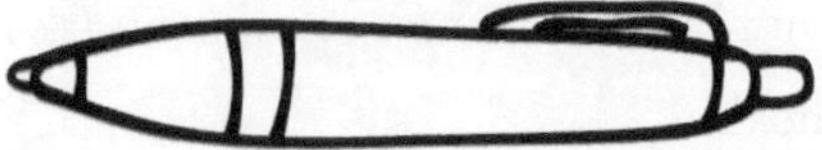

The morning started off quietly, and I was thankful for it. Three hours later, and the whole damn place is packed.

"What can I get for you today, Mr. Mathews?" I ask Ainsley's dad, Jim, as his eyes sparkle with mischief.

"Oh, just a drip coffee, please."

That's how I know something is going on. Every single person in here has ordered a regular drip coffee. I know for a fact half the people in here order complicated, fancy drinks. But not today.

"Coming right up." As I get his coffee together, my mind wanders.

I have this gut feeling that Tennison is planning something big, but I can't quite put my finger on what. The men seem to think they have it handled, but I don't know. I just have a bad feeling about all of this.

"Here you go." I slide Mr. Mathews's coffee to him.

"Where is our dearest Oakley this morning?" he asks.

"He's sick," I throw out without thought. It's not like I can tell everyone what's actually happening. I can't even imagine the panic that would incur.

"Well, I hope he gets to feeling better." He winks and casually walks out the door.

"Willow Marie! Would you come here a second and settle something between Alice and me?" Mabel yells across the room.

This spells trouble. And with the already suspicious activity happening today, I'm keeping close tabs on these two.

"What's up, Miss Mabel?" I ask, plopping down into the free chair at their table.

"Well, Alice here seems to think that Oakley buys all his pastries frozen while I think he makes them all. Perhaps you could settle that for us."

Jesus, these two are ridiculous. It's obviously a ploy to distract me. Keep me occupied. Who knows, but I do know it's absurd.

"Well, everything set out today was in the fridge, but I know he makes almost everything. He makes the sandwiches fresh too, including the bread."

Mabel and Alice look at each other with a knowing look, and I realize I just gave away more than just the freshness of his product. Within half an hour, the whole town will now know that Oakley and I are together in some form.

Crafty gossips. You can't ever let your guard down around them.

"Well, that's wonderful to know. And how about you, dear? Is this just a one-time thing? Or..." Alice trails off.

"I like to help out where I can. If you recall, I have also been known to help out Ledger at the nursery." I smirk.

"Right, of course," Mabel says, giving Alice the evil eye. I'd laugh if it wouldn't offend them.

"What are you two lovely ladies up to today?" I ask, showing them no mercy if they want to play this oblivious game.

"We were just going to relax in here for a while, if that's okay. But if you're closing up, just let us know."

"Perfectly fine." I smile as I get up and start heading back to the counter. I feel everyone's eyes as I walk. Freaking Arlo. It's the only thing I can think of because he knows what's happening with Tennison. He probably started some rumor he knew would lead everyone here.

The door rings overhead and in walk Ledger and Rina.

Lovely, just want I need—overprotective siblings.

"Change professions without telling us?" Rina smirks.

"How can I help you, dear lovely customer." I bat my eyelashes at her.

"We haven't heard from you in a while. Thought we'd stop by and see how things are going," Ledger fills in.

Yeah, might have been hung up with Oakley too hard to send my usual "I'm alive and finished writing" text.

"Interesting, and your first instinct was to come here?" I ask, deflecting.

Ledger's cheeks turn a little rosy, and I roll my lips to stop the laugh.

"Ainsley's dad texted her," he says.

Jim Mathews, that sly little tattle.

"Well, I finished the book yesterday, and I've been taking some time to decompress."

"Decompress, is that what the kids are calling it?" Rina throws out.

"You sound like a dad making his money off of terrible dad jokes," I retort. Not my finest comeback, but my head isn't completely focused today.

"Okay, well, that's fun. Invite him to family dinner this week!" Rina claps.

"So, you finished your book?" Ledger adds, ignoring Rina's shenanigans.

"I did, thank God. I'm so glad it's done. It's officially off to the editor, so now it's a waiting game."

"Proud of you, Will. You're kicking ass, as usual," Ledger says.

After he took over guardianship of Lennox and me, he's been the best role model I think anyone could ask for. So when he says he's proud, he really means it, and he tells me after every single book gets written.

"Still haven't heard why you are here, working behind the counter," Rina continues as if no other part of the conversation happened.

"I'm helping out Oakley, who's ... sick today. I offered, and he agreed, that's all." I'm not lying about us, per se, I'm more lying about the fact that there is a serial torturer in the area going after him. And I'm not supposed to know about that, so he's sick.

And here comes my anxiety.

"Sure, sure," she murmurs.

"How's Arlo?" I ask in retaliation. It's the only thing that shuts her up, and it's a dick move on my part, but I don't want to talk about Oakley. Not when my heart is beating too fast and a bead of sweat is running down my back, all because I'm worried about him.

"Well, this was fun," Ledger cuts in because he knows a full-blown fight usually comes next if we continue our needling. "Let us know if you need anything today. Ainsley and I are just doing administration work."

"And I'll be at my workshop working on that custom order, so just call me."

"Will do. Sorry I didn't text you guys when I finished up the book. This one was rough."

"No worries. We'll see you Sunday, and we can hear all about it?" Rina asks.

"Absolutely. You guys want coffee?" I ask, realizing we've just been standing at the counter, talking.

"Nah, we just came in to see you," Ledger says as he turns around.

Rina hangs back, waiting until he's through the door to spin around.

"I need all the details later of everything going on between you and Oakley. Call me, or I will hunt you down." She spins and is out the door before I can even start laughing.

When I finally stop laughing, my anxiety comes back in full force. Tennison being so close has my hackles raised, even though I'm surrounded by people I know.

I wonder how the guys are doing and if they're any closer to figuring things out. They should talk to Lennox since he knows the damn park better than anyone.

Speaking of Tennison and the park, a memory sparks in my head.

I may not work in the park, like Lennox, but I grew up here and practically lived there when Lennox and I were trying to get some space from our siblings after our parents died.

A beat-up, old cabin sits on the eastern end of the park, where they got the tip about the car. It's hidden away, and you have to know its existence to find it, but it is possible to find it. Lennox and I would go there if we wanted to be alone, and I always brought a book. I'm not even sure if it's still standing, but it's the only actual building there not taken care of. The rest are all official properties that are looked after religiously, and they're at the entrance of the park.

That's it.

I don't even think, I just scramble to pull my phone out and find Oakley's name, hitting dial as I walk back to his office.

The phone rings and rings, and rings with no answer. My panic level is through the roof now. He would answer for me; I know he would.

I switch plans because for, some reason, this stupid little dilapidated cabin feels important to everything. Pulling up Arlo's number next, I call him.

"Everything okay, Willow?" he asks after the second ring.

"Yes, no. No, but I think I have an idea of where Tennison could be hiding out."

"Willow—"

"There's a cabin on the eastern side, almost dead center on the property line. No one knows it's there, and if he found it, it's the perfect spot for..." I can't bring myself to say it.

"We'll look into it. Thanks for the information. And Will?"

"Yeah?"

"He's okay, just on a phone meeting with his old boss about how he should proceed since he technically doesn't work on the force anymore."

"Thank you," I whisper and quickly hang up.

Tears fill my eyes at the relief of just hearing nothing happened. Something as simple as not answering the phone when the unknown is so huge right now makes me think the absolute worst. I need James to be safe.

I need him to come back to me.

CHAPTER TWENTY-SIX
OAKLEY

The only thought running through my head, as my old commander drones on about how I'm not actually working with them, is that I need to catch Tennison so I can come home and tell Willow I love her.

I've been so close to telling her a couple of times, but I held off. It didn't feel like the right time.

And now I'm stuck in a meeting from hell and can't even talk to her.

The other thing pissing me off? This entire conversation with my old boss. If he has it his way, I'd sit my ass here and let "the team" get Tennison. There is no way in hell that I'm not on the front lines with this one. He can berate me, threaten me, or whatever else he wants to do later, but I'm not sitting in this godforsaken office while Woodcroft and the rest of them go after this asshole.

My phone beeps in my ear, and I pull it away to see it's Willow calling me. I almost let out a growl at the fact that I can't answer the damn phone. She doesn't leave me a message, but a minute later I see Sheriff stand up through the window of his office and put his phone to his ear.

He's barely on the phone for a couple of minutes before he hangs up, and pulls out a paper map and starts studying it. Whatever that phone call was gave him something to run with.

"Listen, I promise I will be on my best behavior and not get anyone into more trouble. I know what I'm doing, sir." And then I hang up. Perks of not actually working for him anymore, I guess.

Walking out of the office quickly, I move to stand over the map the sheriff has laid out.

"What'd you find?"

"Not me, Willow." I jolt up at his words. "She said there's a remote cabin in this area that would be the perfect place to hide, so I'm trying to narrow down the area, and find some entrance points and possible exits."

That's my fucking girl.

Woodcroft leans over the table, studying the area.

"Is there a direct path to this?" he asks.

"Probably not anymore. Willow was saying that unless you already know where it is, you won't really be able to find it, but she gave me the general location, so we at least have that. I haven't heard from Lennox yet, but he would be a big help with this too."

"Alright, well, the rest of the team should be here shortly, then we can game-plan," Woodcroft says.

"So, we're supposed to just, what? Sit here and twiddle our thumbs?" Even I can hear the snark in my voice.

"Oak, man. We need back up." Woodcroft isn't fazed by me at all, and I'm thankful for his levelheadedness right now.

"I still think it would be good to come up with a plan before the team gets here. If we're able to solidify things prior, then we can hit the road whenever they show up," Sheriff says.

"I agree. Okay, so if we have an idea of where he is, we could just go find him," Woodcroft says.

"No. He's too smart for that. We need something to give him incentive to come out and play. He likes mind games; we need to play into that. He thinks he always has the upper hand, so we need to feed that."

"Okay, what are you thinking?" Sheriff asks.

"A trap."

"Oak, no," Woodcroft says.

"He wants me; let's give him what he wants. Or at least, the appearance of what he wants."

"This is a fucking terrible idea," Sheriff grumbles.

"Wood and I have been on this case for years. This is the only chance we'll get to be this close to him, and we need to do something drastic. I know how to handle myself. It's not like we'll be throwing some unsuspecting person at him."

"He'll see it a mile away," Woodcroft murmurs.

"No, he won't. He'll think that I'm playing the hero, trying to lessen the impact of his destruction."

The three of us stare at the map in silence. They know I'm right. It's the only way to get a leg up on Tennison.

Woodcroft lets out a sigh. "What exactly are you thinking?"

Three hours later, the U.S. Marshal Task Force Team fills the small space that is the sheriff's office.

We fill them in on our plan of attack, and the five of them stare at Woodcroft like he's completely lost his mind.

"We're technically letting a civilian put himself in danger and lead the mission in order to catch Tennison, am I getting this right?" a guy named Peck asks.

"Sounds about right." Woodcroft arches an eyebrow at him. His edge of authority brokers no room for argument, but that doesn't stop the eyerolls and huffs from happening.

"This is a terrible fucking idea," a new guy says under his breath. I haven't had the opportunity to meet this one yet.

"Do you know why Tennison changed his routine? Do you know why he started traveling?" I ask the newbie.

He meets my eyes with nothing but defiance in them. "No."

"Great, well, let me fill you in then, since you seem to know what the best move is." I stand up and look around the room, making sure everyone is listening. "Tennison changed his routine because of me. He started traveling and leaving a calling card because of me. You want to know why he leaves oak leaves in his cuts now? Because my name is fucking Oakley. If you think for a second that I don't understand the entirety of the situation, you can get the fuck out right now. We need help, but if you're going to roll your eyes and not take this seriously, you're out. I don't need you fucking this up more than it already is."

Sheriff and Woodcroft are sitting in the corner, covering their mouths, doing a piss-poor job of hiding their smiles.

"Anyone else have any comments or concerns?" I ask. A couple of heads shake, and the newbie bows his head, refusing to make eye contact. "Good, so let's move on. We're out of time, and this is the best shot we've had since he got on our radar."

Woodcroft stands up, moving to the front where I am. "Here's what we have so far..."

He fills them in on our very basic plan while my thoughts turn to Willow.

I haven't had time to check in, and it's killing me. But it's not like I have anything I can actually update her on. We're in the planning stage, and I'm sure once we get everything solidified, Wood will want to give everyone an hour or so to prepare and eat before we go after Tennison.

I can talk to her then. Hell, she's just across the street. I can go over there and really show her how I feel about her before I leave. Because I need her to know or at least feel how much she means to me, just in case. *No, we never think like that. No worst-case scenario. We will get Tennison, and I will be coming back to Willow.*

I shake my head to rid myself of the morbid thoughts and focus on what I want to tell her when I finally put Tennison behind me.

I want to tell her I love her, but it also doesn't seem like enough.

She's the air I breathe, the future I never knew I wanted. The future I now know I could never live without. She's the quirky, intelligent as hell sprite that keeps me on my toes.

And I love her.

I know without a shadow of a doubt that I'm in love with Willow Hutton, and now more than ever, I need to close this Tennison chapter of my life. I need to make my world safer so that Willow is never in jeopardy of my past coming back to haunt us.

I still feel that I have a lot to work on, and keeping my appointments with my psychiatrist will help with that, but it feels like a life with Willow is possible. I know she'll help me when I'm struggling, and I'll help her when she's stuck.

Being back in the Task Force mindset is odd. I thought I'd miss it. I thought taking charge and going after the bad guy would make me want to go back, but it's been the opposite. Sure, it's like riding a bike, but I no longer feel the thrill of it. The high of going after a fugitive isn't there anymore. This feels more like a necessary evil. And one I'm not particularly looking forward to.

"Okay, does everyone understand the plan?" Woodcroft's voice pulls me out of my thoughts.

I look around the table and see everyone nodding.

"I've put in a call to our park ranger but haven't heard back from him. I sent him a text, informing him to stay away from the eastern side but keep his eyes open," Sheriff adds.

Lennox.

I know it's the smart thing to do, but it worries me that he's out there with no back up right now.

"When do we leave?" I ask.

"In five minutes," Woodcroft says. "Pack your shit, and let's head out."

Shit. *Shit.* That doesn't give me time to go talk to Willow. As I pack up what little I have, dressing in the extra vest and gear that the team brought with them, I vow to text her while we're driving out.

Good intentions are all well and good, but they don't mean anything when shit hits the fan.

And that's exactly what happens no more than ten minutes later.

CHAPTER TWENTY-SEVEN
WILLOW

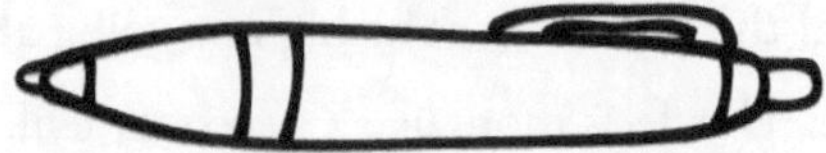

All day, I've been dealing with the residents of Bluebell Falls in all their lively glory.

And now, I'm twenty minutes from closing. Which, in theory, sounds great, except I haven't heard from Oakley all day. I'm not normally one to jump to conclusions, but when I see a couple of SUVs full of guys built like tanks pull up in front of the sheriff's office, I assume shit is hitting the fan. It has to be the task force Oakley used to be on.

And that makes me nervous. And scared. And a little panicky because I haven't heard from Arlo at all since my phone call this morning.

It's fine. I'm sure it's fine. There's no reason to freak out when nothing has happened.

As I'm mentally reassuring myself, I see a man walk around one of the SUVs and jump in the driver seat, followed by someone jumping in the second one as well. They drive off before I can make sense of what I'm seeing.

Quickly looking around, I see the place is empty, so I lock the front door, not worrying about actual closing duties yet. My brain can only focus on one thing right now, and that's trying to not completely lose my shit as my heart cracks in my chest from the unknown.

I plop down in one of the chairs facing the sheriff's office and stare. I don't know what I'm waiting for or expecting to happen, but I'm just hoping for a glimpse of Oakley. Just one little peek that lets me know he's safe.

It's too much to hope for—I know that deep down. He's not the type to sit back and let other people fight his battles, but fuck if I wasn't hoping some higher chain of command would step in and force him to stay put. He isn't a Marshal anymore, after all, so it's not completely unreasonable.

My leg bounces as my eyes stay firm on the door. I'm not even aware that I bring my fingers up to my lips and start chewing on my nails—a habit I only do when I'm especially stressed out.

When I realize I've gnawed off all my nails, I tuck my hands underneath my bouncing legs.

I'm an anxious mess.

Pulling out my phone, I pull up my messages with Oakley and send him a message, crossing my fingers that he sends me something, letting me know he's okay.

Me:

> Closed up shop. It was busy today.

Lame. So fucking lame.

Me:

> Keep me updated if you can. I just want to make sure you're okay.

Is my heart seeping through into my words? Because it sure as hell feels like it.

Knowing there's a chance that Tennison is out there right this second, just waiting for him, is causing me to re-evaluate the way I pushed Oakley to go after him. Logically, it makes sense. But right now? Living in this limbo of having no idea what's happening, if he's okay or not, I wish I never told him to go. There's a real chance I will lose him before I ever get the chance to tell him how I feel.

And how do I feel?

I think I always knew I was capable of loving him. It's probably why I chose to stay away from him for so long. Deep down in my mind, I knew he had some sort of power over me, even if it was just sexual in the beginning.

Now? It feels like it was hopeless to ever think I could keep my heart from beating for him. He takes care of me and somehow knows what I need before I ever even realize it. I want to be just as supportive of him as he is of me, but this is literally killing me. I don't think I've ever felt this anxious because this threat isn't a deadline, isn't disappointing fans. This threat is real. It has life and death consequences. *And I can't lose James. I refuse to.*

I pop up from my chair and start pacing. I don't know if I can just sit here and wait. I know Arlo and Oakley are more than capable, and add in the Marshal's Fugitive Task Force, I know I bring absolutely nothing to the table. My only weapon is my brain, and Lord knows that's a fucking mess right now.

No, going out there, where there is a possible psychopath is a dumb move.

I head upstairs, hoping I can find some sort of distraction.

Neurotically, I move from chair to chair, to the couch, then to the bedroom, trying to distract myself, but it's impossible to stop thinking about all the possibilities.

My phone buzzes in my hand, and I almost throw it with excitement.

Rina:

Want to help me deliver a dining room table?

Me:

No. I mean, I probably should, but I can't be that far away from town. Unless you're delivering it in town, then possibly. I need more details.

I curse my rambling. If I wanted to seem put together and not have her question me, that was the exact opposite approach to take.

Rina:

Okay, lots to unpack here. First, are you okay? Second, it's out of town, so I'll take a raincheck.

Me:

I am … not okay, I think. There's some stuff going down, and Oakley is out saving the world, and I'm so anxiety riddled I can barely think.

Rina:

I can push off the delivery. Do you want me to come and hang out with you?

Me:

Nah, I'm shit company right now.

Me:

> Maybe I'll just send a message to Arlo and hope he gets back to me with an update.

I send the second message without thinking about who I'm talking to, and her response tells me it was the wrong move.

Rina:

> Oh, Mr. High and Mighty is involved? Not shocking. Trouble seems to find him more than not.

Shit. I don't think I can tell her what is actually happening because I'm not even supposed to know. But I also know she didn't always hate him and that they used to be close when they were young. Knowing he might actually be in danger might cause a different reaction.

Me:

> Umm, kind of. It's more like he's helping … where he can …

Cryptic and tells Rina exactly nothing. Good job, Will.

Rina:

> Umm, cool. He can still fuck off. Keep me updated, and if you need a distraction, I'll be back at my workshop after this delivery. So, maybe two hours?

I have no clue what happened between her and Arlo, but it's also not my place to tell Rina his business. Maybe when this is all said and done, this will be a wake-up call for both of them.

I pace around Oakley's small apartment after putting my phone in my pocket.

It takes me five more minutes of pacing to say fuck it.

Maybe I can help, maybe I can catch Tennison unsuspecting, or at the very least, check out the cabin to see if it shows sign of usage.

Is this a stupid idea? Absolutely.

Will Oakley and Arlo probably kill me when they find out? Undoubtedly.

But I can't just sit here doing nothing. What if I can help or find something they missed? I have to try if it means James coming back to me sooner and, most importantly, safe.

Decision made, I make sure I have my phone and keys, and then head out. The cabin is hard to find, and I have doubts that the crew will actually find it without help.

Yeah, this is the right thing to do.

Famous last words.

CHAPTER TWENTY-EIGHT
OAKLEY

The adrenaline is pumping just like in the old days. It's nostalgic, in a way, and I would like it more if Tennison wasn't the cause of everything.

Instead, I'm worried. So fucking worried. Too much can go wrong, and we'll have very little control over things.

It's funny how everything always boils down to control.

The plan, if you even want to call it that, is to send me on the trails. I'm going to head toward the cabin but not get too close, and hope that Tennison is just lurking around. We've been in touch with Lennox, making sure he stays clear of the area we think Tennison is in, but we haven't heard from him since. The bulk of the Task Force is patrolling the rest of the park. It's helping us narrow down things, and it's looking more and more likely that Willow was right about the cabin.

Willow. Just thinking her name is making me second-guess what the boys have deemed the Tennison Trap.

Is this really worth the risk? Of course, I want to catch this asshole. Of course, I want to lock him up for good before he destroys more lives. But having Willow in my life makes me want—no, need—to be less reckless.

Hell, I don't want to be reckless at all. I want to curl up in bed with my little troublemaker as she writes her next great novel. I want to cook for her, take care of her when she is too caught up in work. Fuck, I already miss her.

But I know I need to do this. I'll never be able to fully move on, fully heal unless this job is done.

The rest of the guys are planning to hang back on the edges of the park, hoping that we don't tip off Tennison but being close enough that if shit hits the fan, they'll be there.

This might be the most open-ended plan I've ever worked, but we don't have anything better and we're out of time.

Willow's directions to the cabin were very detailed, so we know exactly where to go and where the trails go around it. We pull up to the entrance closest to town, and I sit in the car for a second while everyone else jumps out.

"You ready to do this?" Woodcroft's voice shatters my thoughts as he climbs in next to me. I feel wrung out and high-strung all at the same time. My nerves feel too sensitive for my body, like my skin is too tight.

"No. Fuck no," I huff out.

"So, it would probably be shitty to ask if you want to come back, huh?"

"Yeah, not happening. I'm not built for this shit anymore."

"I'm happy for you, you know," he says quietly.

"Yeah?" I look over at him.

"Yeah. I don't know a ton about Willow, but she's seems perfect for you, and she's saving our ass on this half-cocked plan we've come up with."

"She's an author and writes thrillers. This entire case is right up her alley." I chuckle at the fact she couldn't stop herself from attempting to help. It's in her curious nature.

"Badass. Well, let's get this fucker, so you can go tell her all the gory details." He slaps my back and disembarks the back seat.

I take one last deep breath and clamber out.

It's time to finish this.

I've been walking on the trail for about twenty minutes, and so far, nothing. I'm making a ton of noise in the hopes it draws attention. Hell, even anyone in the park noticing me could help, although Lennox said he would try to steer people in the opposite direction when we initially talked.

I'm about to round the corner when I spot something on the trail.

A piece of fabric.

No, part of a uniform. I lean down and pick it up, realizing it's a park ranger's shirt.

Lennox.

I search for a clue to solidify my suspicion, but it just looks like a standard uniform. I tap the earpiece the Task Force set me up with.

"I found a ranger's uniform."

"Lennox?" Arlo asks.

"I don't know for sure, but most likely. Has anyone heard from him recently?"

"No. I just tried to call him too." Arlo's tone sounds rigid, and I know he's thinking the same thing I am.

"Try him again," I urge.

"I am. Hold on."

I pace, waiting for a response and when it comes, all I feel is panic.

"No answer. I'm coming to you," Arlo says quickly.

I pace where I'm at, and within two minutes, Arlo is walking toward me. He yanks the shirt out of my hand and holds it up. There are a few cuts in the shirt that I missed initially.

"Shit," I curse.

"We need to go to the cabin. If he has Lennox…" Arlo trails off, not even wanting to say it.

And I can't blame him. Lennox has become one of my closest friends, and I won't even allow myself the possibility of anything bad happening.

We both walk frantically in the direction of that cabin, but I pause when my phone rings.

Unknown Caller.

"This is Oakley," I answer, wondering if it's one of the guys on the Task Force and they have information.

"I think I have something of yours."

I stop in my tracks. *That voice.* It haunts every nightmare I still have. It's a voice that I'm not sure I'll ever be able to unhear as I lie awake at night.

I see Arlo out of the corner of my eye, walking back to me to see what's up.

"What…" I gulp. "What do you want?" I can hear the shake in my voice, and I try my damndest to lock it down. Show no weakness.

I can't show weakness. Not if Lennox is in trouble.

"I think it's time we end this little charade. I thought I would get your attention a lot sooner than I have, and it's become rather … tiresome."

"Why did you need to get my attention?" I ask, trying to bide time. I can feel my breathing growing faster, though, and I know I have limited time before a full-on panic attack hits me square in the chest.

"Oh, my dear Oakley, don't you get it? You're the closest thing to my equal. You've always been the only one who gets close to me; you just were never quite there. And then you left. The fun lessened substantially, and I wasn't prepared for that." He sounds genuinely confused, and I almost laugh. How anyone could consider what he does *fun* is mind-boggling.

"How can I get him back?" I ask as Arlo tries to pull my phone from my ear. He already pulled his out and frantically texted what I assumed was the whole team.

"You know me better than that. You'll get him back when I deem it so. Until then... Come and find me." His manic laughter cuts off as he hangs up, and I fall to my knees as I hyperventilate.

"Fuck. Fuck, are you okay? That was him, wasn't it? Shit, where is he? The team is on the way. What the fuck?" Arlo talks aimlessly as he kneels next to me.

"I—" My voice croaks as I attempt to clear it and breathe through the shortness of beath. "We need to go to the cabin. He won't give up Lennox, but maybe" — I gasp, hunching over — "I can trade for him."

"No. *No*! That's not what we're fucking doing. Just wait for backup, and we'll figure it out."

"No time." I take one last deep breath, pushing everything down before standing up and walking down the path that will lead to the cabin.

"Oakley!" I hear Arlo yell behind me, but I ignore him.

Tennison is right. It's time we finish this.

No matter what it costs me.

"Oakley, Jesus! Just wait." Arlo's voice is getting closer, but I don't stop.

His hand on my shoulder finally stops me, but I'm pissed.

"Just let me fucking go. This is on me; no one else needs to get involved. If I can trade myself for Lennox, then I'll do it, and I'll take this poison from Bluebell Falls so no one else gets hurt."

"Do you fucking hear yourself? How fucking selfish of you. Do you not think you're a part of this town and maybe that's why I give a shit? Do you not think that maybe I've been trying to be a friend to you this whole time?" He shoves me in anger.

We're two angry bulls going head to head, and I know deep down that he's right, but I can't see past the haze, past Tennison and finally ending this once and for all.

"And what about Willow?" he asks softly.

It's the one thing he could say that gets through.

Willow.

"Fuck, man. She'll never forgive me if something happens to Lennox. Hell, I won't forgive myself."

"I know. But I needed two minutes to kill before you went charging in there so backup was a little closer. We'll figure this out together. And whatever comes, we'll handle it. You're a Bluebell Falls resident now, and that means something, okay?"

"Okay," I whisper.

"Let's go catch this fucker," Arlo says with force as we both start walking at a clipped pace.

Arlo double-checks the directions Willow gave us, then heads down an open spot in the trees.

About twenty feet in, we can finally see the outline of a building, and we both start sprinting. It takes us less than two minutes to reach the front door, and I'm trying so hard to keep my shit together.

It's like this immense sense of doom has fallen over me, and I'm fucking scared.

Scared for me. Scared for Lennox. Scared about what's to come.

And I have no control over any of it.

Arlo steps up on the porch silently, and I join him, knowing we're out of time. Reaching out, I grip the door handle in my hand. I can feel myself shaking, feel the dread, but I push it down, like I always used to. And then, I open the door.

Arlo and I enter the cabin one after the other and take a cursory look around, checking for Tennison. But it's hard to see past the man stripped and tied to a chair in the middle of the room.

Lennox.

Bound by rope, with multiple deep cuts down every part of his body I can see.

"Fuck," Arlo curses quietly.

"So lovely of you to join in the fun." Tennison walks out from a shadowed corner with a sinister grin on his face and his knife in one hand as he twirls it around.

CHAPTER TWENTY-NINE
OAKLEY

Alfred Tennison, by all accounts, is average. He's in his mid-fifties, with thinning brown hair, but he is in decent shape for his age. I guess you'd have to be, considering what he does on a regular basis. His glasses sit skewed on his face, like he's rushed this entire setup. Usually, every picture we've ever seen of the man has him put together, not a hair out of place, and blends in seamlessly into any crowd.

He's different right now, unhinged in a way I've never seen him. You couldn't tell by his words, but his appearance tells me this vendetta with me wasn't exactly planned. His clothing hangs off of him, telling me this past year hasn't been good to him.

It also means Tennison is a new level of dangerous, which scares me more than anything.

Lennox tries to lift his head, but he's already weak from the blood loss. My heart clenches painfully in my chest at the sight and the fucking *regret* at having a hand in putting him in this position.

"I'll get you out of here, Len," I whisper.

"Well, he may be getting out, but you certainly aren't. I've come all this way; I plan to talk, get to know you, and who knows, maybe have a little fun while we chat." Tennison's words are sharp as he spins his knife around again.

"No. You were right on the phone." My eyes barely shift from Tennison, tracking as Sheriff takes a step in Lennox's direction. It's a smart move; if I can keep Tennison talking, then maybe Sheriff can get to Lennox and get them both out. "It's time we end this. Talking seems unnecessary, no?"

"It seems you've learned nothing while chasing your tail trying to get to me. Talking is everything, my boy. Tell me, what do these people tell you about me after you've rescued them?"

The hair on my arms rises because I know where he's taking this, but it'll keep him talking and that's important, even if it makes me uncomfortable as hell.

"Do they tell you about the conversations we have? Or do they just tell you my name? Do they tell you how long we play for? Or do they only tell you my name?"

"They tell me your name."

"Precisely. You know why that is?" He tilts head at me in question, and it only makes him look like more of a threat, menacing.

"Why?" I growl.

"Well, let me back up." He slowly walks around Lennox, leaving a clear path for Sheriff. It's clear Tennison doesn't really care about Lennox anymore, and for us, that's the best-case scenario. "Do you know why I don't kill any of them? Why I leave all these witnesses to this so-called crime?"

I stay silent. Why answer him? Why give him power when that's what he thrives on?

"Because if you kill them, you can't watch for years to see the damage you've done. Sure, there are some who have family that's affected, but it's not the same. Being able to check in with the people I've had *chats* with? It's the game that never ends. It's also why they don't ever tell you more information about what happens to them. You see, fear is a wonderful thing. It makes people ... compliant. It really is wonderous what the human body will take when it's in self-protect mode. And the mind is even more fascinating."

I feel sick. Bile is very quickly working its way up my throat, and I'm trying like hell not to show him any weakness, even though that's all I feel right now. My fists clench tight as I see Sheriff out of the corner of my eye cutting Lennox's hands and feet free.

Tennison glances over his shoulder. "I did enjoy our time together. Talk soon, Lennox Hutton," he says before turning his attention back to me. Sheriff quickly gets Lennox out of the cabin, and my shoulders barely sag in relief.

"I'm sure you have questions for me. Please sit," Tennison offers, and I almost laugh.

"No, thanks. I will ask those questions, though." He nods, predicting my response, I assume. "Why me?" I ask the biggest question. I don't even care anymore why he does what he does. I don't care what his future plans are—I don't plan to let him walk out of here alive anyway.

"Simple. You are the one who got the closest. You almost had me a year ago. You remember, don't you?"

My mind floods with my last case on the Task Force.

We had a tip-off that someone saw Tennison on the outskirts of Messena, New York. We raced there, thinking we had finally gotten there in time, only to get a call that police found the victim after a walker had heard screaming.

I wrack my brain, trying to figure out how we were close because that felt like the time we were furthest away from actually catching him.

A blurry vision of a man pointing us in the direction of the cabin floats into my mind, and I rear back.

"The man who directed us. It was you," I whisper.

"I'll admit, it wasn't my best disguise, and I was convinced you saw right through it. You stopped and stared at me for a moment longer than you should have, and I thought the gig was up. I always followed you closer between you and your partner, Mr. Woodcroft, because you always seemed to be closer to finding me. Every single case, you got closer but just never quite reached me. And then you quit," he sneers out in disgust.

He's slowly making his way to me, but I have nowhere to go. I'm trapped because our movement and success in getting Lennox out have shifted me away from the only exit.

"Let me get this straight; you came after me because I was close to finding you and when I quit, you were mad about it?"

A man like Tennison was always going to be deranged, but this feels extreme, even for him.

"You stopped playing the game, Oakley," he says, his voice suddenly getting louder. "I wasn't done yet. I wanted to see who would win. Could I still dodge you? Or would you actually catch me? And we were so close before you went and ruined everything."

My chest physically hurts, knowing that the last year of victims is directly because of me. If I had just stayed, if I had worked harder and caught this bastard, no one else would have gotten hurt. No one else would have to suffer lifelong scars.

Because of me.

Worthless.

Trash.

Not worth the dirt on my shoes.

How did I ever think I was worthy of living a good life?

"I can feel you struggling right now, and it just feels" — he takes a deep breath— "like the end, you know? Feels like the big lead-up. One will win, one will lose. Years of work. Years of trying to find a suitable partner, and it all comes down to this." His smile is deranged, *excited*.

His words pierce my brain, and I finally realize his pattern. He looked for people that could keep up with his brain. Intelligence was the connecting factor. This last puzzle piece should feel triumphant, but I don't know have time to focus on it.

I know I have one chance to take him down. Luckily, the Task Force set me up with all the protective gear I would need to face Tennison, but for whatever reason, it doesn't feel like enough. There are weak spots within the gear, and knowing Tennison, he knows every single one.

"So, how do you want to play this?" I ask. I'm not sure whether I'm trying to agitate him or just trying to get a clear answer.

While I await his answer, I slowly reach behind me and grab the knife that's holstered at the base of my back. It's poetic, really; I could have gone with a gun and made life easy, but taking Tennison down with his own medium feels more like justice.

His eyes snag on my arm as it moves, and he lunges suddenly. Catching me off guard, he knicks my bicep.

"Fuck," I curse as I step back and deflect his arm.

"Come on, now, don't make this easy for me." He lunges again, but this time I catch his arm, holding it in place as I ram my other elbow into the back of his head. Releasing him, he stumbles to the back corner with a smirk on his face. "Much better, thank you."

This time, I lunge at him, but he side-steps it easily.

"What do we think, Oakley, long-lasting psychological effects or death? The first feels so much more fitting, but death is the ultimate win. I can't decide which would be a better fate for you."

"Fuck you," I spit at him and lunge again, this time catching his side. A graze, but I'm getting closer.

His villainous laugh enrages me. I've never felt like I *wanted* to kill someone before, but that's all changed. I don't care how it happens, but Tennison will not leave here alive.

He fakes me out by thrusting his knife again, but moving it just in time to slice open my forearm. Blood spills out, but I can barely feel it.

I move to my left as fast as I can and send my knife backward toward his neck, but I only manage a superficial cut.

"It feels liberating to be cut the way I usually do to others. Makes me feel more alive than I have in a long while," Tennison muses.

I spin around, realizing we just made a circle around the cabin and I missed the fucking exit yet again, when he spears the side of my stomach with his knife. Right where the vest I'm wearing has a gap. It sends me crashing to my knees as the sharp pain radiates through my middle. I reach to cover it in a lame attempt to stem the bleeding when the cabin door is ripped open.

A war cry like I've never heard sounds out, and I realize it's Willow.

My heart plummets. She's not supposed to be here. She's supposed to be safe and sound in my apartment, or literally anywhere but here. *What the fuck is she doing here?*

But my worry is quickly replaced with pride when she swings a baseball bat at Tennison's head. He goes down near the little fireplace, and his eyes roll back in his head—making me aware of how hard Willow actually hit him—before falling to the side. His head hits the sharp corner of the fireplace, and blood pools instantly underneath him. His knife drops to the ground in a sound that signals finality.

"Oh my God. Oh my God. Oh my God." I look up and see Willow starting to shake, the baseball bat falling from her fingers as she stares at the scene. Her face is pale, too pale.

"Hey, hey. It's okay. Everything is okay." I slowly climb to my feet, wincing at the pull on my wound but not giving a shit because Willow needs me.

Her unfocused eyes meet mine and finally clear a little. They trail down the length of my body and then stop when they see me clutching my side.

"Oh fuck, you're hurt." Her eyes well with tears, and mine blur as well.

Everything that could have possibly gone wrong did, and it's all my fault.

She races to me, side-stepping Tennison, and presses her hand to the stab wound. It burns so fiercely I cry out as Willow starts to sob.

"It's okay. We're okay. We're safe," I mumble into her hair as I wrap my arm around her. I see the trail of blood I leave on her from my fucking forearm, and it just makes me angrier at the situation.

The cabin is suddenly flooded with men, and I don't focus on anything except Willow.

"Fuck, brother." Woodcroft stops us at the door.

"We need to get to the hospital," I grunt out. I don't give a shit about me, but we need to check on Lennox.

"Ambulance is right behind us."

"Took you fucking long enough," I growl at him. The pain in his eyes is so quick and so blatant that I almost feel bad. But my logical brain is nowhere to be found right now.

"We tried," he whispers.

"Not fucking good enough." I lead a still-crying Willow outside the cabin just as an ambulance drives up. They usher both of us in, and the drive takes a full half an hour since we need to go to the bigger hospital in Rosedale.

Neither of us says anything as the paramedics work on me. But Willow slowly starts to calm down, holding my hand the entire time.

"I'm sorry," I whisper before they pump meds into me that make me feel sleepy as hell.

If she gives a response, I don't hear it. I just fall into an uneasy sleep, reliving the whole afternoon.

CHAPTER THIRTY
WILLOW

My eyes feel like they're swollen shut, and I'm covered in James's blood.

All I've done for the last hour is cry. I'm currently sitting in the waiting room, waiting for news on James and Lennox, and I'm a fucking wreck. My siblings are here, but they are letting me have my space, thankfully.

I don't even know what I would say to them if I could talk right now. All I keep thinking about is killing Tennison, watching the blood pour from his head after he fell, and then looking up to see James fucking stabbed.

I can't even begin to describe the emotions I'm feeling. Everything from guilt to grief to pride fills me every second I sit here.

And fear.

So much fear.

My brain is coming up with every worst-case scenario for both of them, and none of it equals them surviving. I mean, a stab wound to the stomach has a lot of potential for things to go wrong. And Lennox? God, I don't even know where to begin. I have no idea what shape he was in when Arlo brought him in because Arlo needed to rally with the Fugitive Task Force in a conference room in the hospital. I want to be mad at him, but I can't because it's his job.

You know whose job it wasn't? James fucking Oakley's.

And now he's in surgery.

I'm not angry at James either. I'm just exhausted and so fucking stressed. I don't know how to work through all these emotions right now.

A hand touches my shoulder and I flinch, looking up to see Ledger looking at me with concern in his eyes.

"The doctor wants to talk to us," he says softly. I look around to see the rest of the family standing, waiting for me.

I didn't even hear them call us. Blinking back the tears threatening to fall, I stand up to follow the doctor.

The paramedics that took care of Oakley on the way in talked to me about the effects of being in shock. I can recognize the truth in their words with how I'm feeling right now. The chill has taken control of my body, and the shivering won't stop. I'm wrapped in blankets, but it doesn't matter.

We sit in a bland conference room, one I assume the hospital uses for bad news, and it only makes the tears actually fall.

God, I'm a mess.

"So, an update on Lennox. He's doing as well as can be expected. The main concern was getting more blood into him as he lost a lot during … the incident. Currently, he is in the ICU as a precaution, due to how susceptible he is to infection right now. I'm optimistic that he'll be out by tomorrow and into regular hospital care, but we'll keep you updated. Law enforcement is talking to him at the moment, but when they leave, you'll be able to go visit him one at a time. Physically, he'll recover fine. Mentally, I want to prepare you for a hard road. I don't know many details, but I do know you'll all need to be extremely patient with him.

He could act completely fine but be drowning on the inside. He could show every emotion in the book and take it out on you. I just want to prepare you for a long mental battle for him."

I cover my mouth as a sob breaks free. Ainsley is sitting next to me and pulls me into a hug as the others watch me break down. The doctor, God bless him, just patiently waits while I calm my shit down. It's like I have no control over anything. My emotions, my body ... all of it is working independently of my brain. And all my brain can think is that none of this should have happened. Logically, I know it's a fucked-up way to think, but the what-ifs are adding up and are on a constant loop in my thoughts.

"I don't anticipate Lennox being here for longer than a week. A good majority of the cuts were superficial and will heal in that time, and the deeper ones will have healed enough to let him go home. As long as there is no infection, it should be a relatively fast process."

Ledger nods, continuing to listen. His need to take control shows, and I'm glad someone is able to fully listen.

"As far as James Oakley is concerned..." He pauses. "I'm not really supposed to be telling anything to anyone not family, but he said that Willow is his fiancé, and to talk to you and the family about anything happening."

My heart damn near rips from my chest.

Pain.

I feel so much pain at hearing him calling me James's fiancé because I have no idea if he's even going to make it. And the thought of losing him when I just got him is too much, it's too overwhelming.

"Is he out of surgery?" Rina asks.

"He is, and it was touch and go there for a little bit. The blade nicked his liver and some bigger blood vessels, so there was a lot of bleeding. We ended up needing to take a lobe of his liver before closing him up because it was too damaged. It's still perfectly functional; this just decreases the risk after surgery. So, his risk of infection, sepsis, or even an abscess is drastically lower now. We had to give him some blood as well, but he should be fine once the anesthesia wears off."

"And how long will he have to stay here?" Ainsley asks while still holding me to her side.

"We want to make sure the sutures are good and there's no sign of infection. I'd like to keep him at least a couple more days, but I get the feeling he may fight us on that." He smiles warmly.

Stubborn ass. I'll make him fucking stay here.

The thought almost makes me laugh, but I'm just too terrified. Just because they both made it out of surgery doesn't mean either are out of the woods yet. My pessimistic brain is throwing out every terrible thing I've researched for books as an outcome, and now I want to figure out how to actually shut my brain off. I don't think I can handle my thoughts for much longer.

"I can take one of you up to Lennox right now, and James should be awake shortly. A nurse will come and get you when he is."

The whole group looks at me, and I nod. I might be a mess, but Lennox is my best friend and I need to see the damage. I need to see that killing Tennison was worth it.

I stand up shakily as the doctor ushers me out of the room and to the elevator.

"Are you sure you're okay? We can have a nurse check you out when we get up there."

"I-I-I think it's just shock," I chatter and hiccup through the tears that won't stop falling. "I'm not ph-ph-physically hurt."

He looks at me with concern but nods anyway. I have a feeling he's not just going to let that go, but I don't care about that right now.

The trip to the ICU is a quick one, just a short elevator ride and then through the first doors you see when you get to the floor. Lennox is in the room immediately to the right. I stop outside the door, the huge window making it easy to see Lennox lying in the bed, hooked up to a million machines.

I feel myself weakening, starting to fall to the ground, but I straighten myself up. Attempting to wipe the tears away is much harder to do when they are still trailing down my face, but I take a deep breath, trying to stop the flow.

I need to be strong for him. Unaffected. Just like a regular day, except he's stuck in the hospital. And I will push down all of my shit to make him feel some semblance of normalcy.

Rolling my neck, I finally feel calm enough, although the blanket is still wrapped around me because the chills just won't fucking stop. I scrub my hand over my face one more time and walk into his room.

The smell and sounds will stay with me forever. Antiseptic. Melodic. So fucking sterile.

I walk to his bedside and gently grab the hand that's close to me.

"Hey, Lenny," I whisper. His eyes slowly blink open, and I feel mine well with tears again. "You look good." I give him a small grin, both of us knowing it's not the least bit true.

My eyes trail down his body; only his lower half is covered by a sheet, his legs out in the open too. Most of the cuts aren't covered, left to do some good old-fashioned natural healing. The ones that are covered, I know are the ones that were especially deep. His thighs and torso have the majority of them, and it's painful to see him so *mutilated*.

"I look like shit," he says, his voice gravelly from surgery.

"You do." I nod casually, trying to be my normal self with him. I know if the positions were reversed, I wouldn't want anyone treating me differently, and I know it would piss off Lennox.

"Good news, though. Chicks love scars, so I think you've got this one in the bag," I lamely joke. It falls completely flat, and when I look into his eyes, all I see is a vacancy.

I know nothing will be the same after this. I know Lennox will have the hardest road when he leaves here, but I was hoping so damn hard that his light would still be there. His mischief would still linger in his eyes.

And finding it all gone? It's like a knife to the heart. I don't know how to help him. I don't know how to act or what to say. I feel like one wrong move, and it will make things exponentially worse.

"None of this was your fault, Will. Or Oakley's," he croaks out.

I nod, not meeting his eyes because I don't believe that. I feel like I could have done more. Hell, I could have warned Lennox myself instead of leaving it to the stupid Task Force. They couldn't protect Lennox or James, so I'm not too fond of any of them at the moment.

"Willow," he says, his voice stronger, adamant.

I lock eyes with him, his skin too pale.

"Do not put any of this on your shoulders. Take care of you. Take care of Oakley. I promise I will be okay." He squeezes my hand tight.

I jerk my head in some form of a nod as the tears start to fall again.

This Lennox is different.

And I wonder if I'll ever have the old Lennox back.

"Ma'am," a nurse behind me calls gently.

I look back at her and wait for whatever she needs to tell me.

"Mr. Oakley is awake in his room. And your time is up in here too. We only let visitors stay ten minutes at a time—lessens the risk."

I nod, squeezing Lennox's hand again. "I don't want to leave you," I whisper.

"Go. I'll be here." His voice is dull and has no inflection. It's painful. Something so simple, but it's not the playful Lennox we all know and love, not the unserious and sometimes immature Lennox. I just hope once the bulk of his physical healing happens, he'll be receptive to some help psychologically.

"I'll come see you again soon." I lean down and press a soft kiss to his hairline as the tears fall into his hair.

He gives my hand one last squeeze before letting go and watching me walk out of his room.

The nurse silently leads me back to the elevator and down two floors. It's a totally different world down here, full of life. There's a ton of people, mostly hospital staff that are running around taking care of a multitude of things, but it's completely different than the ICU where it's too quiet.

I'm led to a room around the corner, tucked in the back. There's a handful of muscled men standing vigil outside of James's room, and I can't help but feel utter contempt for them. They should have been more help, should have protected both Lennox and Oakley.

I don't look at any of them, just walk right into the room without thinking and then stop dead in my tracks.

James is lying in the hospital bed, looking weaker than I ever could have imagined. He's hooked up to the same machines Lennox was, and he's covered with a hospital gown. He looks like he's sleeping, so I slowly walk over to him.

That fear when I saw him and Tennison fighting returns with a vengeance. It's like my flight-or-fight response doesn't realize it's all over and now it's time for healing.

I sit in the chair that someone left right next to his bed and try to work through my emotions.

I don't know how to react, what to say, or how he would want me to treat him. And the memory of him calling me his fiancé pounds in my skull, begging to be true, even though I've never seen myself as the type to get married. It just means that he's alive. It means that he's mine, and I won't lose him.

And I'm not sure how he'll feel when he wakes up.

Carefully, I reach out—noticing I'm shaking worse now and my hands feel clammy—and slide my hand into his.

"Trouble," his whispered voice hits me, and I completely break down.

CHAPTER THIRTY-ONE
OAKLEY

Her tears break my heart all over again.

Failure is the only thing running through my body. I should be ecstatic that Tennison is finally gone from this world, but all I can think of is how I failed Lennox. How I failed to protect the family of the woman I love.

It makes me feel less than, and wholly not worthy of her tears.

"I'm sorry," I whisper.

"Nope. We're not doing that. And if you apologize, I think I'm going to poke your damn incision." She laughs through the tears, and I relax a little.

"That would hurt really bad, I think," I grumble.

"Yep."

"How's Lennox?"

"He's..." She completely breaks down again, and the guilt is overwhelming.

She can ask me for the rest of my life to not apologize, but it's my fault. This whole fucked-up situation is my fault, and I'll never be able to atone for that.

"He's physically going to be okay, but how does someone recover mentally from what was done to him?" she whispers.

I can't answer because I don't have an answer. Every victim we've ever talked to struggled every single day. Some succumbed to depression, to the inability to escape the memories. Over the course that I worked on Tennison's case, we lost six people to suicide. It's something I'll never be able to forget, never be able to reconcile.

And if Lennox falls into the same path, I'll never recover. Not for the damage it would do to Willow.

"We'll help him," I barely get out. I don't necessarily feel it's true, not for me. I wholeheartedly believe Willow and her family will help Lennox recover to the best of their ability, but I just don't know where I fit into it all.

Am I even any good for her?

This entire situation is making me second-guess everything. Not how much I love this woman because I think she's the only one I'll ever love like this. But if Lennox never heals, if something far worse happens, in what world would she ever forgive me? Sure, she seems like she doesn't blame me, but will that still be the case in a couple of weeks? In a year?

She puts her forehead on our hands and just cries. My other hand reaches over, putting it on her head in some lame attempt at comfort. Her shoulders shake with her sobs, and my eyes well with tears. I don't feel the pain in my arm or my stomach.

It's ripping my heart into a million pieces that she's in pain and I can't do anything to help. Hell, it hurts more that I know I'm the reason for her heartache.

"Fuck, Will," I barely get out through my own tears. I attempt to scoot over, and it draws her head up.

"Don't move," she scolds.

I ignore her, adjusting myself enough to make room. A little pain from a stab wound won't stop me right now.

Pulling her hand that's still in mine, I lead her up onto the hospital bed with me.

"I don't want to hurt you," she whispers.

"It hurts to not hold you. Just give me this, Will. Please, let me hold you," I beg. She's on my good side anyway, so it's not like she'll hurt my wound. And my forearm is wrapped up in a cushioned bandage.

She leans into my side, gripping the hospital gown as she cries.

"I thought I lost you. When I—" She gasps. "When I walked into the cabin, I just saw you on the ground and I thought you were gone. And then Lennox... Fuck."

I can barely make out her words, but I understand her fear more than anything. I rub her shoulder, and she lets out all of her emotion. I have a strong suspicion she was—or still is—in shock and everything is hitting her all at once.

I don't know how long she cries for, but eventually her tears dry up. She lifts her head up to look at me and wipes away tears I didn't even realize were still falling.

"Can I ask you something?"

"Anything," I tell her.

"Did I kill him?" She whispers it like she's scared of my answer. I know somewhere deep in her brain, she knows logically that she didn't, but wading through her shock proves to be impossible.

"No, Will, you didn't. That was a not-so-unfortunate reaction to him falling. That is one hundred percent not on you."

She nods, but I know she doesn't fully hear me yet.

A nurse comes in, concern in her eyes as she looks at Willow.

"The doctor asked me to come in and check on you," she says softly, her eyes on Willow, not me.

My eyes tear up again with the fact that she's in so much shock the doctors want to intervene.

"I'm good. Totally good." Willow's voice cracks as she continues attempts to sit up.

"I tell you what, if you come with me for maybe half an hour max, we'll check you out and see if we can get you feeling a little bit better. After that, you are welcome to come back. We'll set up a recliner for you to sleep in if you'd like, too."

Willow's gaze shifts from the nurses to mine. I give her a small nod.

"O-Okay." She slowly gets off my bed with help from the nurse before she leads her out of my room.

The nurse meets my eyes over Willow's head, nodding in a subtle way to let me know she'll probably be a lot longer than thirty minutes.

I lean back on the bed, wiping my face one more time. I've seen a lot in my life, but seeing Willow like that is by far the worst. There's nothing I can do to help either. This feeling of helplessness isn't unknown to me, but this feeling of wanting to escape it is new.

A knock at the door makes me lift my head as Woodcroft walks in.

I refuse to hide my glare. Their response was abysmal, and I don't know that anything he says will make me forgive that.

"I'm sorry, Oak," he says quietly.

"What the fuck happened?" I growl.

He sighs as he sits in the chair Willow vacated not all that long ago.

"He sent us on a wild goose chase," he says plainly.

I stare at him, waiting for a better explanation because that tells me nothing.

He lets out a sigh. "He called in an anonymous tip to the line, saying Tennison was on the opposite end of town in some abandoned barn. We followed through because, well, we had to. That's the job. When Arlo called us, we immediately knew what had happened, but it put us just far enough away for shit to go down with no backup."

"You should have known." I don't relent. I can't. I just had Willow sobbing on my chest for God knows how long, and any explanation he gives me is not good enough.

How do I even look at her and tell her this? How do I tell her I got stabbed and she had to save the day because a team of fucking experts got tricked?

How can she even look at me?

Lord knows I'll have trouble looking in the mirror.

"Oak, man, I know this whole thing was fucked up, but it's over."

"Sure, it's over. I just got stabbed, and Lennox is sitting in the ICU. Things will magically be fine because you get to fly back home in a couple of days."

"I'm going to ignore all the shit you just said because you've been through a lot. You're emotional and probably a little high on the good drugs, but believe me, we will be having this conversation again in a few days. I feel shitty enough that we got duped by that fucker and weren't there for you guys." His anger shouldn't shock me, but it does. Subconsciously, I know I'm being a dick, but Willow's breakdown has me so on edge that I don't know how to even express how I'm feeling. Woodcroft is probably feeling the same guilt I am, and it's not fair to put more on him.

"I'm sorry," I whisper. I'm doing a lot of apologizing today, and somehow none of it feels like enough. My eyes burn, trying to keep the tears in, but they fall in defiance.

"Oh, Oak," Woodcroft murmurs before I feel him lean over and hug me.

My shoulders shake with the outpour of emotion.

"I'm no good here," I say through the tears. "I hurt everyone. Willow deserves better than this."

"Shhh. We can talk about it later, but you deserve everything you've built here, okay? Just remember that."

I don't bother disagreeing, I'm too busy letting the events of the day—hell, of the past few years—settle in.

Tennison is dead.

I haven't let myself think that yet, and it feels less relieving than I thought it would.

Years of work. Years of him mentally taking his toll. Years of being on high alert.

And it's just over.

It's strange how, in a matter of hours, everything you've worked for is over. How does a person just move on from something that's held such a large part of their life? Do you forget things ever happened? I know I attempted to do just that by moving here, but it wasn't like I actually forgot everything.

Impossible, if I want to keep Willow in my life, but what else is there? Therapy, sure. I assume I'll be needing it for years to come just to cope, but can you truly move on and be happy? Live a fulfilled life?

They're all questions I have no answers for. I suspect no one does because, as humans, we're all different. We all cope and heal differently. But fuck, it would be nice to have a solid answer for once.

The only thing I can do is question if my place is really here in Bluebell Falls. Can I continue to do more good than harm during this phase of healing? Is love enough to conquer this giant chasm of my own creation?

CHAPTER THIRTY-TWO
WILLOW

Apparently, being in shock is a little more serious than I thought. They hooked me up to an IV and gave me some medication I can't remember the name of, but it calmed my panic and made me fall asleep fast. I woke up a few minutes ago in a little bit of a haze, but now that I've figured out where I am, things have cleared up.

Now, what's hitting me is processing everything—well, attempting to.

Lennox, Oakley, and I are in the hospital. I should be released today, according to the very nice nurse who answered a million of my questions. Tennison is dead. And Lennox needs all of our support.

It's heady. Our sleepy little town hasn't ever had this much excitement, and the fallout from it will affect everyone. The thing I know with absolute certainty is that every single resident will come together to help in whatever way they can.

A knock sounds at my door before it cracks open and Rina's head pops in. She looks exhausted, and I feel terrible for putting more shit on her plate with my freakout. She gives me a small smile as she pushes the door open and comes in, Ledger following behind.

"Good morning," Rina says in a subdued tone, and it almost makes me cry again. She's so strong-willed, and to see her this worn down is hard.

Ledger looks about the same, except I can see the heavy weight of responsibility that's on his shoulders. It's lessened since he got with Ainsley—he was moving more into a brotherly role instead of a parental one—but that's all disappeared now.

"Hi."

"How are you feeling?" Ledger asks.

"Honestly, like I was hit by a truck. Everything is sore, my head is pounding, but they just gave me some meds for that."

"The doctor said you'll probably be out within the next couple of hours, as long as the headache lessens," Rina says.

"Why didn't you tell us?" Ledger asks, sounding hurt. "We should have gotten you help as soon as you got here."

"You didn't know. Hell, the paramedics told me what to look out for, and I just pushed it all aside. I promise, Ledg, this isn't on you." I push myself to sit up a little and wince at how sore I feel. It's weird. I didn't do anything physical yet my whole body feels depleted. The body is so strange, working to protect a person when they need it, in ways you would never think of. I've written about shock before, but now I feel like I did a terrible job of doing it justice.

"How's Lennox doing?" I ask.

"He's talking, in pain, but seems to be doing well. The doctors are optimistic he'll be moving out of the ICU later today," Rina says.

"But how is he doing?" I ask, glad that he'll be out of the ICU but still struggling with everything that will have to happen from there.

"He's…" Ledger lets out a sigh. "He's not talking about it at all. He's answering basic questions about how he physically feels, but he won't talk about anything else. It feels like the physical injuries are nothing compared to whatever that bastard did to Len mentally. Oakley's partner told us a little bit of history with the other victims, and it just seems like everything is going to be hard."

"Fuck." I toss my head back. I was hoping Tennison didn't have enough time to fuck with Lenny's head, but it looks like I'm wrong. "When I get released, I'd like to go talk to him."

"Of course," Rina says quickly. I get the feeling that they hope I can make some magical breakthrough with him, but they'll be sadly disappointed if my gut feeling is right.

I want to ask about Oakley, but I'm not even sure if they've been updated on him. It feels odd to ask about him, and I'm not sure why. He'll just be on my list of visits when I finally break free.

"Knock, knock," a voice rings out from the door. "I'm here with your discharge paperwork."

"You guys don't have to stay," I tell Rina and Ledger.

"Shut up. If we don't get your discharge info now, you sure as hell won't tell us later." Rina gives me a knowing look. She's not wrong.

The three of us listen to the nurse, and within ten minutes, I'm free to go.

Sitting next to Lennox in a regular hospital room is making me feel hopeful. However, the vacancy in his eyes has grown in the last day. He's sitting up in the bed, still shirtless, showing the bulk of the bandages on his chest. The stubble covering his pale face is a reminder it's only been about a day.

"How are you feeling, Lenny?"

"Super good. Feels like I could go for a hike right now." His deadpan joke makes me smile, but I can see he only did it for me.

I open and close my mouth a few times, but I'm not even sure what to say. I don't feel like I need to walk on eggshells around him, but I don't even know how to express all the emotions running through me.

"Thank you." His soft voice pulls me out of my overthinking.

"For what?"

"For taking care of that bastard. He isn't going to hurt anyone anymore because you're a badass."

"Well, I technically didn't kill him." That, I have at least come to terms with since my talk with Oakley. "But I'd be lying if I didn't hope he hates hell."

That gets me a small grin, and I'll take it.

"I don't blame Oakley. I hope he knows that. It could have happened to anyone, but it was Tennison's fault, no one else's."

"I'm scared he's going to put all this blame solely on his shoulders," I whisper, fighting the tears. I don't want to cry anymore.

"He will," he says simply.

I look up at him, trying to figure out how he's so calmly talking about all of this right now.

"I think—" He pauses, trying to gather his thoughts. "I think this is going to fuck me up for a long time. I don't know how I'll ever be able to just … talk about it." "Oh, Len," I whimper. It hurts. He's so calm, so disconnected, and it frightens me. I don't know how to help him.

"I can't say I'll be fine because… Fuck." He tips his head back. "I don't think I'll be fine, Will. This sucks. All of it."

"I know," I barely get out over the sob. "You know I'll be here every step of the way. I'll help you however I can. I'll bug you when you lock yourself away. I'll bring you burgers every day. Whatever you need." I reach out and squeeze his hand, wordlessly giving him as much support as I can.

He squeezes back, and when I look up at him, I see the tears streaming down his face.

We cry together for a while. I'm not sure how long we sit there, but it's cathartic as hell for me. This crying feels helpful, productive. Yesterday's just felt uncontrollable and chaotic, so I like the change of pace.

"How are you doing, Will?" Lennox asks when his tears dry up a little.

"I honestly have no clue. I haven't had a chance to just sit and process everything. After I left you yesterday, I went to Oakley. Then the doctors hijacked me because I was in shock."

"What does that mean?" He's worried, and I'd laugh if this were any other situation. He's still in the hospital yet he's more worried about me.

"Basically, they admitted me, gave me meds that forced me to sleep and calm down."

"Jesus," he mutters.

"It's definitely not something I recommend. But hey, just more material to work with for a future book," I deflect.

"It's okay to not have all the answers, Will. Take time. Figure shit out. Lord knows everyone is going to need time to decompress from everything. You don't owe anyone anything, okay? You don't owe me burgers every day or stopping your life because you feel like you're obligated to help and support me. I'm a big boy. I can handle things, and I promise if I need help, you'll be my first call."

I don't know how to respond to him because I know whatever I say, he won't really hear. He's in the thick of huge trauma, and I believe he wants to think he'll call if he needs help, but there are no guarantees. He knows I'm a call away, and while he's in the hospital, I'll bring him things to take his mind off of the healing he's doing and still needs to do.

For now, that's enough.

We spend the next few minutes talking about what the next steps for him are before the nurse comes in to check his wounds. I leave with the promise to stop by before I go home to sleep.

Wandering the halls of the hospital is eerie. So many stories here, both good and bad. People having babies, people going through the hardest times in their life, all under one roof. It also strangely feels like the perfect place to just think. I eventually find myself in a little seating area off in a secluded part of the hospital with no one in it. I sit in one of the chairs and relax for what feels like the first time in years.

The one thought that hits me with striking clarity is the fact that I'm in love with James Oakley. I know, sooner rather than later, I need to tell him too because if this has taught me anything it's that time isn't a guarantee. Why waste any more time than we already have? And on the off chance he doesn't feel the same, then at least I know. But I truly believe that's not the case.

I know he'll have more demons to conquer because of Tennison, but I'll be right by his side if he'll have me.

Hell, we can make it a year of healing. I can take time off of writing, and we could travel and get away to disconnect from everything that happened here. I'll still be a phone call away for Lennox and able to come back at any point.

This could absolutely work.

My fictitious plans are interrupted as voices get closer.

"What the fuck are you doing?" *Ledger.*

"Leaving." *Oakley.*

"Yeah, no shit. I can see that. What the fuck are you doing to Willow?"

"She doesn't need me here fucking things up for her. She's strong, stronger than she'll ever know."

I don't hear a reply, but I do hear the sound of bone crushing into bone. *Lovely.*

"Maybe that'll knock some fucking sense into you. You don't get to hurt her. You get to man the fuck up and face this shit."

The sound of footsteps walking away is all I hear. I stand up, making my way around the little corner separating us, and find James rubbing his right eye.

"Don't make decisions for me."

He startles, looking up at me with guilt all over his face.

"We will talk about this later, but right now, I need a few hours." My voice is strong, but I can feel the hurt quickly building. It's not that he thinks he isn't good enough; it's not that he was just about to leave, although that fucking kills me. It's the fact that he wasn't even going to talk to me. We talk about everything; nothing is off limits, and for him to just take that decision away is not okay. But I know I need to think things through, think about my response before I lose my shit on him.

I turn on my heel and head toward the elevator.

"Willow..." Oakley calls out.

"Later," I yell over my shoulder, not bothering to look at him. The tears are yet again falling, and I hate it.

All I want to do is stop fucking crying.

Going home and taking a shower, then getting some fresh air with a walk sounds like a good start, though.

CHAPTER THIRTY-THREE
OAKLEY

They want to keep me another two days, but I'm losing my mind just sitting here and thinking.

The nurse has kept me somewhat updated on Willow, but I haven't seen her for myself and it's making me anxious as hell.

But the guilt is still there in full force too. And I'm torn between breaking out and finding her, and just leaving because I'm not even sure what I bring to the table anymore.

"Brought coffee. Probably not as good as yours, but whatever," Woodcroft says as he walks through my hospital door.

"Thanks." I take the offered cup.

We sit in silence as we drink our coffee.

"We gonna talk about it?" Woodcroft asks.

I sigh. "I'm sorry for blaming you guys yesterday. That was fucked-up."

"It was, but I probably would have done the same."

"He played us, just like we assumed he would. We just couldn't plan for the way he actually did it."

"Yup." He pops the P.

"And it was all on me in the end. Tennison was coming after me. He had a vendetta against me, tortured more people to get to me, and nothing good came from any of it."

"Nothing good?" Woodcroft's voice is dangerously low.

"Hell no! I wouldn't be shocked if Willow wants nothing to do with me after all of this."

"Holy fuck," he whispers in exasperation. "You're a dumb shit, you know that?"

I grunt, not responding. It seems like he has shit to say, so might as well let him get it out. Not that it will change anything.

"Tennison is dead. Do you understand that? Years of work, of sacrifice, of hunting, are done. He's gone. That is fucking good, Oak. You creating a life here away from all the bullshit is fucking good, Oak. Our entire career on the Task Force is finally for something, and you're sitting here sulking? Feeling guilty for another, very demented person's actions? We did a good fucking thing here. Yes, shit happened. Yes, what happened to Lennox, to you, was extremely unfortunate, and I wish it never hap-pened. But we *finally* got Tennison. His reign of terror is over. His victims can finally rest easy. Doesn't that mean something?"

He's imploring me to hear him, and I want to, but I don't know how I could ever forgive myself for what happened to Lennox. Yes, I'm happy Tennison is burning in the depths of hell and that victims will get some closure. But I'm still so stuck on his words.

"I always followed you closer between you and your partner because you always seemed to be closer to finding me. Every single case you got closer but just never quite reached me."

I was so close, multiple times, and I just ... wasn't good enough. It literally took Willow telling us about the cabin to get him. He probably would have lured us there regardless, but either way, it wouldn't have been my doing. I did nothing. Not good enough to catch him, instead bringing destruction to a good friend and forever changing his life. How can I not feel guilty? How can I feel any level of happiness right now?

"I just … can't see the positive right now, Kel."

"It's going to take time; sure, I get it. Just please, for the love of God, think about what I said. We finally won. It means something, otherwise what was all of this even for?"

I nod, not agreeing but realizing I'm not in a headspace to argue with him at the moment.

"What's your plan now? I assume you're not going to sit here with your thumb up your ass." He thankfully changes the subject.

"Breaking out then leaving," I grunt.

"Super healthy." He nods.

"Whatever."

"You need help getting home?" he asks.

"No, I'm just going to pack what I can and then head out."

"Wait, you're 'leaving' leaving? Like, leaving town? What the actual fuck, Oak?" He's back to yelling, and I know I deserve it.

"I need to leave. I can't hurt her more," I barely get the last words out because it physically hurts. My heart is crumbling just thinking about leaving Willow, but with everything happening with Lennox, I just don't see how she'll ever see me as James again.

"God, you're such an asshole right now," Woodcroft says on a sigh. "Go home. Don't do anything stupid, and give yourself time to process all this shit. Don't make any decisions right now and fuck up something that's really fucking good for you."

His words don't change my mind; if anything, they reinforce my plan.

Woodcroft starts to stand up then pauses before walking over to me. "Please take the time to think about things, man. And let's not let another year go by without talking to each other again, okay?" He claps my shoulder, looking at me wearily. He knows me well enough to know exactly what I'm planning.

I watch him walk out the door before collapsing back on the bed.

It takes me almost three hours to get the doctor to agree to let me leave, and as soon as the discharge papers are signed, I'm very slowly walking out the door.

I end up taking a wrong turn because when I was wheeled in here, I was hopped up on pain meds, and I end up walking toward a dead end. When I whirl around, I see Ledger shooting daggers at me.

"What the fuck are you doing?"

"Leaving." I tell him simply.

"Yeah, no shit. I can see that. What the fuck are you doing to Willow?"

"She doesn't need me here, fucking things up for her. She's strong, stronger than she'll ever know."

"So, you're just going to walk out and crush her? With all this shit going on?"

I don't see the punch coming, but I should have. It wouldn't have really mattered if I had, though, because I would have let him do it. I deserve it. Hell, I deserve a lot more.

"Maybe that'll knock some fucking sense into you. You don't get to hurt her. You get to man the fuck up and face this shit." He turns and walks away as I stand, reeling in my thoughts.

"Don't make decisions for me." I jolt, looking up at Willow, instantly overwhelmed with guilt. "We will talk about this later, but right now, I need a few hours." She walks toward the elevator that I now see.

"Willow ..." I call after her, although I have no idea what I would say.

"Later," she yells back, not bothering to turn around.

I watch her go. I watch the woman I love walk away from me, and it hits me like a wrecking ball.

What the fuck am I doing?

I scrub my hand over my face and wince at the tender skin around my eye where Ledger punched me.

I spot the nurses station and head toward it, finding the nurse that was assigned to me earlier.

"Excuse me, can you tell me where Lennox Hutton's room is?"

She eyes me for a second, her eyes shifting to my eye before looking at her computer. "Room 312."

"Thanks." I head in the direction of the signs, stopping when I get to his room.

By happenstance, or just the universe helping me out, his room is empty of visitors.

I softly knock on the doorframe, drawing his attention.

"I was wondering if I would see you," he says with absolutely no inflection.

"I can leave if you are companied out ..."

"Nope, you're good. Sit." He gestures to the empty chair next to his bed.

He actually looks better than I thought he would, although he's still in bad shape. Bandages cover a lot of his body, and what isn't covered has smaller nicks to the skin that haven't fully healed yet.

It's harder than I thought it would be to see. It's not the first time I've been in a hospital room with one of Tennison's victims, but this is the first time that I've known them personally and am actually friends with them.

"I feel like 'I'm sorry' doesn't cut it," I say quietly.

"Good pun. I liked it." He smirks.

"Fuck, I'm sorry." I groan.

"Just giving you shit. You know you don't have anything to apologize for, man."

"I have a million things to apologize for. All of this is because of me. Tennison's goal was to get to me, and he did and took you down at the same time. That should have never happened."

"Did ..." He visibly gulps. "Did others get better?" His voice is so timid my heart breaks.

I could tell him a multitude of things. I could tell him it gets better, that I've seen people heal fully, but I can't do that to him. He needs honesty as much as I do right this moment, I think.

"Some. Others, not so much. I learned something while I was in that cabin, though, that might have affected those outcomes. Tennison told me he would visit them ... after the fact. I can't imagine it's easy to heal when your demon keeps coming back to haunt you."

"Jesus." He wipes under his eyes discretely.

"He really fucked everyone up," I murmur.

"Do you think I'll be okay?"

"Yeah, Len. I think so. It'll take work and time, but I think you will." I grab his hand, squeezing it.

He clears his throat, squeezing my hand back before pulling away and wiping his face. "And what about you and Will?"

I scrub my hand over my face again. "I'm not entirely sure. I messed up, badly, and I'm not sure what I should do."

"You want to hear the opinion of someone incapable of punching you, like I'm assuming Ledger did?" He arches his eyebrow.

I trace the edge of my eye and laugh. "I would like that very much."

"Drop the guilt. No matter how it happened, a monster is off the streets because of you and Willow. I would never blame you or hold you in any way responsible, so neither should you. Do whatever you need to do to get your head right, and go after that woman. Don't let your past or this sense of unworthiness take over. You are a good man. Hell, you're a great man. I would trust you with my life ten times over, and that's considering my current position." He motions to his body. "Don't lose her because you can't get out of your head long enough to talk to her. You know how she is; all you need is to be open, and the two of you can overcome anything. Talk to her. Don't give up." He pauses. "If you don't give up, I won't either."

It's like he physically shot me. *If you don't give up, I won't either.*

I nod as the tears fall again.

He has no reason to be on my team, no reason to support me in any way. And yet here he is, making a promise I want to keep. I don't want to give up Willow, just like I never want him to give up on himself, on life.

Somehow, it's the clarity I need. It's not forgiveness because he doesn't feel like I have anything to apologize for.

It's acceptance. That even though everything is extremely hard right now, we push through. We hold on to those who support us, and we fight like hell to survive.

We fight to thrive.

It's like a lightning strike hits me. I jump up from my chair, gripping my side in pain from the damn stab wound I momentarily forgot about.

"I'll be back. Tomorrow, probably," I say hurriedly.

"I'll be here. And Oakley?"

I tilt my head in question.

"Thank you for being honest. Everyone has been too fucking positive, too upbeat. But they don't know." His voice drops low. "They don't know what he does, how he really is."

"Was. How he was, Len."

He nods to me again, a mutual understanding between us. He hasn't said anything to the cops about what actually happened in the cabin, just like the other victims, even though Tennison is gone. Whatever he said to Lennox will stick with him his entire life, and it's something he may never talk about.

He clears his throat again, "Go get your woman."

"Thanks, Len."

I leave without another word.

There will be time. There will be more conversations, more revelations. But for now? It's time I grow some balls and actually talk to Willow.

CHAPTER THIRTY-FOUR
WILLOW

The rideshare I took home from Rosedale thankfully saw the *Do not talk to me* sign on my forehead, so it was blissfully quiet. Fresh air and a walk seemed to have only brought out my emotions more. I've been out here for a couple of hours, and I still feel like I'm all over the place.

Angry. Sad. So fucking sad for so many things. Exhausted. And anything looking remotely like happiness is too far away right now.

How dare James think he can just unilaterally make decisions for both of us. How dare he think now, of all fucking times, is the right time to make a rational decision about anything. Jesus, even I'm aware enough to realize now is not the time to make any sort of choices outside of what to eat. And even that seems like a challenge for me right now.

God, I'm so damn angry at him. But I also understand the way he's thinking. I bet, right now, he's thinking everything is his fault. He's keeping the guilt close like a parka protecting him against snow. The problem is, I have no clue how to pull him out of it.

I told him we would talk later, and I meant that, but before we do, I'd like a starting point.

Thunder cracks overhead, and I look up. Dark clouds are moving in fast, and I nod. Of course it's going to rain. It feels fitting for my mood.

Thirty seconds later, a torrential downpour hits. I spread my arms open, tilting my head up and just let the rain take me. It feels oddly cathartic. It camouflages the tears, and I don't even realize I'm crying until my shoulders start shaking.

Taking one more deep breath, I drop my arms and turn to the direction of my house. No use in staying out here and freezing my ass off as the temperature drops.

The walk takes less than ten minutes, and I cry the whole time. I'm worried. Scared Lennox won't get better, won't heal mentally. I'm scared I've lost James before I ever really had him. I'm scared I won't ever get the chance to tell him how I really feel. I'm worried this will change our family forever and we won't ever recover from it.

I don't think I can handle any of those outcomes, honestly.

I freeze in my tracks as I walk up to my house. There's a bulky figure sitting on my front steps, and my heart is immediately in my throat.

When the man's face lifts from his arms, I take a full breath. *James.*

I open my mouth to be snarky, but a hiccup from crying so much takes its place. He wordlessly holds his arms open, and I immediately go to him. Sitting in his lap and wrapping my arms around him, I instantly feel safe. I feel this release as I hold him tight.

"I'm so fucking sorry." I hear the anguish, hear him breaking down in the crack in his voice.

"Don't do that again. I can't ... I can't" The words won't come out. For once, I don't have the words to articulate how I feel.

"I know. The guilt... God, the guilt overtook everything."

"How long have you been out here?"

"About an hour, maybe? I don't know. After you left, I went and talked to Lennox." We're both quiet, me thinking about how hard that conversation was for him.

"That's pretty big," I mutter.

His surprised chuckle hits me right in the chest, and I smile.

"It was so fucking hard," he whispers.

"But you did it."

"But I did it," he agrees with a sigh. "It helped a lot."

"I'm very thankful." I hug him tighter to me before he grunts in pain. "Shit, your side and your arm. I'm an asshole."

"No, you're not. But I think maybe going inside and getting more comfortable would help." He leans back, looking into my eyes.

My mind turns dirty in a split second. James Oakley dripping wet, with an earnest look in his eyes, is a sight to behold, and I realize just how much I've missed him during all of this.

"Probably don't look at me like you want to rip my clothes off. We have a lot to talk about, and this damn stab wound won't let me fuck you the way I really want to."

"Damn, I missed your mouth." I tip my head back on a groan.

"Up. Now, woman. Shower, then snuggle in bed, so we can talk."

"Did you just use the word 'snuggle'?"

"In the context of doing it with you? I sure as hell did." He says it with no shame, and somehow this little sparring match soothes the last of my chaotic thoughts. We'll get back to us, even if it takes some time.

I carefully untangle my limbs from his and hold my hand out to help him. He groans as he stands up, one hand going to his injured side.

"I'm sorry." I cringe at causing him pain.

"No, it's all good. It's more stiff than anything, I promise."

I eye him with skepticism, especially because I have a vague memory of the doctor saying he was going to have to stay a few days. This is certainly not a few days.

I quickly unlock the door, getting us out of the rain.

We both step in, the sound of the rain quieting behind the closed door. Eyes locked, the electrical current usually between us sparks to life.

"Will…" Oakley warns.

"I know, I know. Shower." I blink out the haze and move toward the bathroom.

I don't even bother with privacy or a sense of modesty. He's seen all of me before, and although I'm sure both of us would absolutely be okay with some sex, I think we both realize that's not actually going to happen tonight. There's too much to work through, and brushing things under the rug isn't an option.

Stripping as I walk, I turn the hot water on and wait. James joins me a minute later, stripping slowly so his stiches don't pull.

"Did you talk them into letting you out early?" I ask, staring at where he got stabbed and seeing the fresh bandage. A flash of Tennison thrusting his knife at him enters my brain, and I squeeze my eyes shut to get rid of it.

"Trouble." His hand grips my shoulder, and my eyes pop open. "I'm fine. I may have left a little early, but what were they really keeping me there for anyway? To monitor the stitches? Look for infection? I can do that, no big deal." He shrugs, and I roll my eyes at him.

"You're a pain in the ass," I tell him as I jump into the shower.

I watch him gently remove the bandage on his wound on his side and arm before carefully moving to the shower. He opens the door and slides in, careful to keep the bad side out of the water. He angles himself perfectly to keep the stitches dry while still being close to me.

My hand reaches up, softly brushing an inch from the injury before I even realize I'm doing it. His hand lands on top of mine, leading my movements and bringing my hand up his ribcage to his heart.

"When you came into that cabin, I felt so much simultaneously. Fear... Fuck, I was so scared to see you there. Pride. You're so fucking fearless, just barging in there with a baseball bat." He shakes his head, with a small smile on his lips. "Then the guilt hit, and it never left. I couldn't pull myself out of it, and I said a lot of stupid shit."

"I get it." My fingers shift against him, feeling his strong heartbeat. "The paramedics, while we were being taken to the hospital, talked to me about the effects of shock. It was weird. I heard them and understood it in principle but didn't understand what it would look like."

"I should have made them take you in before me." He shakes his head, angry at himself.

"Hey," I say sharply, forcing him to look at me. "We're done with the blaming. The what-ifs and should-haves—we're not doing them, okay?"

"Okay," he murmurs before leaning down and pressing a kiss to my lips.

I melt into him.

But it's over too fast.

"I had to, sorry," he says against my lips, and it makes me smile.

"Yeah. I'm really upset about it." I grin.

"Where were we?" he asks.

"Before you decided to kiss me as the ultimate distraction? You feeling guilty and making dumb decisions."

"Right. It just consumed everything. I felt ... so unworthy of everything I've built here. Unworthy of Lennox's friendship, unworthy of Grind Time, and certainly of you. It felt like..." He looks up in thought before looking back at me. "It felt like running was the only option," he says softly.

I swallow back the tears as I nod. I want so badly to be done crying, but I know that's a fool's hope.

"Can I ask you something?" My hand is still absentmindedly moving over his chest.

"Always."

"Did you want to leave?" The tears I prayed wouldn't fall, disobey.

"No. Fuck no. I never want to leave you. I just wanted you to have the best life, and I didn't think that was with me. Unknowingly, I brought all this shit to you, and it's hard to separate that from everything else."

My heart breaks. I know this feeling won't just immediately be gone for him. I know we both will need to be in therapy to really work through the worst of this, but hearing him say he didn't want to leave is enough for me. I don't care how long things take. I don't care how fucking hard it is; it'll be worth it.

His hand moves to lift my chin before cupping it.

"I'm in love with you, and I don't think there's a single thing that would make me ever *want* to be without you."

My breath hitches as a smile spreads across my face. I lean forward, pressing a kiss to his chest, right where his heart is, before pulling back.

"I love you too," I whisper before he leans and crashes into me with a kiss that steals my whole soul.

He pulls back, putting his forehead to mine. "Things are going to be a lot harder before they get better."

"I know."

"But I'll do my absolute best to always be here for you. I know I'll mess up sometimes, though."

"So will I," I tell him.

"I'm sorry. I know you don't want to hear it, but I need to say it one more time. I'm sorry for everything, for leading Tennison here, for the destruction he caused. For doubting you could love me through my worst."

"And I'm sorry for not actually talking to you about all of this before we both went past our breaking point. For scaring you at the cabin. And not staying put at your apartment," I add.

"I honestly don't think you should apologize for that last one. That did way more good than bad," he mutters.

"Possibly, but I'm still sorry it stressed you out."

"No more apologies."

"No more apologies." I say. I press my lips to his one more time before pulling back with a smile. "Now, we actually need to get clean because we're on borrowed time with the hot water."

"Done. I think I'm going to need a bed in two minutes anyway because I'm fucking exhausted," he says.

"I can help with that."

I move to grab my little silicone scrubber before loading it up with soap. I wash him carefully before he snags it from me and reciprocates. I quickly shut off the water before stepping out and grabbing a towel. I hand one to James as he gingerly steps out, and I can tell he's close to collapsing.

"Do you have fresh bandages for those?" I point to his wounds.

"In the hospital bag by the front door."

Huh, didn't even see that.

"Okay, stay here and I'll go grab it." I book it out the living room, thankful for my small house, and return back to my bedroom only to find James spread out onto my bed, buck-ass naked.

"You are a sight to behold. Just saying," I tell him as I walk around the side and start laying out the supplies.

"Absolutely same, Trouble," he says with a smirk.

It takes me a couple of minutes to dress his injuries with his direction, and I look up to see his eyes drooping.

I toss the towel on the floor before crawling into bed next to him.

"I love you," I sigh out as I curl up to his uninjured side.

"I love you too," he barely manages to get out before a soft snore starts.

He's right. It'll be a long, hard road for both of us.

But we'll be okay.

CHAPTER THIRTY-FIVE
OAKLEY

The ringing of my phone startles me out of a deep sleep.

It's reminiscent of only a few days ago when all of our lives changed irrevocably. This sense of déjà vu hits me hard, and I cautiously grab my phone. Willow rolls over, facing me as she blinks her eyes open.

"Tell them to fuck off." Her voice is raspy with sleep and so fucking adorable.

"Wish I could, Trouble." I show her *Kellen Woodcroft Calling* on my phone, and she immediately wakes up and sits up.

"Yeah," I grunt out as I answer.

"Be on the ready. We held them off as long as we could, but the media has descended."

"Fuck," I groan and tip my head back.

"I'm shocked it took this long, honestly."

"I am too. I just forgot this part of the job," I tell him.

"Rosedale is basically covered in news vans right now, and it's only a matter of hours before they head your way. I've already called Sheriff Arlo, and he's preparing the town for the invasion."

"I haven't looked at the news. What's the story they have?" I ask, knowing they won't give them all the details.

"Tennison is dead. The Task Force received an anonymous tip that led to the outskirts of Sam Houston National Park that eventually led to his demise. No other statements will be made." He says it robotically as if he was speaking with the media.

"So, no me, no Lennox, and no Willow?"

"As of right now, no, but you know that information won't be protected. It only takes one person talking."

"I know. I'm not worried about Bluebell Falls talking, more about the hospital staff in Rosedale."

"I'm trying to lock it down, but you know how it is. Someone always falls through the cracks."

"Yeah. Okay, well, call me if something happens. I'll try to prepare as much as possible here. And Kellen?" I ask.

"Yeah?"

"Stop by before you leave, okay?"

"Will do. You sound better, Oak. Does that mean you got your thumb out of your ass?"

I chuckle. "Yeah, that's exactly what it means."

"Tell Willow hi for me. And I'll see you later."

I smile over at Willow, who I assume heard the entire conversation judging by the grin on her face.

"Honeymoon's over." I sigh when my thoughts turn back to the original reason for the call.

"What exactly does the 'media descending' mean?"

"It means the story of Tennison's death is out. And as you can imagine, he's a bit of a national sensation so the interest in the full story will be huge. Every national, regional, local news station will want a piece of the pie."

"Shit." She scrubs her face. "So, what do we do?"

"I call Sheriff and see what needs to be done. I'd love nothing more than to hide out until the hype is over, but I don't know that I'll get that luxury."

"It might be the safest option." She climbs out of bed and heads to the bathroom.

I quickly follow the sway of her naked ass, and I growl in frustration that one, I'm not in any shape to fuck her right now, and two, we have shit to figure out before that's even a consideration.

"Put on some damn clothes so I can focus," I call out.

"What? Am I distracting?" She turns back with a smirk before shutting the door.

Trouble. Too fitting of a nickname if you ask me.

I take my time to put in that call to Sheriff.

"Morning Oakley," he answers with his normal tone. No hint of the turmoil coming to take over our sleepy town.

"I just heard from Woodcroft and wanted to check in, see what I could do to help."

"Well, the busybodies have been informed, so I think whoever decides to show up is in for a rude welcome. Honestly, I think it's probably best to hide out. If they catch your scent or Willow's, they won't let up. If we give them nothing, they'll leave faster. I can make sure you both are stocked up on food, supplies, whatever you need."

My throat works extra hard to swallow. The support and the unquestioning loyalty that I still don't completely feel worthy of are humbling to say the least.

"Will and I are at her house. I have no clue what we have for food, but I can text you later and let you know. I don't want to hide out, but I agree it's the easiest way to get rid of the circus sooner."

"You're a part of the Bluebell Falls family, Oakley. We support each other, and you can bet the people of this town will protect you from whomever decides to stick their noses here."

I clear my throat at the emotions rushing to the surface. "Thanks ,Sheriff," I whisper.

"For the love of God, Oakley, call me Arlo. And while you're hiding out, think about coming to work at the office. Please. I could use your experience."

I chuckle at his continued offer.

"I'll think about it. Thanks, Sheriff Arlo." I smirk, though he can't see it.

"You're a pain in the ass. Text me what you need." He hangs up before I can give a rebuttal, and I laugh out loud. He's a good guy, but he can be grumpy as hell.

"Arlo?" Willow asks from the door I didn't even hear her open. She's put on a pair of shorts and an oversized T-shirt, and I'm almost regretting telling her to cover up.

"Yep. We're officially hiding out. He said he'll bring us anything we need."

"You think hiding out is the right move?"

"I think it's the right move to get everyone out of town faster."

"Okay." She nods. "I have no clue what we have here, so we'll have to do inventory. And I need to check my work email." She cringes. "It's a good thing I finished that book when I did, at least."

"Easy." I swing my legs over and climb out of bed, already feeling a million times better than yesterday. My wounds are starting to itch a little, so I know it's on the road to healing, thankfully.

"Jesus, put some pants on or something." Her murmur makes me smirk.

"Payback sucks, huh?" I chuckle.

She shakes her head, walking into the living room without another word.

A couple of hours later, Willow is sitting at her desk checking emails while I wait for grocery delivery from Sheriff—Arlo.

"Well, I think I just found something to do while we're stuck in here," she says.

"Oh yeah? What's that?" My eyes watch as she starts typing frantically. I don't think I'll ever stop being amazed watching her work.

"I just got back edits on the book." I can't tell from her tone if that's a good thing or a bad thing.

I stand up, only feeling the slight pull of the stitches in my side, and walk over to her. One hand on the back of her chair, the other on her desk, I lean over and try to work out if she's happy or not.

"Walk me through this. Are you happy? Dreading this? What's the process like?" I ask.

She looks up at me with a soft smile on her face.

"It's probably really boring."

"If it has to do with you, it's never boring, Will." I lean a little closer.

"Well, this is only half, but I started skimming them, and honestly? They look amazing. Usually for me, editing is the bane of my existence. There's a ton to work through, usually some huge plot hole I fucked up, and I bank about a full month to make things perfect before sending it off for proofreading. If the notes accompanying the edits are to be believed, it looks pretty good. There's obviously still some smoothing out that needs to happen, but my editor is loving the whole thing, no huge plot holes or rewrites needed."

"That's amazing," I tell her. "How can I help?"

She cringes. "I'm not sure there's a ton to do. If I dive in, you'll pretty much be solo until I'm done."

"I can handle that. I'll make sure you're fed and have plenty of coffee. Just like old times." I wink.

She bursts out laughing. "Like, a week ago?"

"God, I can't believe it's only been a week." I sigh.

"A lot has happened."

"Too much. I'm really worried about Lennox and what happens when they release him, and all these fucking news vans are still here," I confess.

"Yeah, I was thinking about that too. I need to call Ledger and see how things are going there anyways. I'm not sure if Arlo has filled them in on what's going on here or not. but I don't want Lennox to leave the hospital at all if he's going to get bombarded with nosey-ass people."

"I agree." A knock on the front door tells me our food is here. "I'll take care of that. Why don't you call Ledger, so we're all on the same page."

She nods as I head to the front door.

I take a look through the peep hole—you can never be too careful—finding Arlo, so I open the door, ushering him in.

"I've got more in the car, but stay in here." He drops off the armload he was carrying. He spins right around and walks out the door, coming back only a minute later with the rest of the groceries.

"Okay, I couldn't find that fancy coffee thing you were asking for."

"An Areo-press?" I laugh.

"Yeah, we're small town here, man. We don't have fancy shit like that. Why do you think Grind Time is so successful?"

"I thought it was because I cook good food and provide something pretty to look at," I joke.

He blankly stares at me before moving to put food in the refrigerator. "I took the liberty of ordering one online. It'll be here tomorrow. I got rush shipping."

I don't even try to hide my smile. His thoughtfulness, despite his gruff nature, tells me more about him as a person. "I appreciate that. How much do I owe you for everything?" I motion to the counter as we both put groceries away. It takes him far longer because he has no clue where things go.

"It's taken care of," he grunts.

"Arlo..."

"Look, Willow is like a sister to me. Hell, the whole family means a lot to me. I'm just trying to do what I can to make sure everyone is taken care of. And you're not half bad, especially if you join me at the sheriff's office." He sneaks it in so subtly I have to admire his recruitment tactic.

"Well then, I owe you one."

"You don't, but I don't have time to argue. Jim, Mabel, and Alice are down at the station, so we can discuss how we're going to 'take care' of the media."

I really laugh then. The three of them will keep not only Arlo busy but the media as well. Probably send them in circles on some wild goose chase. Honestly, I'd pay to see it.

"Have fun with that. Keep me updated," I tell him.

"Will do. Let me know if you need any other supplies. The coffee thing is getting shipped straight here, so you won't be long without your caffeine." He doesn't wait for a response, the pattern really starting to stand out, before he walks out the front door. I follow him, making sure to lock the door before turning back to go find Willow.

I find her sitting on her bed, looking far too beautiful for words. Her hair is in a messy bun on the top of her head and her blue eyes look exhausted, but she looks happy. I lean against the doorframe as she starts talking.

"Ledger said doctors are aware of the media shit and are planning to keep him until it dies down a little more. Lennox is fucking pissed. I had to talk him out of just walking out when he overheard Ledger talking about it. He's stir crazy. He is literally never inside, so this is basically the worst-case scenario for him." She sighs. "But everyone agrees that you and I need to just hide out and let everything pass. Ledg also wants to do a family dinner in the next few days."

"Family dinner? Is this the same one you talked about a while ago?"

"Yep. Every week, we get together and cook one of our favorite meals. It's been a thing since before our parents died, and Ledger kept it going."

"I love that," I whisper, wanting nothing more than to be included. To be important enough in her life to be considered family.

"It keeps us connected in a time where we're all super busy. I'm not sure when that'll be, but I told Ledger you would be coming. If that's okay with you." Her voice quiet, like she's unsure if I would actually be okay with it.

"I would be fucking honored." Uncrossing my arms, I walk closer to her, caging her in with my arms before she falls back against the bed.

"Yeah?" she squeaks as I press a kiss to her cheek.

"Very fucking honored."

A few kisses turn into a make out session that wreaks havoc on my libido, but Willow stands by letting me heal more, refusing to do anything more. It's sweet she's worrying about me, but if she said it was go time, I'd pop those stitches in a second.

I'll be patient though. This new intimacy we've found outside of sex is amazing too, so it's no hardship. Luckily, we've got some time, and I'll get her to cave eventually.

CHAPTER THIRTY-SIX
WILLOW

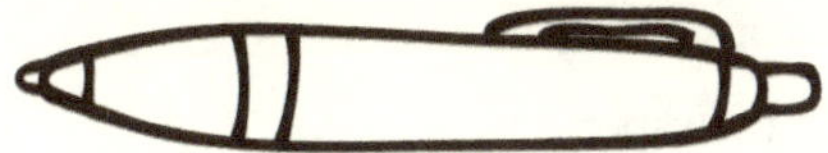

We've been cooped up for almost a week, and I'm about to lose my damn mind.

Edits are almost done and were a great distraction, but being locked in here with James is testing all of my willpower. It feels like he's on this mission to get me to cave, and I've held strong so far. Unfortunately, my edits are coming to an end, and all I can think about is if his stab wound is healed enough.

"What are you thinking so hard about?"

His cocky tone tells me he knows exactly what I'm thinking about as he's wearing nothing but grey sweatpants. I need him to stop knowing so much about what turns me on in a nanosecond because I'm dying.

"How are your stitches?" I ask, looking at the smaller bandage on his side because, let's face it, it's been a week—that's plenty of time for the bulk of healing, right? God, it's like the hours of research I put into books that have shit like this in it have just flown out the window because I'm so fucking horny.

"Good. I did a tele-med appointment with the doctor, and he said they look good. Most of the dissolving ones are already gone, and I'll need to come in to get the surface ones removed. Same for the forearm, but that's pretty much closed up."

Do I look as excited as I feel? Because I feel like my face is about to break from how wide my smile is.

He slowly peels off the bandages, and I see no sign of any stitches and my smile instantly drops.

"What the fuck?" I whisper.

"It's not the first time I've taken out stitches. I cleared it with the doc, I promise," he says with a grin.

I'm not sure why, but I'm annoyed—no, not annoyed, pissed. If he took those out and it causes an infection, I'm going to ... I don't know, punch him in the dick or something.

"Meet me in the bedroom. I'll be there in a second."

He arches an eyebrow at me before sauntering off to my room with a smirk. Yeah, I have a plan, and it's definitely not what he's thinking. I walk to my bedroom and find him lying on his back, sans sweatpants, and I arch my eyebrow at him.

"Wishful thinking?" he asks playfully.

I don't bother with a reply. It isn't wishful thinking, but I doubt he has even thought of what I'm about to do. I know he's as pent up as I am. Walking into my bathroom, I pull the tie off of my robe and go back to my bedroom.

His eyes lock onto the tie and light up. "Hell fucking yes." He sits up, but I stop him.

"Nope. I'm not the one being tied up today, James." I see the second his eyes shutter, and I walk closer to the bed. "If that's not okay, I won't do it," I say softly.

I never want to make him uncomfortable, but push his boundaries like he pushes mine? Sure, but this is more of a one-off anyway because we both know I love being tied up as much as he loves doing it.

"I..." His throat bobs as he swallows hard. "I've never let someone reciprocate."

He doesn't elaborate, and I feel like there's more to it, although I'm not sure what.

"You can tell me no."

He eyes me for a second before his whole face transforms into admiration. "If I let you do this, you know the payback is going to be big, right?"

"Fully expecting that."

"Tie me up, Trouble." He lays his hands above his head in surrender, and it feels like a huge moment. Sure, we've said "I love you", but this feels like a big step too. This is complete trust.

I strip out of my clothes before stepping closer and climbing on the bed. When I straddle his stomach, he groans at the contact.

"Fuuuckkkk, Will."

"Why did you freeze up when I asked to do this?" I loop his wrists through the tie as I ask quietly.

He grunts at the questions but answers anyway. "You're very much using your powers for evil right now." He sighs. "I always wanted to be a Marshal and was pumped when I finally became one. My first time on the task force was really fucking rough. Not as rough as Tennison, but still."

I continue tying him up, making quick work of it before sitting up and shifting back a little as he talks. His hard cock sits at the junction between my legs, and it's almost as tortuous as this week has been.

"It's more about control, not specifically tying you up." His hips tilt as he talks. I don't even think he realizes he's doing it. "I was very young and very eager, so when an undercover case came up, I jumped on it."

He shivers. I put my hand on his heart in hopes it soothes him a little. "We were supposed to catch this woman who killed her husband or boyfriend—hell, I can't even remember who it was now. I was supposed to seduce her, get her to a secluded area so we could safely take her in with little to no drama.

"The whole case shifted something in my head. She ... she attacked me, for a lack of a better word," he says quietly. "Once I had her alone, it was only seconds until the team got there, but she did some good damage. Once we were in the alleyway, it was like she knew what was coming and she jumped on me. Started punching, scratching, anything she could do to harm me. I'm pretty sure I still have scars from her nails on my shoulders. It wasn't even sexual, but it made me realize how much damage a person can do, how much a woman can do when you're vulnerable. I know it sounds crazy that I changed the way I have sex because of one woman. It was scary, though, and my first case on the team. And now I equate staying in control and taking away the use of your arms to staying safe. I stand by that if you hadn't liked it, I would have been fine. You have always been different, and I never second-guess not using restraints with you. It's just a perk that you enjoy them as much as I do."

"Have you had sex since without using restraints?" I ask.

"No."

"Okay," I whisper, thinking this might be a bad idea.

"Willow." His soft voice pulls me out of my head, and I look up at him. "You can literally do anything to me, and I'll be the happiest man on earth. I like control, and I don't think that will ever really go away, but I would be very open to trying new things with you. Seeing what we both like."

"And what if I like the fact that you tie me up and don't want you to stop?"

"Then I will continue to do so. But I think... Everything that's happened is making me reevaluate a lot of things. I don't want to box either of us into this one thing. There's a huge world of things to explore, and I want to do it all with you. I feel ... safe enough to be open to try everything."

My heart pounds in my chest at his words. I don't think I deserve his trust, but I'll be damn sure I do everything in my power to keep it.

"How do you feel right now?" I ask, checking in just like he does to me.

"I feel like my balls are about to explode."

My head tips back in booming laughter, not expecting his response at all.

He tilts his hips again, and my laughter turns into a groan.

"Seriously, James, how do you feel?" I ask again once I gain control of my head.

"I feel good, Trouble. Really fucking good." The honesty in his eyes makes me not overthink anything else. I know he'll stop me if something happens that he's not comfortable with, and the same for me.

I lift up on my knees a little and reach in between us, grabbing his cock and centering myself on him. Locking eyes with him, I sink down onto him slowly but fully. I'm so turned on there's no need for any sort of foreplay.

"Jesus," he breathes out. "Warn a guy." His hips thrust up a little, and I almost laugh, but it feels too damn good.

"This seemed more fitting." I moan as I rock my hips. Not enough movement to get us anywhere but enough to make us both feel it.

"Such trouble," he mutters.

I smile as I lift up and then realize one very important thing I missed.

"Shit. Shit, I forgot a condom. I didn't even think because I'm covered, but I should have run it by you before making the decision." My eyes dance frantically around the room, trying to figure out where I even have condoms.

"Willow." His voice is too calm.

"What?"

"I'm clean. I can show you the tests and shit if you need me too. But I'm clean, and I don't want to ever be with anyone again. I'm all in, so whatever you want is what I want."

"I want you like this," I whisper.

"Take me bare, please. I might have a very, very fast performance, but fuck do you feel incredible." His hips buck again, making me clench.

My hands slide up his stomach, bracing myself and careful to avoid his still healing wound, and up his chest. "Can I ask you something?" His response to the no condom has my thoughts whirling.

"Anything." He tugs at the tie holding him to my bed.

"What do *you* want? You said whatever I want is what you want, but what about the future? What about bigger plans?" I rock on him as I ask.

His hands tug on the restraints again, and I know he wants to touch me. I continue to rock slowly on him as I lean forward and lay on his chest. His shoulders slump, like the contact is exactly what he needed.

"I want you. I don't care if we put titles on things. I don't need to have this big, huge grand life plan. I want you. I want to spend every second I can with you. And whatever comes our way, we'll handle it together.

We'll love each other through it all. If that lands on marriage and kids, perfect. If it doesn't, also perfect."

My eyes well with tears. I don't think I could have found a more perfect man for my quirky soul.

"I've always felt like a man would tie me down." We both chuckle, considering what he usually does to me. "So, I never really dated. I wasn't sure I ever wanted the whole marriage-and-kids' thing. I'm not against it, but at the moment it's not something I feel will complete my life. *You* are something that I feel will complete my life, though. And I like this idea of just living life, going with the flow. And seeing where life takes us together."

"Kiss me. For the love of God, kiss me, woman." His voice is strained, and I look up to see emotion all over his face.

I don't hesitate.

I kiss him like I'll die if don't. I kiss him like it's our form of a marriage contract. I kiss him like I hope I get to until the day I die.

I'm barely moving on him at this point, but it doesn't feel like it matters. I reach up, untying the knot keeping him restrained, needing to feel his hands on me.

Within seconds, his palms are engulfing my jaw and cheeks. The passionate kiss doesn't slow down, even as one of his hands moves down my spine to cup my ass. He starts guiding my movements, making my rocking turn more into bouncing.

Breaking the kiss, he hurriedly tells me, "I need you to sit on my face. I need to feel you come on my tongue."

I don't stop to think, my body moving on instinct as he slides down the bed a little, wrapping his hands around my hips.

The first touch of his tongue has me grinding against him.

"Fuck, James."

He pulls back just long enough to say, "That's right. Say my name, Trouble," before going back.

I can feel myself getting closer and closer. My hands grip the headboard, trying to hold off my orgasm, although I'm not really sure why.

When I feel his finger at my entrance, I know I'm a goner. He knows I love the dual stimulation, and it'll take a matter of seconds before I come, whether I want to or not.

"Yesssss, just like that," I hiss. My head tips back as my orgasm crests over the edge. Wave after wave hits me hard, and I vaguely hear myself crying out with the sheer pleasure of it all.

I collapse against the headboard as Oakley shifts up so I'm straddling his torso.

"You have your fun?" he asks with a smirk, his lips and chin covered in my orgasm.

"I don't know. I might want to try that again some time. Except not have you take over this time," I giggle.

"Whatever you want, Will." It's huge he's even saying that, especially after knowing his history.

While I'm still in that post-orgasmic haze, he grips my ass again, while holding me too him with the other hand before flipping us both over. My smile is wide as I look up at him, with the predatory look on his face I love so much.

"My turn," he whispers before yanking up my arms and holding them in one hand. He doesn't tie me up, but my body arches just the same as if he did.

CHAPTER THIRTY-SEVEN
OAKLEY

Never did I think I would ever trust any woman to tie me up, but I would let Willow do it every single day if it got her off and made her happy.

It was cathartic to give up the control, to let her own my pleasure as much as she owned hers. I know she did it as a way to punish me for taking out my stitches, but what transpired from it was so much more. Talking about our future was just as sexy as taking her bare was.

But now it's my turn.

We've waited a week to reconnect like this, and I'm going to be damn sure she can't walk by the end of it. It's long overdue, and although I understand why she wanted to hold out and wait until I was more healed up, it was hard as fuck to watch her walk around in T-shirts and panties every fucking day.

"How we feeling, Trouble?" I ask.

"So fucking good," she moans as I kiss my way down her collar bone.

I let go of her hands, but she keeps them up, making me smile. I trail mine down the side of her body, her legs already spread to accommodate me, but I grip them and spread them more.

She arches up into me, and I barely keep control of myself.

"Will, you gotta let me work here, or this will be over far too soon. I need to see you completely wrung out for me, dripping and begging me to stop."

"I don't know. I've got a lot of pent-up tension." I look up when I hear the sassiness in her voice.

Arching my eyebrow at her challenge, her smile grows larger.

"Begging for trouble as usual, I see. Okay, if torture is what you're wanting, I'll make that happen for you." I may be two seconds away from coming at any given time, but she just issued a challenge I'm damn sure going to rise to.

I grip her ass in my hands hard before sliding down her body. Her clit is pink and needy even after her last orgasm. My mind is going a million miles a minute, filled with too many ideas and no clue where to start.

Until it snags on one thing. *Edging.* We've done it before but never after having to abstain for a week.

A devilish smirk fills my face, and I can't help the chuckle that erupts from my chest. Her head lifts up to look at me, and I see a twinge of suspicion in her eyes.

"Be nice," she says.

"Nope." I pop the P before licking a line from her ass up to her clit.

"Holy fuck, James," she moans, and it only spurs me on.

Focusing on her clit, I swirl my tongue along the outside, not hitting the spot she really wants me to. Barely gliding my tongue over it once every few circles. When she growls in frustration, I pull it into my lips and suck hard, releasing it just before she goes really wild. The fun thing about Willow is that double stimulation gets her every single time. If I just continue to alternate and not give her both, she'll probably kill me, but it'll keep her on edge until I give her both.

It's wicked mean but so damn fun.

"James fucking Oakley," she growls, and I barely hold back my laughter.

"Patience," I scold.

"I have had patience all fucking week! This is a cruel and unusual punishment, James. Cruel and unusual," she mutters.

God, even in the middle of sex, her sense of humor kills me. She couldn't be more perfect for me.

I slide a finger into her when she's finished chastising me, and her hand goes into my hair. I don't even freeze up; instead, I melt into her touch. The feeling of security is as much a turn-on as her pussy gripping my finger is.

I slide one more finger in, making her grip on my hair tighten, and I have to grind my dick into the edge of the bed to get some relief. *Shit.* I know I'm supposed to be edging her, but it sure as shit feels like I'm torturing myself too.

When I feel her start to pulse around me, I pull them out and scoot back enough to shove my hand around my cock. Her wetness on me makes my hand tighten around her thigh, knowing I'm probably going to leave bruises.

"Holy fuck, that's the hottest thing I've ever seen."

Her whispered words bring my head up, and I stare at her as she watches me pump my cock with her on my fingers. I sit up a little further on my knees, so she has a better view, then move my other hand to her clit again.

Slow circles match the speed I pump into my hand. I can feel her straining; every muscle in her body is so tight, it's like a rubber band waiting to snap. I feel damn close to that myself, but I won't give in until she's boneless.

Her moans are getting loud, and her head is thrashing back and forth against the bed, and I know she's about to scream at me if I don't let her come soon.

I squeeze the tip of my dick hard enough to stave off the too-close-for-comfort orgasm and turn my attention back to my woman.

Bending down, I sweep my tongue through her once again before replacing my finger on her clit. My fingers press into her, hooking up to hit the spot that will send her over the edge quickly, and to my complete surprise, she comes instantly. Wetness flows out of her so fast it puddles underneath her before I can lick it all up.

Smugness like I've never felt hits my chest, knowing I'm the man to do this to her. I'm the man she *trusts* to do this to her.

Her screams echo through the house like a siren's call, and I don't think about what's next or what else I can do. I sit up fast, removing my fingers and slamming my cock into her as she's still riding her orgasm. The pulsating. The heat. It damn near takes me over the edge, but I grit my teeth before reaching down and tugging on my balls harder than I usually would. It pulls me back from the brink just enough to fuck her properly.

And thank god too, because I never want this to end.

I pull out barely an inch before slowly pushing all the way back in, giving her a little stimulation to ride the final wave of her orgasm.

She finally collapses on the bed, breath heavy as a small smile graces her lips.

God she's so fucking beautiful. I take the opportunity to study every inch of her skin. It's not like I haven't done this before, but never like this. Never with a thin layer of sweat making her glisten. Never as her stomach contracts in the aftermath of a powerful orgasm.

My hand slides up her stomach, in between her breasts to her neck. I cup it gently, running my thumb back and forth so I can feel her breath.

"You are fucking magnificent," I breathe out in awe.

Every single day, this woman amazes me, and this moment is no different.

"That... I... What the hell was that?" she says through gasping breaths.

"That was perfection," I murmur.

Her eyes meet mine, and the love I see reflecting back makes my hips thrust involuntarily. Willow moans out, and I bite my lip at the sound.

I bend down, kissing her softly at first as she catches her breath, but before long, her hands are tangled in my hair. The kiss turns messy and out of control in seconds, our need outweighing anything else. One of her hands slides down my back to my ass. She grips it, causing me to shove deeper inside of her. I get the hint and start pumping at a wild pace, our lips never disconnecting.

Her short nails dig into my ass, and the hint of pain sends me into overdrive.

Pulling back from the kiss, I press my forehead to hers as I moan at the pleasure taking hold of me.

"You feel too fucking good. I can't ... I can't hold on, but I need you to come again," I mutter through my heavy breaths.

"I don't know if I can," she whimpers.

I move a hand to her hip, pulling back just enough to slide my hand in between us to reach her clit. My pace never slows, making sure to keep pace so her build-up stays nice and strong.

"I need it, Will. I need you to squeeze me as I come inside of you." I don't tell her I need to be as close as possible because it feels like I need to crawl inside of her to be close enough.

It's a weird feeling, needing someone this much. Wanting someone this much. It's like my soul isn't my own, but that's okay because she's given me hers. It's almost too much, and the emotion of it all threatens to pull me under.

I close my eyes for a second, focusing on the feel of her wrapped around me as her arms circle my neck.

"I love you," she whispers as my eyes open.

"I love you too, Willow. Too damn much, I think," I confess.

"No such thing." She pulls me down and gives me the most tender kiss as I circle her clit harder.

Her orgasm hits strong and with no build-up. No subtle pulsing to warn me; it just pulls us both under with the most powerful orgasm I've ever had in my life.

It goes on for minutes, hours, days—hell, who's to say. It feels like I've lived a whole life in this moment, and it is phenomenal.

I ease off of her clit, staying inside of her as I press my forehead to hers again.

"I'm feeling very poetic right now, which is highly unlike me," I tell her as I attempt to catch my breath.

"I think I'd like to see what a poetic James Oakley sounds like," she murmurs.

"You are more than I could have ever hoped to dream for. I want nothing more than to spend every second with you, no matter what that looks like. It's like I can't get close enough to you."

"I get it. I feel it too. I didn't know it could be like this. This huge emotional dump. I feel like I could just break down into tears." She presses a kiss to my lips, and I hold her tight to me as we leisurely kiss more.

"Do you think it will always be this way?" I whisper.

"You mean, will you edge the fuck out of me so I have an out of body experience in the form of an orgasm and then proceed to give me the best sex of my life? Yeah, babe, I think it'll always be this way."

"Smartass." I smile.

"You like me this way."

"I love you this way."

I don't know how long we lie there, but I do know with Willow by my side, we can make it through anything.

CHAPTER THIRTY-EIGHT
WILLOW

The media circus appears to be dying down, so Ledger calls a family dinner before Lennox is slated to come home.

It's been a week and a half since we've been stuck in here, and as much as I love being locked in with Oakley, I am so ready to get back to our regularly scheduled programming.

He's been getting really antsy too. I'm sure the calls from Arlo and Woodcroft keeping him updated on the media haven't helped a ton. But I'll give him credit; he's been keeping me well fed and hyped up on the lattes I love so much. I'm not sure how he talked Arlo into making that happen, but I'm not asking questions.

Large hands slide around my waist, spanning my stomach, and I melt back into Oakley. "You ready for dinner?" he asks.

"Are you?" I ask with a laugh. The last time he saw any of my siblings, Ledger sucker-punched him.

"Yeah, Ledger and I talked. We're good." He says it so casually. It makes me wonder when he actually had time to talk to my overprotective brother when we've been with each other 24/7.

"You'll eventually have to tell me all about that conversation."

His hand pulls me tight against him, and I tip my head back onto his shoulder.

"Cabin fever is strong, but I almost don't want to leave," he whispers against my temple.

"Same. But people have cleared out ,and Lennox is beyond ready to come home."

"I'm worried about him. He's been putting on a good show for everyone, but I'm concerned that when he gets home and has a lot of alone time, everything will hit him at once," Oakley says.

"I know," I whisper. "He's just so damn headstrong. I don't know if he'll be receptive to help, even if it's just from us."

"Well, we've got to try. That's all we can do."

I nod against his shoulder. I know he's right, but it doesn't make me any less stressed about Lennox's future.

"You ready to head out?" he asks, his thumb brushing back and forth on my stomach, making me absolutely not want to head out.

I sigh. "Not really, but it's time."

He spins me around, pressing soft kisses to each cheek, my forehead, and finally my lips before pulling back and looking at me. "I love you," he murmurs.

"Love you too. Let's go visit the circus."

Ainsley answers the door and pulls me into a tight hug.

"Hello to you too," I grunt.

"We haven't seen you in almost two weeks! We had to sneak into the house in the dead of night a couple of days ago to even get here," she grumbles.

"Might have to put that in my next book," I think out loud.

"Make sure I get the correct credit, Will." She smiles as she pulls back, and I have to laugh. Okay, maybe I did miss this.

"Always."

Oakley clears his throat, and I watch Ainsley's eyes look him up and down before looking at me with a sly smirk and an arched eyebrow.

"Wonderful to see you, Oakley. Please come in." She steps aside, fanning out her arm like Vanna White, and I don't hide my laughter.

"Girl, we need to talk about that later," she says out of the corner of her mouth as Oakley walks past.

"We can talk about it at dinner if you'd like," Oakley calls over his shoulder, and I snort as Ainsley's cheeks turn bright pink.

"Well, that's not embarrassing at all. I thought I was craftier than that." She walks to the kitchen, where Ledger and Rina are leaning on the island.

Ledger stands and holds out his hand to Oakley. "Eye looks good."

Oakley huffs out a laugh. "Yeah, it healed nicely."

"Oh, Jesus, stop the macho-man act, you two. Who's cooking dinner?" I move and give Rina a hug as she smirks at the men.

"I haven't seen Ledg's 'dad act' in a while. This is fun," she whispers to me.

"It's only fun when it's not happening to you." I pull a seltzer and a water out of the fridge and crack it open, tossing the water to Oakley.

"I'm cooking, and I'm making Ainsley's favorite," Ledger says, arching an eyebrow, daring me to question him.

I truly don't care what he cooks for dinner. I'm just happy to get some of his home-cooked food. Although, a certain coffee shop owner sure has been spoiling me on that lately.

Ledger moves to the stove to stir some things in pots as Oakley joins him to help. I smile at how he seamlessly works himself into my family, like he was always meant to be here.

"So, the plan is to bring Lennox home tomorrow. He's being a crotchety asshole to the nurses because he's going crazy sitting in the hospital. The good news is that all the superficial cuts have healed nicely, and the deeper ones are out of the danger zone and healing well. The doctor said he'll need stitches out soon, but we can do that here."

We all nod, happy with the progress this extended hospital stay allowed.

"I am worried about him being alone in that cabin of his," Ledger says.

"I offered to have him stay with me for a little bit, and he immediately said no," I tell him.

"Yeah, I offered too. It probably didn't help that we both asked," Rina adds.

"Shit, I did too. No wonder he wants to be alone," Ledger says.

"Him being alone isn't a bad thing, but I do think it's wise that someone checks up on him daily, or every other day for the next few weeks. He's been through ... a lot, and even if it annoys him, it's better to be cautious," Oakley says. If anyone knows what he went through, it's him. And if there's anyone who's seen the aftermath of Tennison, it's Oakley.

"And what if it pushes him away more?" Rina asks.

"Honestly?" We all nod. "It probably will. He's going to be angry and not understand a lot of the feelings he's feeling. Hell, I still feel that way, and I was never directly attacked." I wince at the thought but also at the fact that he was. He was stabbed, and he's brushing it aside like it's nothing. I'm going to have to take his own advice and use it on him, I think.

"And what do we do when turns that anger onto us? I don't want to push him too far," I say.

"I think it's important to feel him out daily. Just general texts and see how he's doing. You all have different relationships, so one day, he may benefit from joking around" — he looks at me — "or tough love." He looks at Ledger.

"Why do we automatically assume I'm the tough love?" he asks, put out.

The four of us burst out in laughter, and he rolls his eyes. "One punch, and suddenly I'm the hard-ass," he mutters.

"It was a good punch." Oakley grins.

"It fucking hurt like hell. My hand was all swollen," Ledger tells him. My eyes ping pong between them, and I am amazed at their interaction. One little conversation, and now they're joking about the punch. *Men.*

"Fucking men," Rina mutters as Ainsley and I giggle.

"They're ridiculous," Ainsley says, walking over to the double oven and pulling out the garlic bread.

Carbonara. I was trying to figure out which one of Ainsley's favorite foods Ledger was cooking, and I'm not disappointed.

I can practically feel the drool on my chin.

"Do I not feed you well enough?" Oakley's low voice hits me from behind.

"You do, but Ledger makes fresh pasta."

"I could make fresh pasta," he says in a petulant tone.

I rub my lips together to hide my smile before turning around. "You could make the best pasta, James."

"James? Your real name isn't Oakley?" Rina somehow hears with hypersonic hearing.

"James Oakley. I've gone by Oakley for most of my life, though. She's the only one who calls me James." There's a very small threat weaved into his words. Apparently, I will be the only one to call him James.

"Well, okay then." Rina grins at me. "Dinner ready yet, old man?"

"I swear to God, if you don't stop calling me that, I'm not feeding you. I tweak my back one time lifting soil, and you badger me with old comments for weeks," he grumbles.

"Okay, family." Ainsley claps her hands. "Let's eat."

The rest of dinner is filled with our usual banter that I didn't realize I missed so much.

Rina and Oakley are helping clean up when my phone rings. I take a peek with no intention of answering because this is family time, but when I see my editor, Ruby ,calling, I immediately think something is wrong.

Rushing out the back door, I answer on my way out.

"Hey, everything okay?"

"Holy shit, Will. Have you looked online recently?"

"Umm, not after I posted on my socials today, why?"

"Go check how many pre-orders you have." She doesn't answer my question, but I do as she asks anyway. I'm currently trying to push my new book hard on marketing, and because it's so different for me, I just know something bad happened.

I pull up the website and do a double take.

"What the fuck?" I whisper.

"*Put me on!*" I hear Ruby yell through my phone that I'm still currently looking at.

"What happened?" I finally ask.

"The post from this morning blew up. Like, virally blew up. You can't look anywhere without someone talking about it."

"How— What? How did this happen?" I feel frantic and very confused.

"I don't know, babes. It hit perfectly and people kept sharing it, and here we are."

"What do I do?" I mean, I'm successful enough to afford the life I currently live, but I've never seen these kinds of numbers. And that's just the pre-order.

"You keep pushing and marketing, and see how high you can take this."

"But what if it sucks? What if people get it and then absolutely hate it? What if it doesn't live up to the hype?" I whisper. Imposter syndrome never quite goes away, it seems.

"Do you not trust me? Do you think I wouldn't be brutally honest in my edits and let you publish something less than perfect?"

"No!" I tell her quickly.

"Babes, this book is fucking phenomenal. You've earned this." I feel myself nodding, tears filling my eyes at being so overwhelmed.

"I gotta go. Call me. Keep me updated. I love you. Keep kicking ass." Ruby makes a kiss sound through the phone before hanging up.

I hear the door shut behind me, but I'm so confused by this little five-minute conversation that I can't draw my attention to it.

"You're shaking. What happened?" Oakley's voice is hard, like he's ready to go to bat for me, and I love him all the more for it.

"I, uh... That was my editor."

"Was there a problem? I don't understand all the things it takes to, you know, release a book or whatever, but did something happen?"

"I went viral. And that sounds so fucking lame, but look." I shove my phone in his face, the page that shows my pre-orders still up.

"Is that how much you've made? But it's not out yet? I'm confused." His brows are furrowed, trying to understand what he's looking at.

"That's how many people have pre-ordered. Just the number of orders, not how much I'll make. You know, my last book? That pre-order number is double what I've sold total since my last book has been out."

"Holy shit." His eyes are wide as he continues to stare at my phone.

"Yeah," I breathe out.

He hands me back the phone, making sure I have a good grip before he lifts me up and spins me around.

"Bestseller lists, here we come!" he yells into the night, and I can't help but giggle at his enthusiasm.

"What in the hell?" Rina calls from the back door.

"Willow blew up. I mean, her book."

I put my forehead on his shoulder, mine shaking with laughter.

"Hell yes! Amazing job, Will!"

Everyone comes in a huge group hug, and the only thing I can think of is how Lennox is missing.

"Okay, enough about me. It's just pre-order. So much can change between now and release. You guys are picking up Lennox?" I ask Ledger and Ainsley. I can see their looks, but now's not the time to focus on me. We have a brother that needs us.

"Yeah, we'll pick him up and bring him home. How do we want to do the check-ins?" Ledger asks.

"Group chat? That way, it feels how we normally communicate," Rina offers.

"I agree. That way, we don't solely focus on him." I nod.

"Alright. I'll keep you guys updated on everything tomorrow, but otherwise, family dinner next week? Lennox's favorite?"

"Absolutely," I agree.

"Well, we'll talk to you guys tomorrow then," Oakley says as he leads me inside.

Guess we're leaving now, but with the pre-order news and the stress of bringing home Lennox tomorrow, I'm ready to go back to my little cave of a house.

"Love you!" I yell over my shoulder as we head to my car.

There is so much still happening in our lives. I'm just glad I have James here to support me every step of the way.

CHAPTER THIRTY-NINE
OAKLEY

Lennox is getting discharged right now, and between Willow pacing the living room and my head going through every conceivable outcome with him, we're both a ball of anxiety.

"I think I might try and open Grind Time." I stand abruptly. Now that the idea has popped into my head, I actually think it's a good one. Get back to my usual schedule, make coffee for the all the nosey townspeople.

Maybe that's not such a good thing.

"Smart. Sitting around waiting to hear from Ledger isn't doing either of us any favors. Need help?" she asks.

"Honestly, yeah. I told Brittany we'd open back up next week, so I won't have help until then." I like this plan. Not only because I really will need the help, but I'm also not ready to spend a lot of time away from Willow. The past week and a half have spoiled me, and I'm not sure I want to go back to spending our time apart.

"Done!" She speed-walks to her room to get dressed, and I slowly join her, pulling on a pair of jeans and a Henley that Arlo was kind enough to drop off after I realized I would need clothes at some point.

"So, fair warning, when I was in charge of the shop last time, I sucked at making coffee. So maybe I can just be on cashier duty or food duty, or something," she rambles, and I know it's because she's nervous about Lennox.

"I'll take any help you can give, Trouble." I lean down, pressing a kiss to her lips. "Let's go."

I grab her hand and drag her to the door. The fresh air and normalcy at Ledger's house last night have made me anxious to get back to that feeling and to give it to Willow.

Walking to Grind Time gives me the fresh air I was desperate for. The streets are quiet along Main Street, which is unusual for Bluebell Falls. It's not shocking, though; Arlo told me everyone was giving reporters hell all week. They probably feel the opposite of me and want to just relax at home after the eventful week.

I unlock the front door when we finally get there and walk into the eerie silence. It's mid-morning, and normally, this place would be packed.

"It's weird being here in daylight and not having a line out the door," Willow says as she looks around.

"I was just thinking the same thing. I'm not even sure how much food I should bring out. I mean, I didn't even prepare any pastries, so I really only have stuff for paninis." This was a stupid idea. No one is going to show up, and we'll spend all day twiddling our thumbs here instead of at home.

"Somehow, I don't think that'll be an issue." I look up at her and see she's looking out the front windows that face Main Street.

I turn around and see at least ten people bustling across the street. Mabel, Alice, and Ainsley's dad, Jim—which still makes me laugh, knowing he's in league with the gossip queens—hurry their way across the street.

"Shit," I mutter, walking quickly behind the counter to start pulling out all the shit I'll need to fuel the masses.

"Okay. I'll take orders?" Willow says, keeping up with me. I'm impressed she knows exactly where everything is since the only real day she spent behind the counter is the day Lennox ... the day that... When everything went down.

I shake my head of those thoughts. I don't have time to think about that anyway since the bell above the door rings out.

"So good to see you open," Jim calls in his booming voice.

I send a wave up but continue to pull out everything we'll need and turn on the espresso machines.

"So, are the rumors true?"

"Did you really go down there by yourself?"

"How's little Lenny doing?"

All the questions hit Willow at once when she takes her place at the register.

"Umm." I hear her timid voice. She's never timid, so I know she's struggling. Not knowing how to answer is causing her to freeze up.

"When is he coming home?"

"Do you all need anything?"

"Now, Mabel, let the girl breathe," Jim's voice calls out over everyone.

My vision blurs a little, and the angry heat spreads through my chest as I turn around. This group making Willow uncomfortable has my hackles up.

"If you all don't leave her alone and stop asking questions, you can leave. Order your shit." My voice is low and shouldn't be heard over the ruckus of the customers, but somehow, they all hear it.

"Sorry, Oakley," a few people mutter, casting their heads down in shame. They know better, but their curiosity obviously got the better of them.

"Don't apologize to me; apologize to Willow."

A chorus of "I'm sorry" greets both of us as Willow looks over at me, a small smile on her face.

"Thanks. Now, what can I get for you?" Willow asks without a hiccup.

It takes us over an hour to get through the influx of people, most ordering the most basic of coffee orders, so I know they only came in for the gossip. Once we finally have a lull, I step out from behind the counter.

"Alright, show's over, folks. We'll open up full-time again next Monday," I announce, not even feeling the slightest bit bad about it.

"Oakley," I hear Willow whisper behind me, but I wait until everyone is out the door before locking it and turning back to her.

"Yes, Willow?"

"Why did you close? What if someone else needs coffee?" Her eyes are bloodshot, and her hair is falling out of the bun on top of her head.

"First, no one in this town *needs* coffee; they just wanted any information they could get. Second, you are exhausted—hell, I'm exhausted—and this was a bad idea. We should have just gone for a walk and then gone back home." Besides, the adrenaline of everyone bombarding her with questions was too much for me, even if it wasn't for her.

Using this as a distraction for how I'm feeling about Lennox coming home was the wrong move, but nothing to do with it now. Lesson learned; now, we move on.

My old therapist would love that I just said that.

The thought triggers an idea. But first, I need to get Willow home so I can talk this out with her.

"It seemed like a good idea." She sighs. "They really just came in here swinging, huh? This is why I kill them off in my books." She whips out her phone, and I peek over, seeing her writing a note of grievances about everyone who came in here.

I choke out a laugh. "Remind me to stay on your good side. And now I'm going to have to reread your books and guess who everyone is."

"It's a fun game. I'll help you," she says without missing a beat with her notes.

A knock sounds on the front door, and I see Sheriff—Arlo—standing there. I walk over, unlock the door, and usher him in.

"Willow. Oakley." He nods as a greeting.

"Hey, Arlo, need some coffee?" Willow asks.

"I'm good. Thank you, though. I actually came to talk to Oakley." His tone tells me this isn't a social visit, so I motion him over to a table.

I don't ask him what he needs; I wait him out. I know he won't beat around the bush, so there is no need for small talk. He looks over at Will for a moment, arching his eyebrow at me when he turns back.

"She's good," I tell him. Whatever he wants to talk about, she'll find out from me as soon as we leave here anyway. This just takes out the middleman.

"I wanted to formally offer you a job in the sheriff's office. It would be basically a deputy position, but we'd be more equals."

I stare at him in a little bit of shock. Sure, he's offered up casually before but never an official offer.

"You're serious?"

"Absolutely. It's not that we need to fill the position, but I could use a second-in-command. We could take on more of the National Park stuff if needed, things like that."

I look around Grind Time, and it's like time stands still. I see Willow leaning against the corner, her brow furrowed in thought. I see visions of Mabel and Alice shit-talking in the corner. I see Arlo coming in most mornings for an americano, even though I know he has a machine across the street at his office.

"I think," I say slowly. "I think I need to decline." I say the words, and in any other situation, I would be panicking that I just made a rash decision.

But this doesn't feel rash at all. This feels *right*.

"But" — I turn back to Arlo — "I'd be more than happy to be available if things come up that you need help with. Just not full-time. Or even part-time. Just case by case," I offer.

The corner of his mouth tips up in what I would consider a smile from him before he knocks on the wood table. "I'll take that. Thanks, Oakley."

He goes to stand when Willow interrupts.

"They're on the way with Lennox. Thought you both would like to know. Rina said she has to drop him off then run because she has a dinner, so she wants us to meet her there." She says the last part to me.

Arlo checks his watch quickly. "Shit, I lost track of time. Sorry to run, but I've got a ... meeting." He rushes out without another word.

Willow and I raise our eyebrows at each other. Interesting. Definitely something going on there. But that's not my business.

My business is taking Willow to go see Lennox and hope that he's doing okay. Whatever is going on with Rina and Arlo is not something I want to be in the middle of.

Arlo rushes out as Willow laughs.

"Woah boy am I going to have a chat with her later." She shakes her head, mirth lighting up her whole face.

"Alright, little investigator, one problem at a time. Let's go meet Lennox."

We walk to my car because, apparently, Lennox's cabin is a little way on the outskirts. It still only takes us about fifteen minutes to get there, but it's very clear he wants to be on his own out here. There are no neighbors around for miles.

"I want to talk to you about something," I tell her as we park and wait for everyone else.

"What's up?"

"I want to see if my therapist from when I left Marshals has steady openings. Maybe once a week, once every other week. We talked about it before everything went down, but I want to get more serious about it."

"Okay." She nods, putting her hand on my forearm.

"I know I have unresolved shit from when I was still on the Task Force, but I also think everything that happened will hit me eventually, and I want to stay on top of it. I don't want to put you in a position to deal with a partner who doesn't know when he needs help. I want to be proactive."

"You know I would support you no matter what, right? I think talking to your therapist is a great idea, but I also don't want you to think I wouldn't love you just the same if you struggle. Life is not perfect; we're both bound to struggle. Hell, I was just thinking about figuring out how to go about starting with a therapist because I'm starting to get nightmares." She tosses her hands up.

"You're having nightmares?" I didn't know, and guilt hits like a freight train. I missed something.

"Just one, but it was … scary, and I don't want them to become more frequent. That's not the point, though. The point is, I think it's good we're both looking into this. We might feel great right now, but it doesn't mean it will stay that way. What he did … is not something that will go away easily."

"No, it won't," I say quietly.

"Were you worried I wouldn't be receptive?"

"No, not really. It's just not something I've ever felt like I needed to talk about. But we're together and I love you, so I want to include you in decisions I make that affect both of us."

"I really like that," she whispers.

Lifting up as best as she can in the car, she leans over and presses her lips to mine. A car door shutting has us pulling away, the twinkle in her eye telling me being open about wanting to go back to therapy was the right decision.

"You ready for this?" I ask.

"No, I don't really think I am, but he needs us all right now."

I nod, getting out of the car and walking to the door to open it. We meet Rina in the driveway, and she looks like she has something to say.

"He's complaining that we're babying him. When I calmly told him he couldn't drive himself home, he bitched that he could have rideshared. It's like he's a sullen teenager again, and I'm trying to keep my patience but I am about to fail miserably," she says through gritted teeth.

"Well, it's a good thing you need to leave then, huh?" Willow says in a very little-sister tone.

"Sure is." Rina's tone is sugar-sweet, and I know the stress is getting to everyone. The unknown, the unsure of how to treat Lennox is all catching up to everyone.

"Well, I'll go get Lennox." I move quickly to Rina's truck, opening the side door to find a very ticked-off Lennox.

"Tell the women to stand down. I'm not helpless." His voice is flat, albeit annoyed.

"They're worried, and they don't know how to act around you."

He tips his head back on a sigh. He's looking really good today, actually. We haven't seen him outside of video chats, but even the deeper of the cuts have very small bandages on them at this point.

"I know you're right. Fuck, I don't even know how to act around me."

"Hey, it's okay. No one has all the answers right now, and I can not-so-subtly hint to them to chill on their caution level."

"Thank you. For being normal, for treating me like I'm normal."

My heart breaks for him, and it's extremely hard for me to see him so different than the lively man from just a few weeks ago. The one that kicked my ass on the trail. That guilt is pounding hard in my chest again, but I know I can't let it pull me under.

"It'll take time. They'll get there," I tell him, holding the door open, and he slowly swings his legs over the side.

"The hospital set me up with a therapist," he says softly.

"That's good." I'm not sure if he's happy or annoyed with it, so I choose to stay neutral.

"It makes me nervous."

"Yeah, it made me nervous too. Hell, I think it still does."

"Yeah? Does it get easier?"

I once again could lie to him, but I know it would do more damage than good. "No, I honestly don't think it does. You just accept that it's for the greater good and deal with it. And then some other trauma rears its head, and you deal with that."

He chuckles at that before wincing and grabbing his side.

"Easy, man, no need to play the hero. Let's get you inside." I help him out of the truck and then let him take the lead.

Willow already has the house open, and Rina is saluting us as she walks away and takes off. I can't help but laugh at their sibling-ness. I've never had that, so it's super entertaining.

"You pissed her off real good," Willow says, holding the door open.

Lennox just grunts, and Willow looks up at me with a question in her eyes. I shrug, knowing if he doesn't want to talk, I won't be the one to push him. Lennox walks into his large cabin and collapses onto the couch.

"Ledger said he stocked up the kitchen, so you should be good to go on food for a while. Do you want us to hang out for a while?" she offers.

"I think..." He sighs. "I think I just want to be alone for a while." He pats the spot next to him, and Willow joins him on the couch.

"For the last two weeks, at least one of you has been with me damn near 24/7. It's not that I don't appreciate checking in and making sure I'm okay, it's just that it's becoming suffocating. And I say that with love because this is a new normal we all have to work through. I haven't even really had time to process ... everything, and I think it would be good for me to just sit, alone, with my thoughts. Even if it sucks. I promise I'll keep up with the group chat, though."

It's a compromise, and I'm really proud of him for doing it.

"That works. I'm sorry we didn't give you time in the hospital, and I'll tell Ledg and Rina to chill. Love you, Lenny. Call me if you need anything." She hugs him gently before kissing the crown of his head and standing up to walk to me.

"You can call me too. Grind Time is opening back up Monday, so I can have lunch and coffee here whenever, if you want it."

"Thanks, man. Love you too, Will."

I nod to him as Willow hesitates. I put my hand on her back, leading her back to the front door.

"Call anytime, seriously," she says.

"I will, I promise." He looks her in her eyes as he says it, and I feel like it's a good step for him.

Once we finally make it back to the car, Willow breaks down in tears. It's going to be a long journey for not only Lennox but the family as well, but today and getting him home was a good start.

CHAPTER FORTY
WILLOW

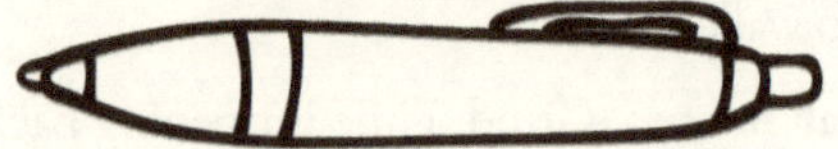

It's been three weeks since our new normal began. Three weeks since we got Lennox home. Three weeks since my book blew up on social media. And three weeks since James and I decided together to work with therapists to help us both process everything that happened with Tennison.

It's been hard on so many levels. My therapy days usually consist of being anxious as hell before the appointment and then crying for most of the day after. James tends to keep to himself more until he feels ready to talk about it. It's been another level of intimacy between the two of us that I never expected. But we're working through it all together.

Today is a fun day, one I look forward to with every book's release. It's dedication day. I started doing a special day where I wrote my dedication and acknowledgments on my second book, and it's the last thing to do before it goes out in the world. It signifies a dream I've had since I was little, and I use this day to soak in that feeling. It's easy to get lost in the business of it all, so for this one day, I let myself be fucking ecstatic at all I've accomplished. I let the imposter syndrome melt away and feel confident that it'll be my best book yet.

Today feels like a different kind of special, though. It's my first romance book, after all.

I write out a couple of different versions and erase them all. Do that a few more times before I stare at my computer for longer than I care to admit.

After what feels like days, a spark finally clicks in my head.

I type it out just as I hear the front door to my house open.

"Well, hello there, beautiful," James says as he walks over to me, bending down to give me a kiss before turning his attention to my computer.

"How was your morning?" I ask.

When he doesn't answer, I turn to look at him and find him staring at my dedication. I feel my cheeks heat, my hands coming up to cover them.

"This is the dedication for the new book?" he asks.

"Yeah," I whisper. I look at it again and try to see it through his eyes.

To love:

Something I've only ever known in the form of family. Something I never thought would come my way. And something that has changed my life completely.

To James:

I didn't know it was possible to love someone this much. You've influenced this book and my life more than you'll ever know. Now you're stuck with me, so tell me you love the book and kiss me.

"I love it," he says then leans down and kisses me again.

"Best dedication yet," I say when he finally pulls back.

"Are you officially done?"

"'Done' done. This gets released in a week, and then it's completely out of my hands."

"God, I can't even imagine writing a whole-ass book and then letting people read it." He shakes his head as he heads to the bedroom.

I quickly get up and follow him because if the routine of the last few weeks has taught me anything, it's time for my man to strip and take a shower.

"It never quite feels real until this point," I murmur as he turns the shower on.

We've become quite domesticated in the last three weeks. In fact, it's something I desperately want to talk to him about, but I want to wait until the time is right.

"Hey." He draws my attention back to his face. I'm certainly not apologizing for watching him undress. "You are a phenomenal woman, and I'm proud of you and I love you."

He never shies away from telling me he loves me. Never lets me forget to be proud of all of my achievements, even the small ones.

"I love you too," I say.

He climbs into the shower, letting the water drip over his head and down his body, thoroughly distracting me.

"How was Grind Time today?" I ask.

"Good for the most part. Mabel is on the war path about something with Arlo, but you know I'm not trying to get in the middle of that."

"We really need to work on your gossip. I need more information. There could be good drama there. Hell, what if it involves Rina?" I have a theory about Arlo and Rina, but it's just as wild as the stories I write, I think.

"You're delusional. Rina hates him."

"Or does she?" I ask before chuckling.

"Anyway, Mabel stayed a good chunk of the day, so I just tried to stay busy and do a shit-ton of prep for tomorrow."

"Well, that's good. Now, you can sleep in." I look at him with a huge smile.

"Sleeping... Sure, Trouble."

I chuckle as he soaps up, mesmerized by both his body and his humor.

"Do you have therapy today?" he asks, oblivious to my ogling.

"Tomorrow. I had another flashback this morning," I tell him quietly.

His head snaps up. "Why didn't you call me?"

"Because my therapist gave me some things to try when they happen, and I wanted to see if it would help."

He nods, and I can see the wheels turning in his head. "Did it help?"

"Surprisingly enough, it did. I mean, I don't expect it to magically absolve me of flashbacks and nightmares, but it's a start, so I'll take it. What about you? You were up too early this morning."

He sighs. "I woke up, and my brain wouldn't shut off. It was running through old cases, not just Tennison, and analyzing all the things I could have done differently."

We talk about everything; nothing has been off limits, and I know he's hesitant to start taking something to help with his anxiety. But things like this have been happening too frequently lately.

He shuts off the water and climbs out, scrubbing the towel over his body before tossing it in the hamper.

"I think I want to start the anxiety meds."

"Yeah?"

"Yeah. I don't want to be dependent on them, but I also need sleep and not have my head running through jobs I no longer work or looking over my shoulder for the next bad thing to happen. It's taking my focus away from the good things, the things I should be enjoying."

I walk up to him, standing on my tiptoes as I palm his cheeks. "I am so fucking proud of you. This is just the start of the process, the hardest part."

"I know, and logically I know it's the best decision. I just want to be able to be the best partner for you, and I don't think I'm doing that at the moment," he whispers against my lips.

"James Oakley, you are the best partner in the world," I tell him with indignation.

"Thank you." He wraps his arm around my waist and picks me up so my legs wrap around his torso.

I lean into his neck, breathing in the scent that's purely James. He calms me in the wild tides. He soothes away turbulent thoughts. Our life is one I wasn't expecting, but now I can't imagine another way.

"I have something I want to talk to you about," I murmur in his ear.

"Is it about tying me up again? Because I could be on board with that."

"What? No! Although, what I just heard was that I get a free pass to tie you up whenever I want, so expect that in the near future, big guy." I nip at his throat.

"Any time, Trouble. Any time. What do you want to talk about?" He sets me down on the bed and pulls on a pair of boxers. Sad, but at least I'll be less distracted this way.

"The apartment above Grind Time, do you rent it?"

"It was included when I bought the shop, so I don't pay rent on it, no."

"How do you feel about a transfer of belongings from one space to another?"

He moves so he's caging me in against the bed. "Are you asking me what I think you are?"

"If you think that I'm asking you to move in, then you're right on the money."

"You know, I've been thinking about this a lot too, but I didn't want to push since we've had so much going on. Ever since we were locked in here for over a week, this is the only place that feels like home, and I want nothing more than to stop acting like I actually live in the apartment." He chuckles.

"Yeah, that's probably a good idea. No reason to use it as a place to hold your shit," I agree with a smile.

"Maybe we can turn it into a writing space for you."

"The whole apartment?"

"Yeah. It'll be like 'bring your girlfriend to work' day, every day." The way he says it so earnestly makes me laugh.

"Will you promise to feed me all the food and lattes?"

He presses a kiss to my cheek. "Absolutely."

"I think I can agree to that. Although, I may have to shift my deadlines because I have a feeling you're going to be more than a little distracting." I smirk before pressing a kiss to his jaw.

"What do you mean? A mid-day quickie wouldn't be inspirational?"

"Hmm, definitely need to adjust my deadlines then." I press a kiss to his lips, and this time, we don't pull away. We kiss like we have all the time in the world. And it finally feels like we do. Sure, we have a lot to still work through, but we both know we'll be there for each other through it all.

"I really want to take things slow tonight, but fuck, all this talk about cohabitation and deadlines is really doing it for me," he murmurs.

Laughter bursts out of me as he trails kisses down my neck. I can feel him laughing as he does.

"Who knew it was that easy to get you going?"

"One look at you is all it takes," he says as he nips at my collarbone. More laughter erupts from me, making it impossible for me to get any words out. "Too cheesy?" he murmurs. "Let me try again."

He lifts up onto his elbows, hovering over me with a serious look in his eyes that stops my laughter in its tracks.

"I am so lucky to call you mine. I am grateful that I get to spend my life with you, going through every bump in the road with you right next to me. I am in awe of you, of your heart, and your mind. You amaze me with your brilliance every single day. I am wholly unworthy of being this lucky, but I'm damn sure going to run with it without looking back."

"And I'm the writer." I sniffle as a few tears fall.

"Maybe you're rubbing off on me."

"You know, I think I had a crush on you since the moment you moved to town. That's why I never came into Grind Time; I thought you would be too much of a distraction." His eyes light up, listening to me. "I was correct in that assumption, but I also think in the last couple of months, I've become the best version of myself because of you. We are an unstoppable force together, and I can't wait to see where the future takes us."

He crushes his lips to mine, and I wrap my arms around him, holding him as tight to me as physically possible. Breaking the kiss a moment later, he rests his forehead against mine.

"I love you." *Kiss.* "And I love our life." *Kiss.*

"I love you too," I whisper before he kisses me again.

We end up being late to open up Grind Time in the morning because he shows me in every way possible how much he loves me.

EPILOGUE
OAKLEY

A year and a half later...

"Order up, Mabel!" I call out to a packed Grind Time.

Willow slides behind me, grabbing my ass as she walks over to the pastry counter and wraps up a croissant for a customer.

"Watch it, Trouble," I warn.

She winks at me as she passes by, and I shake my head, knowing I'll tie her up later for playing grab-ass at work.

"You two are just the sweetest. When are you getting married?" Mabel says as she grabs her coffee.

"Why thank you, Miss Mabel, but nothing on the schedule yet," Willow says sugar sweet. She meets my eyes and gives the look I know all too well means she's about to kill off Mabel in her next book. I have to turn around to hide my laughter.

We talked about the possibility of getting married, but both of us felt it wasn't something we needed or wanted to be together. The gossips in town can't figure us out and frequently bug Willow about it, hence she kills them off all the time.

"Why don't they pester you about this shit?" she grumbles as she stands next to me.

"Because they know I'll withhold paninis if they do."

"How is that fair? I run this damn place with you now. How do they just ignore me when I throw threats like that out?" She throws her hands up in exasperation.

"Because, deep down, they know you're a softie who would never withhold food." I press a kiss to her temple, smiling as she huffs in annoyance.

"You're a softie too. They just don't ever see it."

"And they never will. That is saved for you, Will, and only you."

She looks up at me with nothing but love in her eyes. It's been like this since we finally caved on our attraction to each other, and it's only grown since. Every single day, I think it's impossible to love her more, and I'm proved wrong every single time.

Her fingers intertwine with mine, squeezing my hand in hers.

"I really don't want to leave when you're being so adorable, but I need to get this chapter done." She sighs.

Oh yeah, the apartment upstairs got a complete overhaul. We tore down all the walls, added an area for all of her stock and swag—as she calls it—and made her dream office a reality. She alternates between writing and working at Grind Time with me. When inspiration hits her, she goes upstairs and writes until she can't anymore. It's the perfect setup really, and it's helped her finish four more bestsellers.

That's right, my woman is officially on the bestseller list without an end in sight. The book she wrote during the whole Tennison ordeal bumped her to a level of success I think neither of us were prepared for. It's been a damn whirlwind, but I'm so damn proud of her.

"I'll bring you up a latte once the crowd dies down a little more."

"Add an extra shot please. I'm dragging ass today."

I don't even try to hide my smirk. She's dragging ass because I edged her for over an hour before taking her nice and slow, drawing some intense orgasms out of her.

I subtly reach down and adjust myself in my jeans. Her eyes follow my hand, and a mischievous grin lights up her face.

"I'm game for a repeat *after* I finish this chapter, greedy man."

"Done. I'll have your latte ready in a few." I pull her to me, kissing her in what many would consider inappropriate for the workplace.

She pulls back, patting my chest with a slight blush permeating her cheeks, and heads to the stairs.

God, I love that woman.

The bell above the door dings, pulling my attention away from the sexy-as-sin woman I get to call mine walking up the stairs.

Arlo walks up to the counter with a look on his face I haven't seen in a while.

"Morning, Sheriff," I drawl. I will still call him Sheriff on occasion just to piss him off a little.

"You busy after you close up?"

I straighten my back, going into business mode. "I can be free. What's up?"

"Lost hiker in the park. We have a search party on it but aren't getting anywhere fast. Their family is at the station, and we aren't getting a ton of information out of them, so I was hoping you could stop by and talk to them."

"Yeah. I'll head over when I close down."

"Thanks, man, I appreciate it." He doesn't even ask for a coffee or food, just turns around and heads right back out.

That's been a pleasant surprise as well. I didn't really know what to expect when I told him I would help out on occasion, but it filled a part of my soul I didn't realize I was missing. After many therapy sessions, I came to realize completely shutting off that side of my life was doing more harm than good. Tennison was the exception to every rule, and I still missed the problem-solving, the look on loved ones faces when we got them answers. Arlo has allowed me to keep that, and although the cases have been pretty straightforward, it's still nice to help out where I can.

Willow helped push me a lot with that, allowing me to see that it's still possible to be fulfilled, even if it's only a few times a year.

Latte delivered and interview conducted, which actually led to recovering the lost hiker, I'm now on my way back to Grind Time to check on Willow.

If you would have told me five years ago that I would be loving the slower pace of life, I think I would have died from laughing too hard. But here I am, walking to check on my amazing woman and loving every single second of it.

I hear soft music as I walk up the stairs to the converted apartment, which is unusual. If Willow listens to music, she usually puts on her headphones and immerses herself in it. Instantly, worry hits my chest.

This isn't her norm, so could this be a writer's block? Is she stuck, and she's trying something to unblock herself? Did something happen?

Yeah, the overthinking hasn't gone away in the year and a half since we've been together. If anything, it's worse when it comes to her. I've accepted the fact that I'll always worry about her, no matter the situation, even if she is fully capable of taking care of herself.

"Will?" I call out as I hit the top step and turn the doorknob.

The sight that greets me is nothing short of perfection.

Willow in a little slip of a black dress, candles lit and twinkle lights shining through the whole office.

"What…" I trail off because I don't have words.

"I missed you while you were out saving the world." She walks up to me, wrapping her hands around my neck as best as she can with the height difference.

"I was hardly saving the world, just getting a sketchy family their kid back."

"Well, regardless of how you interpret it, I missed you." She lifts up on her toes to press a kiss to my jaw.

"I missed you too," I murmur. "Did you get your chapter done?"

"I got three chapters done."

"Overachiever."

"You were gone a while."

"And yet you still had time to set this all up." I smile into her temple.

"I wanted to surprise you."

"Mission complete, then."

We start swaying to the soft music in the background, holding each other and being completely in the moment.

"I can't believe this is my life some days," she says.

"Me either, but I've stopped questioning it."

I circle her around the open space in the office, slow-dancing and pressing kisses to every inch of skin I can reach.

A moan reaches my ears, and I groan in her ear. "Make sounds like that, and I'll take you over your desk."

"I'm good with that plan." She nips my shoulder.

I haul her up into my arms, walking toward the desk that is conveniently already cleared off.

"You plan for this, Trouble?"

"I may have been hopeful."

"It's good to be hopeful." I set her down on the desktop, pressing on her chest so she lies flat. I drop to my knees, groaning as they crack. Willow's laughter permeates the air, and I bite her thigh as I laugh.

"I'll still show you a good time," I tell her after I soothe the bite.

"Don't I know it. Maybe I should have a little padded mat for our knees next time." She bursts out laughing, and all I can think is how much I love this woman. There's never a boring day. There's never a day where we don't have fun together.

"I'll order one later. Now, hush, so I can get you off properly."

"You like it when I'm loud." Her loud shriek hit my ears as I shove her panties to the side and show her just how loud I can make her.

I lean back, letting her head lift up to see what I'm doing.

"I love you, Will. So damn much."

"I love you too, James. Now, make me come, so you can take me home and really fuck me properly."

"Yes, ma'am."

I show her smart mouth exactly why she keeps me around and then take her home and love her all night long.

This life of ours is something special, and I can't wait to see what's next.

ACKNOWLEDGEMENTS

This is where I tend to ramble, so bear with me!

Michelle: As per usual, this book wouldn't even happen without you! Our friendship has become one of my favorite things.

Emi: Thank you for helping turn this into the best book possible.

Nina: I owe you so many thanks! You've changed and helped my writing for the better and now you're stuck with me.

Kait and Joscelyn, my Betas: THANK YOU! From brainstorming, to making sure things are flowing the way they need to, you are both so invaluable. Your friendship is unparalleled and I'm so grateful you are both in my life.

The Hubs: You are endless inspiration. You push me to put myself first and give me time to do what I love. I love you endlessly.

My readers: THANK YOU! I will never be able to thank you enough for the support. Every time you share my books, talk about my books, or shoot me a message about my books it makes my whole life! I hope you enjoyed For the Thrill of It and I can't wait to show you what's next!

ALSO BY

The Catalyst Series

<u>The Beginning</u>

Meet the women of The Catalyst Series a decade before the series takes place!

<u>The Detour</u>

Bea and Riggs

<u>The List</u>

Penelope and Andy

<u>The Case</u>

Larkin and Theo

<u>The Vacation</u>

Jane and Pierce

Bluebell Falls

<u>Second First Impression</u>
Ainsley and Ledger

Be sure to join my newsletter to stay up to date on new releases and all other things me!

http://www.samanthamthomas.com

If you enjoyed For the Thrill of It, please think about leaving a review! I would be so grateful to you!

Review Here